Dancing in the Dark

BOB STRAUSS

iUniverse LLC
Bloomington

DANCING IN THE DARK

*This is a work of fiction. All of the characters, names, incidents,
organizations, and dialogue in this novel are either the products
of the author's imagination or are used fictitiously.*

iUniverse books may be ordered through booksellers or by contacting:

*iUniverse LLC
1663 Liberty Drive
Bloomington, IN 47403
www.iuniverse.com
1-800-Authors (1-800-288-4677)*

*ISBN: 978-1-4917-0979-5 (sc)
ISBN: 978-1-4917-0980-1 (hc)
ISBN: 978-1-4917-0981-8 (e)*

Library of Congress Control Number: 2013917354

Printed in the United States of America.

iUniverse rev. date: 03/25/2014

I dedicate this novel to my wife, Ruth Ehrenkranz Strauss, who taught me the true meaning of love.

CHAPTER 1
Jennifer Slater

D r. Harry Salinger, a psychotherapist, looked out the window of his ground floor office as he awaited the arrival of his next patient. The street was empty except for a middle-aged woman walking a small poodle across the way. It was unusual to find things so quiet on a Manhattan street in the middle of a warm sunny afternoon. It was also unusual for Jennifer Slater to be late. As a rule he could rely on her promptness. His thoughts turned to her; he admitted to himself that he looked forward to seeing her and hoped that she would not be too late. Looking nervously at his watch, he realized that her forty-five minutes of therapy were now reduced to just over forty.

He recognized his feelings toward her. For one she was very pretty, and he was too experienced an analyst to believe that it didn't matter. He pictured her as though he couldn't wait to see her before him. She would be dressed in tight designer jeans or slacks that accentuated the contours of her long, slender body and ample, well-toned buttocks. He never missed a quick glance at those. They stood out, demanding attention, making a statement.

His fascination left him feeling slightly disreputable, a feeling that he was never quite able to shake. In one of his more self-effacing moments, he'd speculated (to himself, of course) that he had the makings of a first-rate lecher. He reminded himself that sexual feelings were only human, a part of life, even

1

for therapists. He needed to cut himself some slack; a feeling was only a feeling after all. There was nothing wrong with it.

When she arrived, she would be wearing her extraordinarily thick jet-black hair pulled back from her forehead, neatly tied behind by a ribbon and then cascading broadly across the small of her back. Would he call her beautiful? He thought about that. She was certainly unusual looking. He loved her eyes, a shade of gray, or were they actually blue? He wondered why he was having these thoughts now. When he first encountered her some eight years ago, she was just as pretty, but he never gave her appearance a second thought. Of course his wife had been alive then, and perhaps that made all the difference. Were these erotic thoughts simply a matter of horniness, or loneliness, or some other as yet unknown need?

Nevertheless, other pretty women were coming to him who did not engender the same feeling. So clearly there was something else. *It's our relationship*, he thought. Over time they had become comfortable with each other, and—especially on her part—quite free. She said whatever came to mind, that little censor that came between the thought and the verbalization of the thought having apparently long since perished. Jennifer had a way of teasing him in a subtle, occasionally not-so-subtle, manner, with just a hint, a suggestion, of possibility. After the death of his wife, Harry had been sexually inactive for years, and it pleased and flattered him that she might entertain, even in her imagination, such a possibility. He was not tempted, but he was titillated. He seemed to need it, although he knew, from a strictly professional standpoint, that it wasn't a good thing to need anything from a patient except timely payments.

At other times their sessions were like verbal duels. Jennifer could be difficult and combative. At her worst she could be absolutely oppositional, disagreeing with everything he proposed. From session to session his feelings toward her underwent a change. They might be angry or avuncular or sexual. Of course he would never act on the latter. It was also true that he was never bored with her or indifferent.

Harry thought about the eventuality of her terminating therapy. He knew that would not happen soon; she still had much work ahead, particularly in the area of romantic engagements. Nonetheless, she had made great progress, and it was bound to happen. He would no doubt feel a loss, since he enjoyed the work with her so much. Having experienced severe losses in his life, Harry knew all about loss. His mother had died when he was still a teenager, his wife when he was a still young fifty-four. Cancer took both of them. This loss would not be so bad. She was a patient, after all, not a mother, or wife, or lover, or even a friend. Yet never seeing her again would be bad enough. The thought left him feeling sad.

Jennifer flew in without knocking, offering no excuse for her lateness, throwing herself on a chair opposite him as though she owned it. She looked quickly at the couch on the side of the room, a soft taupe leather feature that dominated the office. "Would you prefer the couch?" Harry inquired. She declined.

Today she shunned the tight jeans, favoring a short skirt with bare legs, her feet lodged in a pair of sandals. A soft cotton top covered her torso. She appeared quite at home. He noticed the whiteness of her skin along the length of her crossed legs. His eyes returned to her face as she began to speak.

"Isn't it an odd thing about life, Harry, that the more you need the less you get? I'm wondering whether there's something that tips men off, some aura, or glint in the eye, or whatever. Then you get treated like you're some kind of desperado, like you're a grasping, clinging, pathetic soul, and men avoid you like you're carrying bubonic plague! Maybe it's best to go through life not needing anything or anyone, the way I used to be."

Knowing her as well as he did, Harry was not in the least surprised by this dramatic opening declaration. Nevertheless, he felt called upon to react to Jennifer's words. Resorting to his vast storehouse of experience, as well as his shrewdness and psychological expertise, he formulated the perfect response.

"Uh huh," he said.

"It's not that I'm feeling needy; it's more like I'm feeling lack."

Harry waited for a follow up but was greeted with silence. *She's keeping me in suspense*, he thought. "And you lack ...?" Harry asked, coming yet a step closer to uttering a complete sentence.

"I don't know," Jennifer replied, a preamble to disclosing that she did know. "I think everything was easier before I went into therapy. I didn't want anything then, so the stakes were so much lower. I never let anyone get to me. If a guy liked me too much, I dumped him so fast he didn't know what hit him. Man, I could be a heartless bitch! It was a fun time," she added lightly, if a little sadistically.

As she talked, Harry played with arithmetic in his head: a happy patient enters therapy. Her troubles begin (a subtraction); life becomes complicated and disappointing, especially when contrasted with the ease of life before therapy (another subtraction); all of which equals an implication of years wasted, money thrown away (a highly negative result). Of late Jennifer had been difficult with Harry, ignoring his suggestions, contradicting his opinions, quarreling with his interpretations, generally annoying.

"Then I started seeing you, Harry, and I learned about *more*, wanting *more*, like intimacy, love, marriage, kids." She sounded very disapproving, as though he had been training her to commit a series of crimes.

"I did that to you?" Harry asked in a voice suggestive of mock incredulity.

"So what do I have now?" she continued, ignoring his comment as though it were perfectly irrelevant. "It's obvious. The more you want, the less you get—no boyfriend, no sex, no fun. It's hard to believe that I'm better off than in the days when I was just screwing around."

In barely more than a sentence Jennifer neatly, with cutting edge precision, negated eight years of hard work in therapy. Was Harry miffed? Was he annoyed at having his strenuous efforts over the years so cavalierly dismissed? Did he feel at least a trace of irritation in the face of this infuriating ingratitude? Not in the least. In fact he was pleased. He could readily recall how timid and fearful she had been at the beginning of her therapy. She would nervously and incessantly prattle on, as though the greatest danger was a moment of silence. Then, whenever she relented to give him a little space to talk, when she dared to direct a question to him, she eagerly attended each of Harry's words, as if it were originating from the Oracle itself. Oh, the power she endowed him with! It was a weakness in her self-regard, he knew. Now here she was, comfortably tweaking him, secretly teasing him, and gently chiding him for the absence of fulfillment in her life. It took ego strength to challenge him, to think for herself (even if wrong). Perceived in this benign light, Harry could take pride in her growth. As for her lack of fulfillment, he took no responsibility for that. Who gets to be fulfilled these days? Harry could speak volumes regarding that. To his way of thinking, fulfillment was as much a matter of luck as anything else. And after all, he hadn't promised her a rose garden.

At this particular moment however, he needed to find a proper response. He understood this new Jennifer loved a quarrel and would happily engage in verbal combat with him, given the slightest opening. And no matter how lucid and sound his argument might be, it would be to no avail. She would never concede his principal contention—that her therapy had not been a waste and that she had made great personal strides. For every point made, there would be a counterpoint, a universal *but* that would defeat his efforts. He was determined not to engage with her. He would try a different angle.

"I've been a big disappointment to you," he said.

Jennifer hesitated.

Harry hesitated. How would she respond? Would she agree, pronouncing him a failure as a therapist? Would she disagree, defending him by blaming herself, or fate, or men?

"Thanks to you I gave up my old life. You know what I mean—full of wild, thrilling sex," she stated firmly. "Although admittedly superficial," she added parenthetically.

Harry smiled. If she had had a life of "wild, thrilling sex" she had kept it from him, so the statement fell happily under the rubric of Gross Exaggeration, whether it was deliberate or merely the production of a wild, thrilling imagination.

"Then I met Allan. I thought it would please you that at last I was in a serious relationship. Instead you disapproved because you hated Allan."

"When did I ever express an opinion about Allan?"

"I don't know, Harry. Where would I get the notion that you didn't exactly like Allan?"

Jennifer had now adopted Harry's technique: answer a question by asking a question. *Imitation is the highest form of flattery*, he told himself.

"Why did you care what I thought, Jennifer?"

"What patient doesn't care what her therapist thinks? I was always trying to please you."

You could have fooled me, thought Harry.

"But I think I've gotten off my original point," Jennifer said without waiting for Harry's response. "Now that I've learned to expect more, to look for intimacy, to use your nauseating word," she said, spending considerable time distinctly pronouncing the word *nauseating*, "it's not there for me. You think Allan was bad? The guys I've been meeting make Allan look like a saint! They're all turkeys, their brains mired in football and Rambo-style movies. They couldn't tell you the difference between a feeling and a fantasy! You've gotten me to want more, but there isn't any more. Sometimes I feel like regressing, going back to my old ways, keeping things light, having sex for fun only, no strings attached."

"That's okay with me, Jennifer, if you think that will help."

"Really? You wouldn't be critical of me?"

"I think you're confusing me with your mother."

"Perhaps there's something to be said for low expectations-no disappointments likely. Maybe fun's all there is. Maybe the rest is bullshit. I know so many girls who have broken up with their boyfriends. Anyway, I like having bad-girl thoughts. Don't you ever have bad-boy thoughts, Harry? Don't you ever have nasty sex fantasies, like screwing a pretty patient?" A slight mischievous smile appeared on her lips.

Harry held his tongue; he was a master at holding his tongue.

"Do you?" she asked in her most insistent, seductive voice.

Harry once again turned to his feelings for Jennifer. Had they met today, for the first time and in a different capacity, would he be tempted? Would she? At thirty she was almost half his age, but stranger things had been known to happen. Harry was a demon for physical exercise, and his hard, muscular body showed it. At fifty-eight there was not even a hint of a paunch, and he still had a full head of hair, although now a very dignified white. For a time after his wife's death he had let appearances go, but he was back now, rushing to the health club, running almost every day, feeling strength and health returning to his body. Whatever he thought his chances with Jennifer might have been, he was realistic. It was permissible for a therapist to have a sexual fantasy about a patient; acting on it was decidedly not permissible. Even the fantasy gave him a slightly disreputable feeling. He pushed it away from his mind.

"You've got your provocateur's hat on today, Jennifer. What other bad-girl thoughts are you having?"

"Answer a question with a question—the usual shrink smokescreen," she said in her best sarcastic voice.

Look who's talking.

"Well, for one I thought about calling Allan," she said, suddenly turning compliant. "I felt depressed and reached for the phone. Some people take meds when they're depressed; some people go shopping; I get on the phone. Saves a lot of money. But you already know that. God! Is there anything you don't know about me? Whatever happened to privacy? I stopped myself from calling Allan, but it was a close call."

"I'm curious. Why call him when you're depressed? As I recall, he was often the cause of your depressions."

"That may be so, but life was always exciting with him. You

see what I mean though? You're always pointing out the bad things about the relationship."

True enough; then again, there was a lot to point out.

"So if the truth is not what you want to hear, should I withhold telling you? Why, by the way, did you stop yourself from calling Allan?"

"Pride," she said after a short reflection. "He hasn't called me, so it would be like I was the needier one."

Harry gave Jennifer a C for that answer. He would have preferred some recognition of how dreadful a boyfriend Allan was; that he would disappear for weeks without calling or responding to her messages, ultimately offering the reiterated excuse that he had been "depressed"; how he had been so unreliable, so inconsistent, and, most of all, how he had broken so many promises he made to her. Her answer seemed to leave the door open for renewal of the relationship.

"Do you want him to call?"

"Yes and no. How's that for an ambiguous answer? Yes, it would feel good to hear from him, proof that he was still thinking about me. It would mean he hasn't found someone else. And no, because I don't want to start thinking about him again; you know the old longing. What would be the point? Been there, done that."

"Still, what would you do if he did call you?" He held his breath, waiting for her answer.

"You know, I like your office, Harry; it's warm and cozy. I always have liked it. I see you favor earth colors, dark brown and green, with a little tinge of deep red, like midfall. I imagine it's a reflection of you. Now why can't I find a guy like you—steady, sensitive, caring, mature?"

"Old."

"Handsome."

What should Harry say to her? Should he note her rather obvious change of subject? Should he insist on her answering the question? Would she see Allan if he called, and if yes, then why? But it was clear she wasn't ready to address the question, so he decided on a different tactic.

"I'm glad you told me about the almost-phone call," Harry said.

"Why is that?"

"It's always better to talk about feelings than to act on them."

"Yes, I know; that's your philosophy of life. But just because that's your belief doesn't make it right. Talking about feelings before you act on them sort of strips life of spontaneity, don't you think? Sometimes going with a feeling because your heart tells you it's right is a good thing. That's what I think."

This heart-above-head comment concerned him. He knew she had an unfortunate propensity to act on impulse with men. Were her words a harbinger of the future? Certainly she had made progress over the years, but what was happening now? Or was this just another harmless example of her prickly self, that little oppositional imp that seemed to be materializing with greater frequency during their sessions? Yes, he thought her emerging ability to take him on was a sign of strength, but was he wrong about that? Could it be something else, a retreat from health, part and parcel of the one-step forward, one-step back syndrome? Or was there something else, something he was missing? Could it have to do with *her feelings* toward him? What were those feelings, and why hadn't he explored that with her? What was he afraid of? In an instant he knew. He was afraid of the truth. Any truth would pose a problem. Did she really think he was handsome? He moved away from that thought and explored instead her last statement. When he notified her that the session was at an end, he felt an incompleteness.

When Jennifer left the office, Harry noticed a cheery jauntiness in her parting salutation. It was as if she had scored a breakthrough, when none that he could detect actually occurred. Perhaps he had helped her in some mysterious way, or perhaps not. It was so typical of his experience with patients.

Despite all the years of his practice, they still managed to confound and surprise him.

And what about his erotic thoughts about her? What was that about? She was his patient, and as such there was a great insurmountable wall between them. Although an invisible wall, it was still very much there, like dark matter in the universe. Still, it was just a feeling. No therapist ever got sued or lost his license because of a sexual feeling. But this had not happened before, so why was it happening now? What was his problem? Or was there a problem?

CHAPTER 2

Harry and Amanda

Despite himself Harry could not refrain from watching Jennifer as she crossed the street in front of his office, watching the slow sway of hips and buttocks as she strode away. No sooner was she out of sight than he looked at his watch, hurriedly grabbed his jacket, and rushed out. Harry had a scheduled date with Amanda Blake at a trendy restaurant near Lincoln Center, within walking distance of both their offices. Was it a date? *Not exactly*, Harry thought. That was the issue for him, whether they might cross that ever-so-slender invisible line between student and lover.

When he arrived, she was waiting, having secured a table for two in a quiet corner. Harry gave her a decidedly nonsexual kiss as he settled down opposite her. He looked at her and immediately noticed how attractive she looked. She wore a light tan suit with a thin silk blouse open at the neck. She embodied perfect trimness and neatness: not a dark blond hair out of place, not a blemish on her smooth golden skin. In a certain respect she was the physical opposite of Jennifer, much shorter in stature, with skin a shade or two lighter than Jennifer's. There was a fifteen-year difference between the two women, a fact that was not lost on Harry. He could accommodate the difference between himself and Amanda much more readily than with Jennifer.

He responded to an ordinary question of Amanda's by bringing up an aspect of his session with Jennifer, omitting entirely the feelings he was having regarding Jennifer. Amanda was also a therapist, although still a student, and they commonly discussed their experiences during the therapeutic hour. This was a new fact in their relationship. When Amanda had been his student, he never spoke of his own patients. Then again, at that time they never met for lunch.

"Perhaps we expect too much from our patients," Amanda suggested. "And weren't you the one who taught me to expect nothing more than their coming on time and paying on time?" she said with a teasing twinkle in her eye. Amanda spoke above the clatter of dishes and hum of nearby voices.

"Yes, but we have to allow ourselves to be human," Harry parried, a forefinger in the air and a teasing smile on his lips. Instantly he thought about his all-too-human feelings toward Jennifer, but he forced himself to return his attention to his companion. He needed to not think about Jennifer when he was with this lovely "friend."

Amanda had progressed at warp speed since the days when Harry first became her training supervisor at the Psychoanalytic Center. How long had it been, four years? It had to be, since it was coterminous with Sarah's death. Harry had taken two months off from his private practice and from various obligations at the Center, not long enough to recover from the loss of a beloved wife but his longest time away from work in thirty years. He had begun supervising Amanda soon after his premature return.

Harry had been simply unprepared to deal with life again, with patient's problems, with quotidian chores, with the supervisory and administrative functions at the Center that had been once again thrust on him, as though nothing very much had happened. In fact he was a shattered man whose world had been radically transformed. In those days he lost his sense of purpose, of any kind of a future. With Sarah's death, nothing mattered to him. It was as though all meaning had been ripped from his life. The years since had been a struggle to regain something—was it hope?

"Jennifer can be a pain in the ass, but she keeps me on my toes. She's the one patient I love to hate and hate to love, but I do—sometimes against my will—I do. She keeps an underlying sweetness and vulnerability carefully hidden; but I've caught occasional glimpses, so she hasn't fooled me. At times I've enjoyed her sense of humor, and, you know, for me it's quite a blessing to be able to laugh again."

"It's nice to see you laugh, Harry. And you know you've gotten handsomer in the time I've known you."

"I have?"

"When I first met you, you were so drawn and gaunt. I knew you had recently lost your wife; that was common knowledge at the Center. Look at you now. I can see you're taking better care of yourself, and I love that you've allowed your hair to grow long. It gives you a touch of the bohemian, an air of unconventionality."

"This white mane? I was thinking of coloring it."

"Don't you dare! It's you, and there's nothing wrong with it. I like the color."

What was he to make of all this flattery? In the last year Amanda had become increasingly direct with him, making inquiries regarding his state of mind, treating him like a close friend with whom she could be completely honest. Since he'd finished supervising her, the formality of an unequal professional relationship was no longer required. He was beginning to think something more than friendship might be available to him. The thought stirred something that had lain dormant for a long time. He shrank from it instead of welcoming it. It put too much at risk, but he seemed incapable of shrugging it off. Why was it so much easier to entertain thoughts about Jennifer, when possibly a more available woman was at hand?

"Well, thank you, Amanda. Your opinions mean a lot to me. Do you know that?"

She smiled.

"Four years is an awfully long time to mourn, so I'm not giving myself too much credit for finally coming around. It's an odd thing to be attached to someone who's no longer here; not very rewarding, you know?"

"Perhaps you have to let yourself attach to someone new," Amanda suggested as she lifted a cup of coffee to her lips; her eyes peered over the cup, fastening on his.

Harry looked across the table at his companion. After confining his sexual being to one woman for nearly three decades, he had lost the definition of flirting. Actually, he had lost something of even greater significance, namely his sense of his value in the eyes of women. The years had aged him, of course; the lines in his face had deepened. In fact, he was not very far from sixty, a number that still held some shock value. He dreaded that approaching decade with its somber aura of over-the-hill, superannuated old age. Such was Harry's state of mind when Amanda subverted his inner calm by suggesting, "Perhaps you have to let yourself attach to someone new." And who might that someone be? There was enough vagueness to leave him in a state of uncertainty.

Harry wanted his response to be purposeful and direct, wanted to discover immediately whether there was a possibility that … if she could … well, where he stood with her. Harry's brain was willing, but his heart wavered.

"Do you have a candidate for me?" he at last ventured, instantly recognizing the barely hidden timidity behind that elliptical question. He had matched her ambiguity with his own.

"And do your work for you? You need to take the initiative, Harry, and go after what you want."

"What if what I want doesn't want me?"

"You'll never know unless you try," she said; she appeared to lean toward him, elbows resting on the table.

He knew she had given him a second chance to emerge from the closet, to state his interest. What was he most afraid of—that she would say yes, or no?

"Yes, you're right, you're right. But I have to let go of the past first. I've been imprisoned by it. Sarah's dead. All that's left of her is in the grave. Yet I still think about her every day." Having said this, Harry recognized that he had somewhat contradicted what he had said earlier about separating from the memory of his late wife.

"It's understandable," Amanda said soothingly. "It's different for you. My marriage ended with bitterness and mutual recrimination; it was easy to disengage from that. Divorce was a liberating experience, like an albatross was lifted from my neck. Your marriage ended tragically. I can only imagine how awful that must have been."

"You know what the problem is? Letting go is like losing her all over again. Can you understand that?"

"Of course I can," Amanda said after a brief silence. "In a way I envy you."

That remark struck him as bizarre. He was talking about enduring an interminable mourning. What was there to envy? Harry tried to measure his response. The last thing he wanted was to alienate this woman.

"Really? I think my situation is less than enviable," he said.

The waiter interrupted, asking whether they wanted anything else. Amanda requested another cup of coffee.

"I mean, you had something of inestimable value, a wonderful marriage with a wife you adored, a happy family life. I never had that."

It was true. He and Sarah had a romance that endured all the vicissitudes of life: the birth of Brad and Katie, the struggle to build a private practice while living on a shoe-string budget, the expensive and scary childhood illnesses, the inordinate cost of college educations. They'd remained in love through it all, perfect partners who thoroughly knew each other's heart and mind. Theirs was a tranquil union of kindred souls, with few, if any, secrets from each other.

"But you must have loved Bill once, at least when you married him. Weren't you ever in love?" Harry asked curiously.

Amanda shrugged. "Bill never gave me a chance to love him; he was never around. He was too busy making money, climbing the corporate ladder. It took time for it to seep in that I wasn't that important in his scheme of things, although he would deny it, and the kids weren't either. Sadly, even when he was home, which was not often, he was largely absent. It's a strange irony, Harry, that his ambition, his sheer drive to succeed, was what attracted me to him. Be careful what you wish for."

"It seems grim to me."

"Does it?" she asked rhetorically, with a small laugh. "That's not the half of it. Since all his energies were channeled into his career, there was little left for the bedroom, so I was starved in that regard too. I sensed that his infrequent efforts were perfunctory and obligatory. There was no passion at all. Mostly I had to initiate sex, and there was never a guarantee that he would go along. More often than not, he didn't. In our marriage he was the one with the proverbial headaches. I suppose I should have been angry about it, but I was consumed with self-blame. I was ageing; I had lost the glow of youthful beauty. I put on some weight. Perhaps I wasn't attractive to him any longer. That was my thinking."

Harry scoffed at the idea. "I can't believe that. You're still a handsome woman. In fact, you're the best-looking woman at the Center, despite the fact that many of them are younger than you."

"Yes, but they're all so homely," Amanda said, grinning.

She had a point there. "You're a hard woman to compliment."

"Life has given me the best compliment."

"Meaning?"

"Being single has been a revelation."

"Yes, and that is?"

"Men want to have sex with me. At times it's even annoying."

This should have come as no surprise to Harry. Amanda was a very sexy woman. But the fact that she would so openly and casually imply that she had been (and possibly still was) sexually active excited him. It was positive proof that she was not the Madonna. He was seized by an impulse to reach across the table, close the gap between them, and kiss her. Of course, he did no such thing. It would not have been his style. A simple word or two might have done the trick. But what evidence was there that she was actually sending him an invitation? Perhaps she was just being honest. Had he dared to say something, he certainly would have discovered the truth. It would not have required a cascade of words; a few straightforward ones would do. "What about me?" probably would have done the trick. Did he want to know? He remained fastened to his seat, immobile and frozen in hesitation.

It was a moment, and the moment passed.

Sensing his discomfort, Amanda asked whether she had embarrassed him.

Harry laughed, and his body relaxed.

"I'm not a prude," he said, "and I haven't the slightest doubt that men want to have sex with you. The mystery is that you could ever have doubted it."

She gave him a long look but said nothing.

Another moment passed; another moment wasted.

"Okay, enough about me and my shocking revelations. Now I have a question for you, Harry. Are you dating? Are you seeing any one?"

The question caught Harry by surprise. Their friendship had been largely a collegial one. Occasionally they would discuss their children or other family matters. But this was a very personal matter; their love lives, such as they were, had been off the table. This question seemed to Harry like a rather sudden violation of that unspoken rule.

"Not at the moment," he answered, a half-truth concealing the reality that for four years there had been no one.

"Were you seeing someone?"

"Not recently."

"Have you had *any* dates since Sarah's death?"

The woman was taking no prisoners. Should he tell the truth? Was it a low thing to lie about this? Harry hated to lie. But in this case he also hated to tell the truth.

"Of course."

"Have you had sex?" Good lord! She was on to him. How did she know? Was she a mind reader? What a bold woman! Thank God he was not a blusher! Harry was a little unsettled by her directness, and more than a little embarrassed. How would it look if he told her the truth? Still, one lie was enough for him. There had to be a way to avoid telling the truth without lying. He thought about saying it was none of her business, but wouldn't that be an implied admission that he had indeed been inactive?

"Amanda, I've been a widower for four years. What do you think?"

Amanda shrugged, looking at him archly. She seemed dubious.

"What about you?" he asked, a desperate attempt to shift the subject away from himself. He felt she was looking right through him.

"Yes, I've had a sexual partner. Does that surprise you?"

"Of course not." Harry struggled to keep his face an inscrutable screen. "How did we get into this discussion?" Behind the screen was a feeling of dejection. *So she's with someone.* He thought she might have been opening the door for him. Now it appeared she was being a concerned friend, nothing more. *I'm too old for her,* he told himself.

"I think it's about time we did. At last we're having a real talk."

At that moment, as if to add emphasis to her last words, someone dropped a plate on the other side of the room. Its sharp clang when it struck the floor startled Harry. Amanda barely flinched.

"Would you like anything else?" their waiter asked.

"Just the check," Harry said. "I have to get back," he said to Amanda. He was feeling unhinged, confused, perplexed. He found her last words indecipherable but was afraid to request an explanation.

"You know, Harry, the next time we have lunch or dinner we should have wine."

"Why?" Harry asked. The woman totally threw him. "I don't usually drink alcohol when I'm working."

"*In vino veritas*," she said simply.

Did she suggest dinner?

They sat in companionable silence while the waiter prepared the check. Harry felt Amanda's eyes on him, scrutinizing him closely.

"I didn't mean to make you uncomfortable, Harry," she said.

Harry took a quick sip of water and said he hadn't felt uncomfortable, although he certainly had. In fact, he still did. In a flash they had parted from the safety of their sanitized relationship, arriving at this new, uncertain thing. What was it now? Harry was unable to define it. The check came, he paid (it was his turn), and they went their separate ways to their respective offices.

Back in the security of his office Harry had a lot to ponder. Fortunately Russ was his next patient, a man who had not arrived promptly for a year. That would give Harry some extra time to sort things out. How should he interpret Amanda's behavior? It had been a sharp departure from previous conversations. Never had she been so revealing about her personal life, and never had she been so aggressive in ferreting out his. And the inquiry about sex? What did that signify? Was there a chance for him, or was she in a settled relationship? She'd never spoken about anyone before.

Harry could be clear about one thing only. Over the last year he had begun to pay more attention to Amanda's physical presence, the features of her face—those lively green eyes—and the shape of her body. From time to time he caught himself daydreaming about her, as though those unwanted mental events had slipped past his power of self-control. His good and much admired friend and colleague Dr. Israel Gross was on to Harry's interest in Amanda. It was not that Harry told him as much; Izzy was a shrewd guy, and Harry talked too much about her. It was "Amanda said this" and "Amanda said that" and "Amanda was wearing this" and "Amanda looked like that." Izzy took a dim view of the matter. A stickler for proper boundaries and restrictions, Izzy cautioned Harry that their colleagues at the Center frowned upon supervisors sleeping with their students. In reality Harry no longer supervised Amanda's work, Izzy did. It was a fact that failed to quiet Izzy's concern about a pas de deux. "Once a supervisor, always a supervisor," he said.

"It's all a moot question, Izzy, since I doubt she has any interest in me at all," Harry said to reassure his friend.

"What makes you say that?"

"Look at the age difference; she's forty-five, I'm fifty-eight."

"Harry, in all the years I've known you, I never realized what a blithering ninny you are!"

Harry was unconvinced. What did Izzy know, that wizened, seventy-eight-year old, married-forever fuddy-duddy? Even so, his words now gave Harry pause. Harry, hidden away in his office, was in a virtual panic of indecision. What should he do? Had he waited too long to come forward with his desires? Had he lost his opportunity? He was drawn to her, more powerfully now that he knew she was in to sex. Who was she sleeping with? Was it someone Harry knew, someone from the Center with less angst than Izzy about sleeping with a former student? *Wait a minute. She used the past tense.* She said she had *had* a lover. So maybe she was now available? And if she were, was he ready to love again, really ready? Most of all he needed time, time to form a plan, reach a conclusion, or at the very least to clear his head. Perhaps another ten minutes would do.

Fortunately Russ ... *Oops, there's the buzzer. Shit! It's Russ! And on time, after a year of consistent tardiness! That son of a bitch!* For the moment Harry had completely forgotten about Jennifer.

CHAPTER 3

Jennifer and Meg

Every Wednesday at noon Jennifer Slater met her best friend, Meg Simon, whom she had known since her college days at Wesleyan. They would quickly purchase take-out lunches and sit in a vest-pocket park not far from where they both worked. Only sickness, inclement weather, or winter interrupted this time-honored ritual. The two women sat side by side on a stone bench. They were looking straight ahead, although from time to time one would turn to glance at the other.

In these meetings conversation easily superseded eating. On this unexpectedly balmy spring day conversation acquired a discrete purpose. They were discussing the engagement party that Jennifer was planning for Meg, going over the names of the invited and, perhaps even more importantly, the uninvited. Having drawn up the list of the saved and doomed, Jennifer suddenly noted in alarm that too few men had made the list. The immense consequences of such a blunder weighed heavily on her mind. To Jennifer's chagrin, Meg appeared blithely unconcerned. Observing that it was not a singles party, she said she wanted only close friends, regardless of gender.

"Meg, every gathering that includes at least one single guy is a singles party as far as I'm concerned."

Meg giggled. She often giggled at things her friend said. It partly explained Jennifer's affection for her.

"How well I know," Meg said. "Be that as it may, I'm looking

21

at this forthcoming event in a certain context, shall we say. Something like it's my party and I'll cry if I want to."

"Meaning?" Jennifer asked.

"I want only people I'm close to, and since I have many more girlfriends than guy friends, it is only logical—if painfully regrettable to you—that there'll be more women there."

"Well, I hope you're feeling my pain," Jennifer rejoined. Persuaded that Meg's point was incontrovertible, she returned to the essential task of demolishing the sandwich that sat on her lap. When Meg mentioned how eagerly she was anticipating her party, it jogged Jennifer's memory. She needed clarity about something pertaining to the guest list. A member of the charmed circle, one Annie Giraud, had inquired whether she could bring her brother, Jacques, who was not a close friend. The sandwich returned to Jennifer's lap. Here was an opportunity to add at least one guy to the list, but Meg's approval was required.

Meg thought a minute. She appeared to be engaged in some serious mental calculation.

"That's a tough one, huh?" Jennifer asked.

"Ordinarily I'd say no, he shouldn't be invited, because I don't know him very well, although he seems decent enough. But there's another consideration. I'm doing some math, and I'm coming up with an interesting equation.

"What?"

"Jennifer plus Jacques = couple. True, your personalities are dissimilar, but that could turn out to be beneficial. Perhaps he can convey to you a bit of his gravitas, and you can convey to him a bit of your lightness of being."

"And I've been looking everywhere for gravitas. I'm even trying to be depressed about my happy-go-lucky lightness of being. No luck there."

"And your names even start with the same letter. That has to be a favorable sign."

Jennifer, ever the pessimist despite the appearance of enthusiasm, was unconvinced.

"What does he look like?"

"Tall—very, very tall. Let's see—you're what, five eleven? He's got to have five or six inches on you."

"Really? It would be nice to have a tall boyfriend for a change. I was at least a full iota taller than Allan. I think that was the cause of my late-onset slouching. Then again, height isn't everything."

"It isn't? I thought it was for you."

"No, he needs to have other excellent traits.

"Like what?"

"He needs to be continent."

"God! You're so demanding," Meg said with notable emphasis.

"Is he cute?"

"I think so, but then there are others ..."

"Others? What do they say?"

"They say he's adorable," Meg answered in a nonchalant way.

"Oh, well," Jennifer exclaimed, throwing her hands in the air in resignation, "who are we to believe?"

"I think we should invite him."

"Yes, we should," Jennifer pronounced definitively. "With such a scarcity of eligible men I'll have to fight off all the single women."

"That was never a problem for you before," Meg noted dryly.

Jennifer lapsed into thoughtfulness. The moment required a change from this light banter to more serious matters. There was something she had been meaning to ask her friend, but the time never seemed right. Meg approached her impending marriage with a tranquility that seemed unnatural to Jennifer. For some reason it made Jennifer uncomfortable. Was it proper to say anything? Why stir things up now, with the wedding already deep into the planning stage? On the other hand, she had a need to not hold back her concerns with her dearest friend.

"How are you—" she began tentatively.

"What?"

"How are you feeling about getting married?"

"Excited, happy."

Okay, that was a start, although not exactly what Jennifer was looking for.

"How can you not be at least a little nervous?" In Meg's place, she imagined she would be paralyzed with fear.

"Oh, I suppose I'm a little nervous—you know, the usual stuff."

At last, something meaningful might emerge. Jennifer rushed in. "You mean about Dan?"

"About Dan? No, not at all. I mean about the wedding. Why are you bringing up Dan?"

"I didn't exactly mean that," Jennifer responded, beating a hasty retreat. "It's more about getting married, that's what I mean."

"What about it?"

"Don't you find it scary, at least a little bit?"

Meg became pensive. "You know, Jen, I've always dreamed of getting married. And now that I found the man, which, as you know, involved kissing a lot of frogs, no. It's not scary at all. Not finding this man, now *that* would have been scary."

That sounded definitive enough, but somehow Jennifer's unease refused to evaporate. She wanted further clarification.

"Look, I think Dan is the right guy—don't get me wrong. You know I'm very fond of him. But something you told me a few months ago stuck in my mind, and I'm wondering about it. You told me that sex with Dan wasn't good." There. It finally came out. But did it come out wrong?

"I never said that."

"You did."

"No, I said the sex wasn't as good as it had been with Michael."

"So. Doesn't that bother you? It seems as though you don't really care." *How could it not be a source of worry?*

"Not a bit."

Jennifer swiveled to face Meg directly. She had finished her lunch and held the discarded paper on her lap.

"Are you serious?"

"You know, Jen, while I'm not denying the importance of sex, there are other things that matter as much, maybe even more.

"Like what?"

"Like character, like trust, like a loving heart." Meg paused. "Sex is a mystery," she said mysteriously.

"Yes, it is," Jennifer said firmly. "What the fuck are you talking about?"

"Why is it that I could have fantastic sex with someone I wasn't close to but less so with someone I love?"

"I have a worse problem," Jennifer announced.

"Really? What?" Meg now turned to face Jennifer.

Jennifer could see that she'd gotten Meg's full attention, that her friend was genuinely intrigued. "With me, the more I *dislike* the guy the better the sex," Jennifer said.

"That's why you like to be with losers."

"You're probably right," Jennifer answered softly, although she was stung by her friend's remark. "Even so, that was a shitty thing to say."

"I'm sorry. Look, you frustrate me. I want this for you, this very thing. I want you to stop playing games and find a good guy."

"You're sounding more and more like my mother. Is it possible that marriage isn't right for everyone?"

"I'm not getting into this argument with you. You could do better than Allan, a lot better."

"I'm sure you're right. But at the time he was the only game in town. Something always trumps nothing." Jennifer was silent for a moment, and then she spoke again.

"Look, Meg, as you already know, it isn't easy. I've met so many losers. They don't even rise to the level of mediocrity. Shit! When I meet someone mediocre, I think he's special.

Everything is relative, you know. The most attractive and sexy man I know is about twice my age."

"Who?"

"Harry, my therapist. If he wasn't my therapist I could cheerfully jump into bed with him."

"Did you ever tell him that?"

"No, why would I? It would be a waste of time. I'm paying for the time."

A look of sadness appeared on Meg's face. Jennifer picked up on it and it altered her mood.

"I'm sorry," Jennifer said.

"For what?"

"For bringing all this shit up. I've got to keep in mind that we're not alike. The idea of marriage freaks me out."

"If I had your parents, given the wretchedness of their marriage, I'd probably feel the same way."

"But you don't feel the same way, and if this is going to make you happy, this marriage, it's what I want for you."

"That's my girl. It does make me happy, Jen."

"Can we change the subject now? Talking about sex and marriage is so boring."

"If only there was something else that really mattered, like … like …"

"Like baseball."

"Yes, like that."

Time had run out on their luncheon date. After discarding the remains of their lunches and wishing one another a good day, they returned to their respective jobs. Jennifer regretted bringing up the subject of marriage. There was another aspect to the matter that Jennifer was barely aware of herself that was now coming into sharper focus. She knew she had feelings about Meg's approaching marriage, and they weren't all positive. It wasn't about Meg's choice. Dan was a good man, and he was crazy about his fiancé. Her concern was more about herself. Things would change with Meg, she knew. When women married, their friendships changed. There was less time, less intensity. Jennifer would miss that terribly. They'd been single together for so long. Half of their conversation was about the men they were dating, usually about their disappointment with men. Now what? Jennifer was finally ready to acknowledge to herself a wish that this marriage would not happen. Yet marriage to Dan was what Meg needed, so Jennifer had to watch herself. Perhaps that was the problem today. She hadn't been watching herself. "My friend needs me to celebrate her impending marriage," she said to herself, eyes filling with tears. At that moment she felt herself to be an awful and selfish person. She worried about the future.

CHAPTER 4

Harry and Jacques

Jacques Giraud, long-legged and lanky, stumbled into Harry's office and marched toward his chair (not the couch) like a man on a mission. Harry was fond of Jacques. In particular he was impressed with the young man's intensity and how seriously he took the work they were doing together. He was pleased by the obvious influence he had with Jacques, how the young man struggled to absorb the lessons of therapy, which, although not always successful, revealed strong motivation. He liked Jacques's character; he was not only intense, he was also deeply honest and good at heart. In a world of narcissistic men and women, self-involved and self-aggrandizing—the world that Harry's profession compelled him to navigate—here was a different sort of human being.

Jacques sat upright in a leather chair opposite Harry. He was so tall his knees were virtually at the level of Harry's eyes, perhaps partly accounted for by the fact that Harry rarely sat up straight. Jacques arrived with good news. He had just received notice of his promotion to associate professor and his tenure at Rutgers University. Harry offered his warm congratulations.

"You've worked hard for this, and you truly deserve it. Even though I know you had your worries, I never actually doubted that they would give you tenure. They were not going to let someone with your ability go."

"I'm happy about it, of course, but you know, it's not where I really want to be."

Harry knew that Jacques had spent his undergraduate years at Harvard and his graduate years at Princeton, and he was motivated to reach higher. "I know that, Jacques, but it's a significant achievement and a good omen for your future."

"Well, it's an achievement. I'll call it a 'significant achievement' when I get to the kind of university I want to be at."

Minimizing his success was an old, bad habit of Jacques's, as Harry well knew. "Raining on your parade again? Only a week ago you were fearful of being passed over and having to leave without another position in hand."

"That's true. I am very relieved."

"And Jacques, it's not Podunk Community College; it's a state university, and it's your first tenured promotion. So how is it not significant? Congratulations, man, well done!"

Jacques smiled. "May I change the subject?" he asked.

"No, you may not. I want you to stay with the feeling, 'Associate professor, tenure, yes!' At least *I'm* going to celebrate it."

"Okay, Harry, let's open the champagne."

"Small triumphs are important," he told Jacques.

"Duly noted, and I do feel happy. But I've been thinking."

How many times had Harry heard Jacques begin a sentence with those words? Harry wished the man would think less and feel more.

"About my relationships with women."

"Yes?" Harry leaned back in his chair, the fingers of his hands laced together, as if preparing for a long slog.

"I've never been close to anyone, not once, not with my stepmothers or any of my girlfriends."

"You never felt close to Barbara?"

"I suppose over two years there were times ... but there was a hell of a lot more propinquity than intimacy. You pointed out how much she resembled my second stepmother, giving me the feeling that I wasn't her priority, that work, friends, and whatever came before me. Why didn't I see that? I wasted so much time. "

Harry listened and tried to read between the lines. What was the underlying message?

"Should I have been more direct with you?"

"Why are you always blaming yourself, Harry?"

Actually, he wasn't. It was a question he could have directed to Jacques.

"No, it wasn't your job to tell me how to live my life. I just kept right on ignoring what I was feeling, missing the handwriting on the wall, chasing a foolish fantasy that she would eventually come around. My head was up my ass and my brains followed."

Jacques had a facility for self-attack. Harry had a facility for not allowing him to go there.

"Pretty harsh, Jacques. You did finally get it, and you acted on it. As I recall, you did break up with her."

"Yeah, after two years."

"You live and learn."

"Only after you practically begged me to."

Harry's memory differed markedly.

"I don't deserve that credit. You used your own good judgment and walked away."

"No, I used your good judgment and walked away. Without you I'd still be with her, disastrously I think."

This was not an unusual exchange between the two serious men: Harry trying to support Jacques with Jacques turning it aside and giving all credit to Harry.

"You're getting down on yourself, aren't you? What's that all about?"

"Why didn't I confront Barbara sooner? Why did I let her get away with so much shit?"

An excellent question, Harry thought.

"What's the answer?"

"I haven't a clue."

Should I give him one? Harry thought. *Should I wait?*

"Could you confront your father?"

"About his working so hard?"

"About having so little time for you."

"No, how could I? He was doing it for me and Annie."

Harry was skeptical. "Really? Most people work excessively hard because they want to. It's what they do best. That's okay, except when they short-change those who love and need them. What about me—can you confront me?"

"About what?"

"Oh, I don't know. Aren't you ever angry with me?"

"Why should I be? You've been great for me."

"I don't know; it took me two years to help you leave Barbara."

"Not your fault."

"I could have pushed harder. I'm too soft on you."

"Sorry, Harry, but I can't be angry with you about this. I refused to see her blemishes. I closed my eyes to reality. So how is that your fault?"

As Jacques talked, his face was animated by frequent frowns. His hands were in perpetual motion, used for emphasis or to express perplexity.

Harry decided to change course. "Why a need for reassessing this now?"

"Because I'm beginning to think I'm a fuck-up when it comes to the ladies. I make poor choices, pick ambivalent, difficult women. And maybe the other side of the coin is throwing away the good ones. You know, I never told you about this, but about six years ago I met a girl named Alexis. She was pretty, she was smart, and she was crazy about me. Do you know what happened?"

Harry took a wild guess. "You dumped her."

"Exactly. I couldn't begin to tell you why. The reasons I gave myself were a crock of shit. I keep thinking about her, with some regret."

Harry had no argument with this. It was in fact a good thing that Jacques was examining that behavior. "So what are you feeling?"

"I'm feeling hopeless. I'm worried that I'm going to repeat this pattern over and over again. I'm worried that the next girlfriend will be as bad as the last one, and I'll make the same mistakes with her."

Harry felt annoyed with Jacques. "You know what I'm feeling, Jacques?"

Jacques shrugged.

"I'm feeling pretty inconsequential. It's as if I'm not part of the calculus. You're hopeless and I'm useless, can't help you with your fuck-ups. I'm just going to sit here and watch you repeat terrible mistakes."

Jacques appeared taken aback by this unintended consequence. "I didn't mean to say that, Harry. I'm pretty confident that you'll ask the right questions. But will I pay attention to you?"

"Okay, so let's go with that. Let's say your next girlfriend is a real clunker. I see it, you don't. What should I do?"

"You're asking me to tell you your job?" Jacques stretched out his hands and turned his palms up. He looked a tad confused.

"Yes. Help me out here. The message I'm getting from you is that I wasn't effective enough regarding Barbara. I know you blame yourself for that, but I'm feeling that I shouldn't get off the hook. We're in this together. How are we going to do this better?"

Jacques gave that very thoughtful consideration. The two sat in silence as the younger one cogitated. Jacques's eyes were cast down in the direction of his shoes until it was time to speak. "I think you'll need to remind me of this session, because I'm pretty dense. You might even have to slap me around a bit, you know, knock some sense into me."

"I have your permission then?"

"Yes. It might prove necessary. I really want to fall in love with the *right* girl."

"You've got a deal. I'll do it!"

Jacques laughed.

CHAPTER 5

Roof Garden Party

On a clear, sparkling Sunday early in the month of June, a small group of bright and sophisticated young women were seated in a circle on the high roof garden of a doorman building in Manhattan. It was Jennifer Slater's building, and it was Jennifer's engagement party for Meg and Dan. As Jennifer's capacity for preparing food was limited to boiling water, the party was catered. The festivities began at two in the afternoon. By four, most, if not quite all of the invited guests had arrived. About fifty guests sat or stood in small clusters scattered along the length and breath of an extensive roof. The area was fitted with groups of wooden chairs, which surrounded large coffee tables. Each cluster of people, chairs, and tables were separated from one another by a space of approximately thirty feet, far enough in the open air to provide a modicum of privacy to each group. It was the perfect setting for a party, with spectacular views of Central Park and the line of stately buildings that graced Upper Fifth Avenue on the East Side.

The circle of friends consisted of Jennifer and Meg, Hillary and Daryl, and Annie Giraud. With the exception of Annie, introduced to the others by Meg a year earlier and still on the periphery of the circle, the friends had known one another since college, or even earlier. They were familiar with each other's tics and idiosyncrasies; in short, it was a quite comfortable group of intimates. It was perfectly natural and even expectable that at some point during the party they would congregate and lose themselves in a discussion that, as often as not, would involve men. For the last few minutes the topic of conversation that engrossed the five young women was: *why are men afraid of commitment?* Annie, the youngest member, happily in her midtwenties, sought information from the one member of the group who wore the mantle of "expert."

"How did you do it, Meg? How did you convince Dan to commit?"

"It's a long story," Meg said in a voice suggestive more of levity than seriousness. "Dan did put up the usual guy resistance. You all know the dreary story—all the crap about needing 'space.' Then the answer came to me in a flash—you know, one of those eureka moments. Why not out-phobe the commitment phobe? So I began to ask for more space than *he* wanted. You see, girls, guys love a challenge. They go for the kind of girl who's hard to get. The harder she is to get, the more they prize her. After a while I had the poor man in a complete daze. So that's how I bedazzled him." Meg deliberately mispronounced the word *bedazzled* to rhyme with *daze*.

"But that's so unromantic. That's gamesmanship," Hillary protested. Hillary was the idealist of the group.

"Romance is an illusion," Jennifer retorted. "It all comes down to power." Jennifer was the group cynic.

"You're a cynic," Hillary said.

"I'm a realist. It's all about who has the upper hand."

Annie requested an explanation.

"It's simple; someone is going to be needier. That's the person who doesn't have the power."

"So why don't we just withhold sex? That way the guy's got to be the needier one," Daryl suggested.

"*You* withhold sex?" Jennifer said. It was a strictly rhetorical question.

"You know, we never have gotten around to answering the original question," said Annie. "Which is why men fear commitment."

"To be fair to the guys—" Daryl began, interrupted by cries of "No, no!"

"To be fair to the guys," she repeated, "not all of them have a fear of commitment. The ones who have a shitty relationship with their mother give the most trouble."

"A distinct majority of all men," Meg said.

"Hold on," said Jennifer after downing the remnants of her wine. "Is there anyone here who thinks women have no problem with commitment? Allow me to refine that question: is there anyone among us, beside Meg, who has actually made a commitment?"

"Sure," Daryl said, "I made a commitment to my last boyfriend."

"Bullshit, Daryl, bull ... shit," Jennifer said. "Making a commitment to a commitment-phobic asshole like you did doesn't count. It is null and void. When you make a commitment to a guy who's ready to commit, that's when it counts."

"What about you, Jennifer, are you ready for that?" Annie asked.

Jennifer was not surprised by the question, since she and Annie were only acquaintances. "I want to be, but I find the idea kind of scary."

"Why is that?" asked Annie.

"Well, Annie, it took eight years of therapy to figure out that I have the fear in the first place; it will probably take another eight years to figure out why. At any rate, my therapist doesn't seem to be in any rush. I'll say only this: it seems to me that you can't really know a person; I mean truly know his character. Choosing a guy to be your one and only is like throwing dice. It's a crapshoot. I know that explanation doesn't run very deep, but it's all I can come up with right now. By the way, what about your brother? Where is he, and where *is* he?"

"He said he'd be late. He *said* he'd be late."

"No, I mean where is he regarding this thorny issue of commitment?"

"Jacques? Jacques is a girlie man. He can hardly wait to find the right girl, settle down, and start a family. When he falls, he'll fall hard. I'm afraid he's too susceptible."

"How come he's still single then?" Hillary wanted to know.

"He's focused on his career, all work and hardly any play. So he's had limited experience. The last couple of years he's gotten more serious about meeting someone. Speaking of the devil, there he is now."

Annie rose to rush over to her brother, who had just arrived. He looked around for her, seeing her only as she approached. Jennifer stared intently to satisfy a growing curiosity. He was indeed very tall (all to the good), but in other ways not particularly impressive. With his too-formal cotton summer jacket and necktie, he had the look of a typically starchy academic. All the other men at the party had open collars and wore their shirtsleeves rolled up, as befitted such a warm day. His dark horn-rimmed glasses and slight stoop, plus the gravity of his expression, which looked as though he were entertaining thoughts regarding the meaning of life, gave him the aspect of an over serious intellectual. Too much gravitas! His nose was a little too prominent (even at a distance Jennifer could tell), his dark hair too perfectly in place (she preferred the slightly shaggy, unkempt look), his eyebrows in dire need of a trim, his ears much too large. Jennifer absorbed all this vital information in a matter of seconds and had sliced the man up: pigeonholed, neatly defined, and dismissed. Jennifer was in no rush to meet Jacques. *So much for Meg's talent as a matchmaker!*

"I wonder what the guys are talking about," Meg said as she glanced toward the nearest all-male group. The women took turns guessing the answer.

"Sports," said Daryl.

"Best beer," said Hillary.

"Most violent action film," said Meg."

"Ten best ways to avoid making a commitment," said Daryl."

Before long the little group of friends began to circulate. Jennifer's first objective was to studiously avoid speaking to her nemesis, her *bête noire*, her *persona non grata*, Felicia Star. She was almost as pretty, just as tall, more seductive with men. She was standing with Meg's fiancé and two other nondescript men a mere twenty feet away. Felicia possessed that bony, starved look that men inexplicably adored. Jennifer might have tolerated that most annoying fact were there no other reason for her marked antipathy toward the woman. Having met in a course on creative writing at Wesleyan, they had once been good friends. Both English Lit majors, they had found themselves sharing classes on several occasions. In her senior year Jennifer was dating the very desirable Ron Campbell, editor of the college newspaper, top gun on the school's debating team, and reputed "hunk." Felicia was dating a tide-her-over Mr. Nobody, a brainy but dull dweeb, in Felicia's declared opinion. Felicia suggested double dating. With considerable ill humor, Jennifer then witnessed her friend's overt flirtation with Ron. That would have harmlessly passed were it not for the fact that Ron and Felicia were seen walking arm in arm only two weeks after he broke up with Jennifer. "All's fair in love and war," was Felicia's response to Jennifer's accusation of boyfriend stealing. "Besides, I did you a favor. Obviously he didn't like you so much, or I wouldn't have been able to take him."

"Oh, you weren't trying to do me any favor; you were just thinking of yourself. I would never have done that to you, or to any friend. So you may consider our friendship over." And with that firm statement Jennifer had walked away.

Because Meg had insisted, she'd invited Felicia to the party, against her better judgment. Meg knew her from childhood; because her parents were close friends with Felicia's, it was impossible to not invite her.

Jennifer had protested, using her nickname for Felicia. "Fellatio is so phony, so affected. She's competitive and envious and self-important, an all-American bitch," Jennifer had declaimed to Meg, but to no avail.

"You're holding that against her?" was Meg's facetious (and disappointing) reply.

Jennifer moved far away from Felicia at the party and spent

her time flitting from one conversation to another until she crossed paths with Hillary. Hillary was excited.

"I just met a fabulous guy."

"Really? Who? Where?"

"He left. He had to meet a friend at a movie. He asked for my number."

"What movie?"

"I don't know. What difference does that make, Jen?"

"It tells you about his tastes. Suppose he's going to see *Son of Godzilla*? Would you want to date a guy who would go to a movie like that?"

"Jen, you're too much. This guy has brains and taste."

"Promise?"

"I promise."

"Okay, tell me about him. What's his name?"

"Doug Rothstein. You must know him—you invited him."

"Yes, I do. Seems like a very likeable, interesting guy. You should definitely check him out."

"How come you never checked him out?"

"Too short."

Hillary was ten inches shorter than Jennifer. His short stature made no difference to her.

Jennifer's eyes shifted from her friend to Annie and her brother. They were in conversation, their eyes pointed in her direction. As her eyes met Jacques's he turned slightly to face his sister. It was not an unfamiliar occurrence for others to talk about Jen or look at her from a distance. In fact she expected it, and sometimes she complained about it to whoever would listen. "Oh, to be short, fat, and ugly, and so, so, *obscure*," she once said to Meg.

"Sure, and then you'd complain about that."

Jennifer wondered what Annie was saying about her. Would she disclose that little snippet of conversation they'd had only a short time ago, the one about Jennifer's fear of commitment?

Jacques and Annie began to walk toward her. As they approached, Jennifer averted her eyes and turned to face

Hillary. When they arrived, Annie introduced her brother. Jacques complimented Jennifer on the party and remarked what a great place it was for it. "Ordered the weather too, did you? You've done well for Meg."

Jennifer thanked him but said nothing more. She knew instantly that he was interested in her. If men only knew how they give themselves away. A certain tension radiated from his body, and something about his speech seemed forced, as though he were struggling to find something—anything—to say. She felt in control at once.

"I understand you're a book editor, Jennifer. What kind of books?" His eyes never left hers.

"Fiction. Quality fiction."

"As opposed to junk fiction?" Jacques asked, trying his hand at a little humor.

Jennifer thought he was trying too hard. "Junk is okay, as long as it's quality junk," she answered, her voice self-assured.

"Quality junk? That has a funny ring to it."

"Don't you just love an oxymoron?" Jennifer said brightly, easily. She turned to Annie. "I think you're getting a burn, Annie. Your face is a little red. I believe Daryl has some lotion. She's so light-skinned. I'll get it for you."

"I'll get it," Annie quickly replied.

"That's okay. I need to speak with her anyway. Nice meeting you, Jacques. See you later, Hill," she said to Hillary, who had been watching the conversation quietly. And with a slight nod in Jacques's direction she glided away toward a distant group, where Daryl was conversing with Meg and her fiancé.

When Jennifer moved to the open bar later, Hillary approached her again.

"What if he doesn't call?"

Jennifer was pouring a container of orange juice into a glass filled with ice. Hillary, recognizing Jennifer's superior experience, tended to use Jennifer as an advisor on matters of the heart.

"Who?"

"Doug Rothstein."

"Why don't you wait ten days and then ask me again."

"Okay, but then should I call him?"

"No, you wait another ten days."

"And then?"

"Then you follow Jennifer Slater's first rule."

"Which is?"

"You say to yourself, fuck 'em!"

Hillary was clearly unhappy with that. "Don't you think I should call him at least once?"

"What for?"

"To show him that I'm interested."

"He knows that already. If he doesn't call, he's not interested, so what do you gain by calling, except maybe a little humiliation? No guy is worth that. Why are we talking about this now, Hill? He likes you. That's why he asked for your number. He will call."

"Okay, but suppose it takes him a month?"

"A month? That's practically a lifetime. Why are you asking?"

"Because it's happened to me before."

"If he takes that long, you give him a very hard time."

"How?"

"You pretend to draw a blank when he tells you his name. He tells you how he met you. You tell him you met several guys at that party, and you ask him what he looks like. He'll describe himself, but he won't mention that he's short."

"He's not so short. He didn't look short to me."

"That's because you're only five feet. Everyone looks tall to you. I must look like a Cyclops."

"I'm over five feet," Hillary protested.

"Did I just insult you? I didn't intend to. Hey, we're opposite sides of the same coin. I worried about every inch I grew, and you worried about every inch you didn't grow. I know how you feel, and I also know how Rothstein must feel. He is at most five feet six, and that's giving him the benefit of the doubt."

"How do you know he won't tell me he's short?"

"Short guys never do. It's not one of their favorite topics. So after he describes himself you say, 'Oh yeah, now I remember—the short guy.'"

"How will that help me with him?"

"Guys think more highly of girls who squeeze their nuts."

"I don't think I can do that."

"Why not?"

"Because I know what it's like to be short."

The remark stunned Jennifer and momentarily left her mute. She reached out and touched her friend's arm. "You know, I think some day you'll make a better person out of me. That's my hope, Hill, that some of your goodness will eventually rub off. Forget my advice. What would you like to say to him?"

"I would like to say that I was disappointed that he waited so long."

"Then that's what you should say."

"But he may not like that."

"Then that's when Jennifer's fuck-'em rule applies. Listen, girl, you have to be yourself. That's why taking my advice won't work." As Jennifer said this she instantly recognized its absolute validity. They were different people, and Jennifer could not elude the feeling that she would be better off being more like Hillary.

The conversation continued and broadened into an investigation of Hillary's low self-esteem, and Jennifer noted an unpleasant sight in her peripheral vision. Felicia was talking to Jacques. The temptress must have swooped down upon the unsuspecting would-be victim while Jennifer was engaged elsewhere. Initially she thought very little of it; it was probably a chance encounter, nothing more. She didn't think Felicia would be interested in Jacques. She liked handsome men with some money and a certain savoir-faire. But as the minutes rolled by she grew increasingly alarmed. They might be coupling off! That thought made all the difference. He might be far from the man of her dreams, but his attractiveness increased geometrically with each minute that he spent with that treacherous viper. Jolted into action, she strode with firm purpose over to the new "couple."

"Hello again," Jennifer said breezily to Jacques. She waved hello to Felicia. Jacques offered a faint smile and a slight nod. She immediately picked up on his coolness. Felicia frowned. Jennifer had no idea what the two were talking about, and she could not have cared less.

"I understand you're a professor of English literature," Jennifer said.

"Yes, I teach the nineteenth-century novel. Have the two of you met?"

"Oh yes," Felicia swiftly replied, winking at Jennifer. "We were in the same year at Wesleyan, and we did some heavy carousing together, etcetera, etcetera."

"And we will never reveal the true meaning of that etcetera," Jennifer added.

"I'm all envy," Jacques said. "I wish I had sown some wild oats in college. I was too preoccupied with books and studies."

"We read our books too," Jennifer said, "but we reserved a little time to be wild."

"I hear you still are," Felicia said.

Jennifer experienced a sudden urge to retaliate. If Jacques had not been present, she might have said, "I'll bet a thousand bucks you've dropped your thong far more than I have." The words were virtually begging to spring from her lips. Exercising self-restraint, Jennifer turned from Felicia to address Jacques, who had been looking from one to the other.

"How does it feel to be face to face with a genuine, bona fide wild girl?"

"I'd say it makes you more interesting."

Jennifer didn't know how to take that. She was more interesting than what? Than she had been before? She sensed that she had lost ground with Jacques and might have a problem making it up.

"Jacques teaches a course on Jane Austen," Felicia said, seeming to be in a hurry to change the subject.

"Well, that must be popular."

"Very popular with the girls, much less so with the boys. I think Austen's focus on relationships bores them."

"Not this boy, apparently," Jennifer said, pointing at Jacques's chest.

"Yes, but it puts me at odds with my gender. I think maybe I should be teaching novels about serial killers instead of chick lit. When I went to a Super Bowl party last winter and told some of the guys that I teach Jane Austen, they looked at me like I was from outer space."

"Well, you are a bit of a freak, you know. The next thing, you'll be telling us that you prefer reading a novel to going to a Super Bowl party," Jennifer said.

"It's true, and it's very sad for me," Jacques answered, pretending to look sad. "Felicia and I were talking about Austen's novel *Mansfield Park* before you came over. Since that's one of the novels I teach I was interested in her point of view. Have you read it?"

"I have, yes, but at least three or four years ago. What is your view of it?" she asked Felicia as she turned toward her. Felicia was no slouch when it came to books. As a literary agent, books were her stock in trade.

"It's my least favorite of the three Austen novels I've read."

"Really? I thought it was wonderful. What didn't you like about it?"

"The leading character, Fanny Price. I couldn't identify with her. She was a bland and timid Austen heroine. Perhaps that says something about Jane Austen. I know she was the moral center of the story, but I found her terribly boring."

"Jane Austen's mother agreed with you," Jacques said. "She referred to Fanny as insipid. And she was nobody's fool."

To Jennifer's surprise Jacques seemed to be agreeing with Felicia.

"But that's the fun of the book," Jennifer protested. "Austen created a heroine with flaws. She's a bore who can distinguish between right and wrong and whose heart is in the right place.

And that contrasts with the other key character, Mary— Uh oh, what was her name?"

"Mary Crawford," Jacques replied.

"Yes, thank you—Mary Crawford, who is witty, interesting, and full of life. I loved that character, even though she was shallow."

"You always had a preference for style over substance," Felicia said.

"It's true I don't run as deep as you, but my preference is actually for style *and* substance. I was about to say that while Mary is a fascinating woman, she is not able to distinguish right from wrong. That's the contrast with Fanny. If only Fanny had Mary's personality and Mary had Fanny's moral perspective, then you would have the perfect woman."

Jacques, appearing uneasy, spoke up.

"You know I've been looking for just such a woman, but my therapist says I'm whistling in the dark."

"What a cynical professor. There are perfect women everywhere," Felicia said.

Jennifer took that as sarcasm, although it occurred to her that Felicia might be referring to herself. Jennifer looked at Jacques. He was smiling and looking directly at Felicia. *Have I lost the game?* She had a sinking feeling that he liked Felicia and imagined the two of them going off together. How would that feel? She had actually begun to like him and to believe that her negative first impression had been hasty. Judging too quickly was a nasty habit of hers, and as much as she tried to change it, she continued to fall into it. Was this another example?

"What about you, Jacques? You haven't expressed any opinion about the novel," Jennifer said.

"I think you both have excellent points."

Jennifer didn't think Felicia's point was excellent at all. Was he partial toward her?

"But you shouldn't judge a novel by whether you like or don't like the characters," he continued. "Do the characters seem real? Do they behave consistently through the novel? Has the author plumbed the depths of her characters? I could go on, but then you'd find me tedious. I'll just say that in my opinion *Mansfield Park* is indeed a great novel, which, by the way, is why I teach it. I should add that there are some who disagree."

Yes! Maybe I still have a chance, thought Jennifer.

At that moment Meg arrived, announcing that she and Dan were planning to leave.

"Me too—I have to go," Felicia said. "Would you happen to be going downtown?" she asked Jacques.

"Actually, I need Jacques to help us with the engagement gifts. We have to carry them to Dan's car," Jennifer said quickly.

"I'll be glad to help too," Felicia said.

"Oh, no, that won't be necessary. Jacques's sister volunteered to help, so we have five. More than enough."

"Well, it was a pleasure meeting you, Jacques," Felicia said, removing her oversized sunglasses for the first time. "I hope we have an opportunity to meet again. And if you recommend a book to read from one of your courses, I'll promise to do that." Felicia extended her hand to Jacques. He took it and gave it two vigorous shakes. Jennifer held her breath, her eyes glued to Jacques.

"It was fun. I'm sure we will meet again," Jacques said.

Jennifer exhaled. "It was fun for me too," Jennifer said to Felicia. Then she walked away with Jacques and Meg.

Jennifer was too superb a tactician to prematurely celebrate a tactical success. There were other ways for Jacques to secure Felicia's telephone number. Nor would she put it past Felicia to find an excuse to call Jacques. Jennifer's fervent imagination invented a make-believe scene:

"Jacques, it's Felicia. I got your number from Meg. The reason for my call is you mentioned that you teach a course on Dickens. I have a friend in graduate school who has to write a paper on Dickens's *David Copperfield*. Would it be okay if she called you to talk about it? Great. How have you been?"

That bitch. Jennifer considered the imagined telephone call as good as made. She would have to take steps to secure Jacques's interest.

After the engagement gifts had been loaded into Dan's car and the couple departed, Annie jumped into a cab that also sped off. Jacques and Jennifer stood on the sidewalk. It was still light outside, the lion's share of the evening before them. Jennifer looked at her companion. He seemed disinclined to talk and a trifle uneasy. Perhaps he was thinking about Felicia and feeling trapped. Had she really bested her old enemy, or only outmaneuvered her? For once her intuition deserted her. She needed to find the answer to that question. Having begun to like Jacques and feeling responsible for his seeming aloofness, she needed to know exactly where she stood with him.

CHAPTER 6

Jennifer and Jacques

It was not typical for Jennifer to be at such a loss regarding a man's intentions. Jacques's posture, his mute inscrutability were no help to her. There they stood on the sidewalk in front of Jennifer's building, sixteen floors below the roof garden where they first met, facing one another and saying nothing. His silence made her uneasy.

"I actually live here, Jacques. Would you like to come up for a drink?

"I'd love to," Jacques said, his face brightening sweetly. To Jennifer, it was a very reassuring look. Perhaps she hadn't blown it after all. She felt instantly better.

"Come," Jennifer said, extending her hand to him. He took her hand in his and allowed her to guide him past the doorman to the elevator and up to her apartment on the third floor. They entered a small foyer and then immediately were in the living room. The room, an unusual oval shape, had furniture that was tasteful and obviously expensive. Twentieth-century art decorated walls painted a light shade of lime green.

Jacques's eyes alighted on the art. "Who's this artist?" he asked, pointing to a lithograph with abstract lines sketched in black and white.

"That's an Ellsworth Kelly," she said.

"What is it?"

"What do you think?"

"Frankly, it looks like an anus."

"Well, you're close. I believe it's the leaf of a melon. You have quite an imagination, Jacques."

"Failed every Rorschach test I ever took. Wow! That's a Warhol," Jacques said in some wonder, pointing to a piece next to the Kelly. "That's got to be worth a few bucks."

"Sure, but it's not the most valuable piece here." She took him over to an adjacent wall.

"Jean-Michele Basquiat," Jacques read. "It looks like the sort of thing a kid could have painted."

"Well, a painting's value is not strictly dependent on its quality. In the case of Basquiat, his life story enhances the value."

Jacques looked at Jennifer in an inquiring way.

"He was a high school dropout, never received any art instruction, but managed to convince a famous art dealer to let him live and work in his home in Venice. Basquiat had a girlfriend who went by the name of Madonna who lived with him. Of course, that was before anyone ever heard of her. Perhaps most important of all, he died very young, I think before he reached thirty."

"Why's that so important?"

"There's not a lot of his stuff out there."

"How do you know so much about this?"

"Stepfather. This all belongs to him."

Jacques turned from the art to the room itself. The aged oak floor was decorated with the muted earth colors of a Persian rug. A lovely marble fireplace graced one wall, and the artificial logs that lay in a container on the side conveyed that the fireplace worked. Moldings along the edges of the ceiling demonstrated a quiet, charming age.

"Is this a rental?"

"It's a condo."

"How many rooms do you have?"

"Seven."

"Excuse me. Did you say you were an editor for a publishing house, or did you say you owned the publishing house?"

Jennifer laughed. "It's my stepfather's condo, and most of the stuff in it is his too, except for a few odds and ends. The living room couch is mine. That's the only major object that belongs to me."

"So he lets you stay here temporarily?"

"Not exactly, no. He's a very rich man, as you may have already guessed. He once owned a fleet of tugboats, sold it for an astounding amount, and became an art dealer, his one true love. He and my mom have a house in Greenwich that's like a palace and another apartment in Soho, a fabulous loft. If you think this place is nice, you should see their loft; it's an architect's dream. So this is mine, although he still owns it. He's promised it as a wedding gift. There's no mortgage, only maintenance, which I pay. How's that for an inducement to wed?"

"Let's get married then."

"Hey, I'll give it careful consideration. Why don't you sit and make yourself at home? Can I get you something? Coffee, tea, beer?"

Jacques opted for decaffeinated coffee and followed her to the kitchen to help her prepare it. The kitchen, which possessed expensive, up-to-date utilities, was large enough to accommodate a table, although there was none; marble counters and oak cabinets gave the room a modern look. The apartment was a combination of the very old and the new.

"Do you like teaching?" she asked as she leaned against the stove. It was the only sound against the drip-drip of the coffee machine.

Jacques, standing just a few feet from her, replied, "I love teaching. I love scholarship and writing too."

"Teaching is one thing I never thought of doing. I don't know why it never appealed to me."

"Maybe you don't realize how much there is to it. Helping students to read critically instead of just for entertainment is quite a challenge. They enter my class not understanding the difference between great literature and mediocre literature. So they learn to read with a discerning eye, to appreciate nuance and subtlety, to read between the lines to catch the author's intent and meaning. It's the sort of thing that will serve them throughout their lives. They learn to think about values, about what really matters."

"Okay," she laughed, and she threw her hands up as if to say, "Enough."

"Sorry," he apologized. "I have this bad habit of overselling. I lapse into my professorial ways."

"No need to apologize; I'm convinced. You see, in my line of work one doesn't often get to read what you would call great literature. The stuff I get to read is either good, which I define as publishable, or not good. The lion's share falls into the latter category. If I read one manuscript a year that I deem to be truly great, I consider myself fortunate."

The coffee ready, they adjourned to the living room, bringing along cups, saucers, spoons, a pitcher of milk, and sugar. He removed his jacket and hung it on the back of a chair. She deliberately avoided offering to hang it in a closet. That would give the impression of a lengthier stay than she intended. They sat on opposite ends of Jennifer's one possession, a beige Ultrasuede couch. She drew her legs on to the couch after flipping off her shoes and demurely pulled the hem of her dress as far over her knees as it went. She held her legs modestly together. She had not the slightest urge to tempt him.

After they settled and began sipping their coffee, Jacques spoke. "May I ask you a personal question?"

She made a gesture of consent.

"What was going on between you and Felicia?"

"I was wondering whether you noticed."

"How could I not? It was pretty clear."

"We were good friends in college, until she stole my boyfriend from me. We've been very cold to one another since." Jennifer decided to keep it simple; no need for sordid details.

"I understand your anger, but not hers. She was the perpetrator. I would think she'd feel guilt, not anger."

"You'll have to ask her about that," she said, forgoing an opportunity to savage Felicia. "By the way, did I interrupt something between the two of you? Did you want to take her home?"

"I'm where I want to be," he said.

"Oh." Now she was sure. The look on his face, the slight smile, the intensity of those large brown eyes behind the glasses that said much more than words could. The question now was what to do about it. There was something very nice about him; his earnestness and directness were endearing characteristics. She had a sense that nothing was camouflaged with him; it was all out there, in front. It was refreshingly different and new. But did she like him enough? She remembered the first time she met Allan, how turned on and eager she felt. She could hardly wait to see him again. Just thinking about him sent tingles up and down her spine. With Jacques it was not nearly the same. Her feelings were more friendly. She had the feeling that she could never fall in love with him, no matter how much she liked him.

"This is going to be a short evening," she told him. "I have an early morning meeting tomorrow, so I need to turn in at an ungodly early hour." It was a lie, but she knew it would do. She did not want him to have the wrong idea about her.

"That's fine," Jacques responded, a curious smile crossing his face. "I have an early class. You know, I actually took a dislike to Felicia. I felt she was insulting to you in a crude kind of way. At the time I figured she was pissed at you for something, but of course I had no idea what that was. In fact, when we were leaving, I was headed in the same direction as she was, downtown to the Path train, so I would have been stuck with her if you hadn't saved my life." Jacques said this with an amused smile on his face.

She liked him more. "Tell the truth, Jacques; you didn't like her because of her opinion of Jane Austen's novel."

"God! You see right through me," he said with smiling eyes. "Another personal question?" he asked.

"It seems those are the only ones you ask."

"Just say no if I get too intrusive. My question is a little bit off the beaten path. It has nothing to do with Felicia or anything else we've been talking about. It's just a curiosity I have."

"Okay, go for it."

"How come there's no mortgage on this apartment? I'm green with envy."

"Are you telling me that you're not interested in me for myself; it's just my apartment that you're after?"

"Hey, this is Manhattan. Apartments are more important than people."

She laughed. He had a sense of humor.

"Pops always pays in full with cash. Saves him a lot of money. I don't take after him."

"Who does?"

As the last light of day fled from the room, a dark shadow settled across Jacques's face, and the living room took on a tenebrous gloom. She rose to bring a candle over to the coffee table, continuing the conversation as she lit the wick. She returned to her place on the couch, carefully retaining exactly the same distance from him as before. Jacques's face was now bathed in the golden glow of candlelight, which softened his features. She thought he looked *almost* handsome.

"I take it you're close to Pops?"

"Absolutely. He's a fabulous man. Best of all, he adores me. When I first met him, I gave him a hard time. I wasn't going to let him in because I already had a father. But he never gave up, and eventually he wore me down. I think I speak to him more often than to my mother. I'm actually closer to him in a way than to my dad, although I love Dad too. I'm a lucky girl having two fathers for the price of one."

"Two good men in your life. Do you have room for one more?"

"Haven't made room so far."

Jacques frowned and changed his position on the couch. "How old were you when your parents divorced?"

"Whatever happened to small talk?"

"For me this is small talk," Jacques said.

"And what do you call talking about the weather?"

"I call it talking about nothing at all."

Jennifer conceded the point. "I was twelve, almost thirteen, and Pops appeared a year later."

"Not a great way to begin your teens."

"Actually, their divorce was a relief. I know that surprises people. Everyone thinks I should have been traumatized. I was traumatized—by the marriage, that is. All they ever did was quarrel; and my mom could get really mean when she was angry. She was on his back all the time. So when he decided to split I thought it was good for him."

"It's pretty clear who you favor."

"I suppose that is pretty clear. Growing up, he was my buddy. I felt he understood me, and even when he didn't he tried. Mother was another story. We didn't get along; you might say it was love-hate. Dad was more accepting of my misdeeds, and I knew his heart was in the right place. I didn't feel that way about my mom. She was just so judgmental."

As she talked, Jacques gave her the impression of rapt attention. That was one of the things she noticed about him. He seemed to hang on her every word.

"What misdeeds?" he asked with a mischievous grin.

"None of your business," she said with a laugh.

"I'll get it out of you."

"Not."

"Have you ever heard of water boarding?"

She laughed.

"Didn't you ever have good times with your mother?"

"Not that I can remember. What I remember are the diatribes. I had fun with my father," she said. "He was a great tennis player, captain of his college team. And after college he worked as tennis pro at a country club for a couple of years. He taught me to love the game."

"So you must be good."

"For sure," she boasted.

"I'm a pretty fair player myself. We should play some time."

She shook her head. "I don't recommend it."

"Why?"

"Guys don't generally like being soundly thrashed by a girl. You know, the macho thing; they feel castrated. It's kind of pathetic."

It was his turn to laugh. "I'll make a deal with you," he said as he reached out and lightly touched her arm. It was the first time he had touched her. She was not alarmed.

"Oh, yes, please. I love deals."

"I'll risk castration if you risk humiliation."

"You're on!" Those little words told a story. She realized that she was agreeing to see him again. She realized as well that it was no unwitting blunder. *I want to see him again.* How had that happened? She was enjoying his company, although it wasn't a romantic thing; that had not changed for her. She liked him and felt at ease with him. He was intense, to be sure, more so than she had experienced before, but she judged him to be a man of substance, sincere and well-intended. As time went by he seemed more relaxed, less starchy. His sense of humor made an appearance. Besides, she didn't have any male friends. Until now she'd never thought of men that way. They were either prospective loves or they were nothing.

She asked him whether he wanted more coffee, and when he answered affirmatively she left for the kitchen to prepare it.

"You might do something productive while I'm making your coffee," she called out to him.

He asked what that was.

"Like practice your tennis. God knows you'll need to."

"Pretty sure of yourself, aren't you?" he called back.

"Uh huh."

When she returned with his coffee, she found him standing up, practicing his backhand with a pretend racket. She laughed so hard she nearly spilled the coffee.

"So are you very athletic?" she asked.

He replied that he had been on the track team in college. He was a good athlete, but not a great one.

"Did you ever go horseback riding?" she asked.

"No. In my family we bet on horses, we don't ride them."

She enjoyed his response. "We did that too. Dad used to take me to the racetrack. It was always so exciting. Oh, I loved it. I think I've got a little bit of the gambler in my soul. Some of my best memories are about our times at the track. He was always in such a great mood."

"Have you been there recently?"

"No, not in quite a while. Dad's remarried and lives in New Jersey, in Cape May. His wife has no interest in it. Even if she did it wouldn't be the same. Three's a crowd, you know."

"I'm guessing you're not too fond of her."

"She's a total bore. All she talks about are bad movies and celebrity gossip."

"What does your father see in her?"

"I think it's mostly sex. She's barely over five feet, but she's all tits and ass—just his type.

"You know, you look sad when you talk about him."

That surprised her. She had not been aware of any particular feelings. She averted her eyes, as though concealing something. She stared at her toes instead. They were painted a light shade of pink.

"You miss going to the track with him, don't you?"

Now *he* looked sad.

"That and other things," she said softly.

"Do you get to see him much?"

"Not too much. Barbara—that's my stepmother—doesn't like coming to New York; it's too noisy and confusing for her. And she has no interest in silly things like great museums, art, or theater," she said sarcastically. "So I take myself down there a couple of times a year." She sensed that she was revealing a little more than she wanted to. He was just so easy to talk to. She noticed that his ears weren't really that large for a big man.

Talking about her stepmother usually put her in a bad mood, and she was beginning to fall into one.

"I'd like to take you to the track. Will you let me?"

She raised her head to look directly into his face. He meant it; she had no doubt about that. She had a premonition that he meant everything he said, unlike most guys she knew.

"Sure, but only if you promise to go horseback riding with me first," she said in a voice indicative of a sudden lightening of mood. Seeing his hesitation, she urged him to consider it. It would be fun, she reassured him.

"Your dad taught you that too?"

She nodded.

"I didn't think there were any more stables in the city."

"There are, just not in Manhattan."

He nodded. "So let me understand this, Jennifer. You will come to the track with me, but only on condition that I put my life in grave jeopardy first. Is that the bargain?"

"Excuse me, but are you implying that I'm not worth risking your life for?"

He laughed. "You're on!" he said.

That brought a smile to her face. Her mood lifted further. She could never get guys to go riding with her. Allan refused to even discuss it. Meg and her other friends had no interest. She went a few times by herself, but it wasn't as much fun. She was a gregarious woman and wanted company.

They were silent for a time while he sipped his coffee. He looked at her and smiled coyly, and she recognized that she had already committed to three dates: tennis, racetrack, and horseback riding. They had come a long way since she invited him to her apartment. Of course, she could always change her mind. There was no real commitment. The problem for her was that she looked forward to spending the time with him. There was something indefinable about him. What was it? She thought it was a safety factor. Yes, that was it, she felt safe with him. She was sure that he was absolutely in to her. But why? Was it a purely physical thing, a strong sexual attraction that drew him to her? Then that would make him like other men, not really interested in her, the person, the woman, the human being. Yet he did seem interested in her.

As they talked Jennifer was dimly aware of the passage of time; the evening had gone on far later than she originally intended. Since he made no move to leave, it was up to her to bring down the curtain on this particular little theater. But the time never seemed quite right; the conversation was too engaging, the man too guilelessly charming, to break it off. Deeper into the night, she became aware that she needed to break things off. It wouldn't be good to give him the wrong idea. If only he looked like Allan, she might have taken him to bed.

"What a lovely time I've had," she told him as he stood at the door.

"Me too. And I'm serious about that date at the races."

"Only after I've throttled you at tennis."

They prattled on, seemingly reluctant to say goodnight. She wondered whether he planned to kiss her.

"Well, I guess I'd better go."

She nodded.

He moved toward her and stopped. She took a step toward him, stepping out of the doorway. She smiled at him, and he kissed her on the lips. He lingered there only a second or two.

"I'll call soon," he said.

She knew he would, and he did.

CHAPTER 7

To Have Nerve or to Have It Not

All those lunches twice weekly, three weeks running, had finally paid off. "Let me make dinner for you," Amanda said memorably one rainy afternoon. Harry could vividly recall the mixture of excitement and nervousness he felt. Were those two very separate emotions somehow connected? Could the one have evoked the other? When was the last time he felt this excited about a woman? The emotion felt foreign, almost out of place. As he walked back to his office, hunched into his raincoat and holding a wobbly umbrella, he thought about Amanda's invitation. What did it really signify? Was he getting ahead of himself here, reading into it something that wasn't actually there? That question endlessly gnawed at him. So unsure was Harry that he ran the question by Herbie, his older brother.

"Looks good," Herbie said in his perfectly succinct way. "Seize the day." Good old Herbie, ever the optimist, had served as a surrogate father ever since Harry's real father had left the family when Harry was fourteen.

Harry was in his small West Village apartment, preparing to dress for his trip to Amanda's Upper East Side brownstone residence. What to wear? The seemingly simple matter became a prime source of indecision. Should he go formal or casual? Formal, which meant at the very least a tie, could reflect badly, old and old-fashioned. To be sure, casual was better, particularly in this warm weather, but he wanted to take care not to dress too young. That could be interpreted as pretentious. Needless to say, a fifty-eight-year-old man should not dress like a teenager. *Scrap the jeans.*

Each new item of apparel provoked a new agony of doubt and indecision. Should he wear a white shirt? Should it have long sleeves or short? And then there was the matter of two days growth of stubble. Should he shave? Would Amanda see through the affectation of rugged manliness, or would she think him ruggedly handsome? Getting ready was taking too damned long; time was running out. That too suggested a question: should he arrive on time or fashionably late? And how late was that? Didn't a dinner invitation when a meal was being readied require promptness?

Harry sat down on his bed, a look of dismay crossing his face. He thought of Sarah, his late wife. How strange it was to be thinking of another woman, to be excited by the thought of her, of being with her, of making love to Amanda. No, not making love—fucking. "Unreal," he said aloud. He felt he was about to commit adultery, as foolish as that sounded. He wished it could be Sarah, wished she were alive and they could start over, that it could be like it was the first time. In his way he kept her alive. How often did he conduct make-believe conversations with his dead wife? As a self-aware man, it seemed to him that he needed her almost as much in death as in life. This continual imaginary dialogue in some ineffable way aided him in navigating life's strains and stresses. She was so practical, so hardheaded and smart. She was his ghost consultant. What would she think about Amanda?

"There's something I need from you, sweetheart," she said toward the very end of her life. "I need you to go on now, to find your happiness. I need you to keep on dancing for both of us." He'd broken down then. Possibly her words reminded him of her imminent death, something he had fought mightily to deny. Possibly it was her selflessness, the most salient feature of her character, that came shining through her words, only to remind him of how much he was about to lose.

And what would she have said about the concern voiced by Izzy, that iconic figure of an analyst's analyst? A sexual connection between mentor and student was frowned upon in Harry's professional circle. Matters of the heart (and bed) typically become public information before long, for people love to gossip, and secrets have a way of being exposed. What would Sarah think of that?

He pulled himself away from the thought, away from the sadness. *No sense going there now.* Every memory of her, even the sweetest ones, was imbued with the bitterness of loss. Despite the pain, he was trapped in the memories.

Now it was time to think about Amanda. When was the last time he had a home-cooked meal? He couldn't remember. Harry always loved to cook, had in fact made many a meal for his wife and himself. Now he never cooked. Her death removed the purpose from it. "You've got to stop," he told himself forcefully. "Stop thinking about Sarah." Perhaps he wasn't anxious about his clothes after all. Perhaps the thought of being with Amanda was displaced on to what he should wear. Amanda. Would it really happen, or was he fooling himself? Did he want it to happen? Did she actually want it to happen? *A dinner invitation is hardly proof positive.* Harry had a sense of something major impending, for good or for ill. How would he feel at the end of the evening? He began dressing more quickly, as if the recognition of where his anxiety truly belonged helped break a barrier.

On the train to Amanda's he almost traveled past his stop. He leaped from his seat at the last moment to bolt through the open doors just before they closed. "Get a grip," he told himself. "It's not like you're going to your doom." These pep talks sometimes helped; sometimes they didn't. He wished he had dated before this, wished he had coerced himself to meet women. Maybe even to have had sex, just to prove to himself that it was possible without falling apart with guilt, to prove to himself that he could still do it, that the equipment worked with another woman. Wouldn't this be easier if he had done that?

She greeted him with a warm smile and a kiss on the lips. The odd mixture of excitement and nerves reappeared. Would it ever leave him? She wore a knee-length beige dress that becomingly accentuated her perfect figure: the slender waist, broader hips, and shapely, muscular legs. Clearly the woman worked out. The loveliness of her appearance was no help to his nerves. He thought of what to say to her. Could he compliment her without appearing too obvious? The last thing he wanted was to make her uncomfortable, to have her regret making the dinner invitation.

"You look so handsome," she said to him, her smile brightening further.

"Thank you," he said, startled by the unexpected compliment, and then he weakly offered, "You look wonderful yourself."

"Would you like to open that?" she said referring to the bottle of wine he had offered to her. He nodded and followed her into the kitchen. Kitchen, dining area, and living room were open, giving the viewer a sense of ample space. In a house this old, the space was clearly a somewhat recent renovation.

"What a lovely place you have," Harry said. As he stepped into the kitchen he immediately picked up the fragrance of roasting veal. She thanked him as she handed over a corkscrew.

"Why don't you open that in the dining room and pour us both a glass. I have a few more things to do here, but everything will be ready shortly."

"You're evicting me from the kitchen?"

"Well, yes, I am. It's too hot and too small a space."

"You think it's too small a space for two people?"

She looked at him. "Yes, a bit."

He shook his head.

"That's a problem?" she asked.

"The old fear of intimacy," he drawled. His eyes drifted downward and his head slowly shook from side to side, as if a gesture of resigned pity.

Her spontaneous laugh told him she understood he was

joking. Humor worked for Harry. It loosened him up and allowed him to take himself less seriously. In fact, her laugh brought about a marked diminution of tension. He wondered whether the word *intimacy* sounded like a tiny flirtation. Would it be wrong if it did?

"I hope you like an Australian shiraz," he said as he started to leave the kitchen.

"I'm not much of a wine buff, Harry. I couldn't tell the difference between that and anything else."

Harry walked into the dining area and opened the wine; he set it down on the table without filling the glasses. He felt good that he had made her laugh. He looked across at the hostess working so efficiently in the kitchen. Her back was turned toward him, affording him an unobstructed view of her lissome figure, the outlines of which were clearly discernible within the tight dress. As he watched, his mind conjured a picture of her standing naked, moving here and there, hips and buttocks in graceful motion as she completed the preparations for the meal. He stayed with the reverie, momentarily losing himself in it. It took him to a different emotional place from the one he had only recently inhabited; fears, doubts, conflicts all vanished, until he was jolted from the fantastical vision by unexpected words.

"What are you smiling about, Harry?" She had turned and caught him off guard.

"I was imagining you naked and thinking what a fabulous, sexy ass you have," were the words he never spoke. He could never be that bold, that outrageous. (What if he had been? How would she have reacted? Would she have been scandalized? Embarrassed? Appalled? Pleased? He didn't have a clue.)

"I was imagining what I was about to receive."

"You mean ... dinner?"

"It smells so good." He thought it was an odd question for her to ask. What else could it be about beside dinner? He thought about the way she posed the question. Was she flirting with him, or was he foolishly reading significance into an ordinary, innocent question? Yet her hesitation between the words *mean* and *dinner* gave him pause. Perhaps there was a tacit "or me?" there? Just the possibility of it put him on edge.

She arrived shortly with their food. He poured the wine.

It may have been a delicious meal, but Harry was oblivious to the taste of the food, although he complimented her. Throughout the meal they talked about many things, about their grown children, about parenting and its terrors and confusions; they talked about their work, about its terrors and confusions, but they did not talk about what Harry wanted to talk about. *Ah, that tiresome elephant in the room.*

When the meal finished, Amanda began clearing the table.

"May I help you with that?" he felt called upon to ask.

"Mmm. Can I risk the intimacy? Okay, I'll be daring," she teased.

She is adorable.

They piled the dishes in the sink. He began to rinse. As he handed each dish over to her he stole a look. She noticed and smiled shyly at him as she placed the dishes in the dishwasher: a friendly smile, a seductive smile? How should he read it? They were a cooperating team as they continued to clean dishes and counters and then put things away in cupboards. How often had he shared these tasks with Sarah? Their house in the country contained a much larger kitchen, but they were often side by side, working away, cooking or cleaning, or sometimes just talking, their faces inches apart, as they waited for something to get done, whether it was water to boil or eggs to be cooked. How strange it seemed to be with someone other than Sarah.

"Thank you for helping," Amanda said.

"Thank you for coping with your fear of intimacy," he countered.

"It was tough. Shall we?" She pointed to the other room.

They settled on the large couch in the living room. Harry poured more wine for both of them. "Don't worry, I won't spill it."

"What makes you think I'd be worried?"

"Sarah always used to worry about that—you know, wine stains, especially red wine."

"Well, perhaps your couch was more expensive than mine."

Harry doubted that.

After a few moments of awkward silence, she asked him about his most interesting session of the week. This was a little tradition they had during their twice-weekly lunches. One would describe a recent "interesting" session, and in the following meeting the other would take a turn. It was Harry's turn. As he had many patients, he needed to think carefully about which one to present. In time he found the perfect session to relate.

"This session is interesting, Amanda, because I didn't do what I should have done. Tom's a twenty-five-year-old man, handsome as can be, who I've been seeing a little over a year. He tells me about having picked up a twenty-year-old girl in a bar, whom he took home to bed. Here's the issue for me: when he talked about the sex, he described it in great detail. It falls under the category of too much information. I don't really need to know the how and where and how often."

"Such a dilemma!" she said with that Amanda touch of irony.

"But it is a dilemma. I should have asked him how it helps to describe their fornications, and why in such minute detail. Does he want something from me: approval or admiration, for instance? Or was I being tested in some way?"

"And you didn't ask?"

Harry shook his head.

"Because?"

"Because I underwent a metamorphosis from therapist into voyeur. I'm mesmerized by the graphic images he was spinning for me, and I want him to continue. In other words I'm not inclined to interrupt."

He waited to see Amanda's reaction. What would she think? Would she be critical of him? All of a sudden he worried he had chosen the wrong case to present.

She chuckled. "So what were those graphic images?"

Did she really want to know? Could he tell her? They were gross. "Now you're being the voyeur."

She chuckled again, louder and more unrestrained than before. "Well, I suppose I'm just as human as you."

He hadn't supposed that. Harry was beginning to sense that he possessed a residue of prudery in his psyche. He couldn't bring himself to reveal Tom's descriptions.

"I'm not sure you made a mistake, Harry. I think it's simply that Tom trusted you and felt closer to you by describing what happened. It's a guy thing, you know. It brings you off the pedestal and down to his level, where you are just buddies."

"You may be right, but until he confesses that, it's only a theory. I still think I should have inquired."

"Did you envy him?"

The question threw him. If he admitted envy, it would tell her something about himself that he wasn't prepared to have her know.

"Envy him?" He stalled.

She smiled. It seemed she was looking right through him.

"No, not really."

She gave him a look that said, "I don't believe you," but she said nothing.

She had provided him with an opening, and Harry knew it. There were so many things he could have said that would have blown his cover. There were so many ways to show that he desired her. Why was he vacillating? Harry was paralyzed. His answer had been evasive and dishonest.

As he left Amanda's apartment an hour later, each step he took seemed to bring his spirits down a little further. He felt a deflated sense of disappointment. Why was he such a coward? What was he afraid of? If not Amanda, who? Before he hailed a cab, a memory from his undergraduate years flashed in his brain. His college roommate had left a present for him on the desk of his dorm room. It was a white button with a legend in purple scrawled across it.

So many girls
So little nerve

CHAPTER 8
Slater versus Slater

Jennifer had heaped so much derision on her mother, Emily Slater, her disdainful words echoing down the corridors of old, half-forgotten therapy sessions, that Harry girded himself for her coming as if he were about to grapple with the devil himself. He knew that she would be difficult and relentless; that she would be defensive to the point of giving no ground; that her point of view would prove to be immutable, impervious to facts, feelings, or logic; that it would be an exercise in futility and frustration. What then was to be gained? Jennifer stated that it would be easier to speak her mind to this formidable ogre with Harry in the room. While her expectations were low, she thought it might be of some therapeutic value to express feelings that she'd never dared to say before. So what if her mother was her usual opaque self? As for him, Harry thought it might be informative for him to see Emily Slater in action with her daughter, and Jennifer with her as well.

It was a surprise then when Emily arrived with her daughter, offering ingratiating smiles, kind words, and flattering phrases, such as, "I've heard so many good things about you," and "So glad to at last meet you," and "Jennifer thinks the world of you."

I was expecting Darth Vader, the Destroyer of Worlds, Harry thought to himself. *Instead I get Little Red Riding Hood!* Not that he was taken in by Emily's front; he understood that she was merely propitiating what Harry sometimes referred to

69

(tongue in cheek) as "the Great God of Therapy." He shook her proffered hand and said a simple hello.

Harry looked her over. He guessed her to be in her late forties, although a simple calculation (Jennifer was thirty) told him that she must be older. He was surprised at how attractive she was; Jennifer never commented on her mother's looks. She was only a little shorter and almost as slender as her daughter; Emily had dyed blond hair and put a good amount of makeup to excellent use. She wore a stylish gray suit with a tight skirt that stopped just above her knees, exposing very shapely legs. Harry thought she looked well tailored and expensive. He was impressed and quietly admitted to himself that she was sexy.

They sat on the couch in tense silence for a minute, until Emily commented about how warm and comfortable his office looked. Harry found the comment seductive. He prided himself on the special attractiveness of his work environment. It was a large space with charming casement windows that looked out to a street of century-old, well-kept brownstones. Over the years, as he prospered he replaced cheap, nondescript furniture with more attractive contemporary units. A brown sisal rug with Ultrasuede trim lay on the floor. The couch, with its large pillows, was a soft taupe color, plush and inviting. To some therapists décor meant little. Utility was all that mattered, and the cheaper the better; that was not Harry's style. He found Emily's remark gratifying.

Harry suggested that Jennifer should begin.

"Mother, let me tell you why I wanted you to come. I feel distant from you, Mom, like there's some emotional barrier that keeps us from ever being close. I sometimes feel I'm not good enough for you, that I'm a disappointment. In fact, I've always felt that way."

Good. Good beginning, cards on the table. Harry was pleased. He also noted that Jennifer's comment was a statement of feeling and not a verbal assault on her mother; no blame had been allocated. He had urged her to take a calm, reasoned approach and to avoid intemperate criticism. She seemed to be taking his advice.

"Not at all, Jen. I can't imagine why you feel that way."

"Well, you're kind of critical of me," Jennifer said. Responding to her mother's head shake, she continued, "Okay. For instance, you won't let up on the fact that I'm not married."

"But I don't mind that you're not married. I mind that you don't want to get married. Is that wrong of me?" Emily addressed this question directly to Harry. "Should I not want this for Jennifer, that she find a husband settle down, have a family life instead of jumping from man to man?"

"Mrs. Slater, I prefer that you speak directly to Jennifer. Think of me as listening and noticing, a neutral observer, so to speak."

"Maybe I don't want to have a marriage like you had with Dad."

"So I made a mistake. I married a loser. I did okay the second time, didn't I? She adores her stepfather," she said needlessly to Harry, who already possessed that information.

"Don't talk about my father that way, okay? You always do that, and you know I hate it."

"What I'm saying, Jennifer, is that it's better to love in vain than not to love at all."

Harry smiled at this, remembering that Jennifer had once said her mother loved to quote little aphorisms. "She's just not herself until she's uttered some mindless daily platitude," Jennifer said. "Some people need that strong cup of coffee to get started. My mom's caffeine is a homey little saying; she's 'a stitch in time saves nine' kind of a girl."

"I don't think it's good for you to be promiscuous," Emily added.

"I'm not promiscuous," Jennifer said, bristling at the remark. Her voice had taken on a decided edge. "I enjoy sex, but I don't jump from bed to bed."

"Sex is an overrated pleasure if you ask me," Emily rejoined. Turning toward Harry, she said, "She enjoys sex so much she started having it when she was fourteen years old. Fourteen years old, and with a twenty-three-year-old boy, no less!"

Harry was taken aback. In eight years of therapy Jennifer had withheld that little piece of datum. Was it shame that fostered her reticence? On the other hand, he thought the remark retaliatory and inappropriate. Emily was scoring points against her daughter, Little Red Riding Hood no more.

"Did you ever think that screaming at me that I was a slut and taking away all my freedom and privileges was not the best thing to do? Did you ever wonder why I was doing it? Did you ever think of getting me help?"

Harry noted the change of tone. It was, however, purely reactive. He would not blame her for it.

"Excuse me, but how could I afford it? It wasn't easy for me," Emily said, once again turning toward Harry. "When Charles left, I had to find work. Charles was always pleading poverty, always behind in his child support payments. I had only a high school education and no skills. So I took a job as a receptionist in a dentist's office. I could hardly make ends meet. I was so stressed. All I needed," she said, now addressing her daughter again in a tone far sharper than the one she'd used with Harry, "was for you to get pregnant at thirteen."

"Fourteen, Mom, remember? I didn't get pregnant, if you recall. All I wanted was a little understanding, but that was beyond your capability, Mother, wasn't it? I was depressed when Dad left; I felt lonely and unloved. That's what I was looking for, some love and understanding."

This was a complaint Harry had heard many times over the course of Jennifer's treatment. He was very curious about how Emily would reply.

"Not from me. From that stupid jerk, Tommy, or whatever his name was."

"No, not from you. Why should I? All I ever got from you was criticism."

"Well, someone had to set some limits with you. Your precious father certainly wasn't."

"He didn't have to set limits because you set too many."

"Oh, yes, go ahead, defend him." To Harry she said, "He can do no wrong in her eyes, and she can do no wrong in his."

"What about Tommy—did your father know about him?" Harry asked.

"His name was Teddy, and yes, Mom made sure that he knew. I guess you thought that he would side with you, huh, Mom?"

"When did he ever side with me?"

"He didn't?" Harry asked in a surprised voice.

"He wasn't judgmental like Mom; he wasn't worried about the sex. He wanted to be sure that I understood about birth control."

"How did that make you feel?"

"It felt like I got a figurative hug. It was a wonderful antidote to Mom's judgmental approach."

Harry leaned forward and turned his head toward Jennifer. It was clear to both women that he was about to speak.

"I'm sure you did feel better. And I know you needed to be understood. But if it were your thirteen—I mean fourteen-—year-old daughter, is that how you would handle it? Have as much sex as you want, kid, just be sure the guys use condoms. Your mother may have been too harsh, but your dad was too permissive."

Jennifer frowned but withheld a response.

Harry considered asking for her reaction to his words, but Emily spoke first.

"She talks about me criticizing her, but let me tell you, she was pretty good about dishing it out herself," Emily said in a voice that contained a stern note.

"I criticized you? When did that happen? The only memory I have is fending you off. I think you're confusing self-defense with criticism."

"No, you blamed me for everything."

"Like what? Give me an example."

"Like … like … you think I don't know that you blamed me for breaking up the marriage?"

"You *were* to blame, Mom. You made it impossible for him; you were such a bitch. You treated him the way you treated me, like he could do nothing right. If he left the toilet seat up, if he came home late, always the complaints, the whining. He just wasn't good enough for you, was he? But he wasn't a dependent kid like me. He stood up for himself; that's why he left. If you had been more loving, he would have stayed."

"And maybe if *he* had been more loving, *I* would have been more loving."

Harry was jolted by the tears that suddenly appeared in Emily's eyes.

"Were you angry with your husband before he left?"

"Yes."

"What happened?"

"He stopped loving me."

"So it wasn't about the toilet seat or his coming home late, was it?"

"He came home late because there was another woman."

"What? What are you talking about, Mom?" Jennifer sounded disbelieving and irate.

"Do you think I would lie about that? You should ask him then. It had been going on for years. He openly admitted it; it was no secret at all."

"He wouldn't let her go?" Harry asked.

"No, he let me go instead."

Harry looked across at Jennifer, whose face had turned a ghostly white, as though all the blood had been drained from it.

"I'm in shock. Mom, why didn't you ever tell me about this?"

"What good would it have done? You had already left me. You were *his* daughter."

Jennifer looked very upset.

"Who was she?" she asked.

"Does it matter now, dear? Her name was Alice. I actually met her once, after he had left."

"Oh, my God! I remember her, a red-haired woman."

"You kept this a secret so long, Emily—why reveal it now?" Harry asked.

"I used to feel ashamed of it, like it was my fault. I thought it was my failure, that I wasn't good enough for him. I feel differently now."

"Is that why you didn't tell Jennifer, because you were blaming yourself?"

"I suppose," Emily said after a slight hesitation. "I thought she would think it was my fault too."

"Oh, Mom." Jennifer began to cry.

Emily, taken by surprise, looked at Harry. The expression on her face seemed to say, "What should I do?"

Harry directed his gaze to Jennifer, and if he noticed the older woman looking to him for assistance, he paid no attention to it.

Emily moved closer to Jennifer and put her arm around her.

"You should have told me. I didn't know," Jennifer said in a strangled voice. She groped for and obtained her mother's hand.

Harry felt both sadness and hope. At the beginning of the session he was prepared to dislike Emily Slater. That thought disappeared. Perhaps all of them had turned a corner.

"What are you feeling?" he asked Jennifer.

While she dabbed her eyes with a tissue scooped from a nearby box, she seemed to be contemplating an answer. She looked at her mother and then at Harry.

"Shock. Confusion."

"Uh huh. And ..."

"I don't want to judge their marriage, who was responsible for what."

"Haven't you already done so?"

"Yes, she has," Emily added immediately. She vigorously nodded her head. "Her father can do no wrong in her eyes. Even now she's probably thinking that I drove him to infidelity. Aren't you, Jennie?" She said this in a soft and unchallenging voice.

Harry had never heard that nickname, and he wondered why he was hearing it now.

"No, I'm not," she said, removing her hand from her mother's. The gesture did not escape Harry's notice. "What he did was repugnant, no matter what he might say to justify it."

"He'll tell you how awful I was, how miserable he was, and what a sacrifice it was for him to stay. And he'll tell you that he only stayed because you were so young. I know him so well. I know how he gets on your good side, gets you to feel sorry for him."

This was dangerous territory, as Harry well knew. He hoped it would somehow come out well, but he was on edge. He awaited its unraveling, understanding that this conversation needed to play out.

"I'm not as naïve as you think, Mom. I know Dad is no angel. But he gave me something you weren't able to give. He gave me understanding; he gave me sympathy. He never criticized me; he never put me down."

"Yes, because he needed you on his side, and he wanted to feel that he was the good one. He turned me into the bad cop. Someone had to set limits, to make rules and enforce them. You could have been a wild animal as far as he was concerned, so long as it didn't land on him. And you're right, he didn't put you down. He never said a negative word to you. On the other hand, he did abandon you. When he left me, he left you too." There was bitterness in Emily's voice.

"And he left me with all the bills. It was six months before I got a dime in child's support. Did you know that?"

"Of course I knew that; you said so earlier. You never stopped reminding me of it. Did it ever occur to you that he didn't have the money?"

"Didn't have the money? That was because he was spending it on that bimbo."

"You don't know that. You have no evidence for that."

"That's right, you always defend him. The judge figured he had enough to pay a little child support, but apparently you know better."

Jennifer looked like someone who had been backed into a corner. She was like an army in full retreat, the space remaining to stand upon diminishing by the minute. Emily was accomplishing what Harry could not do in all the years of his work with Jennifer. She was successfully assaulting the citadel that her daughter had built around Charles Slater to defend his reputation in her own eyes. He was impressed with how formidable a woman Emily Slater was and how well prepared she had been for this session. He thought this was all good, that Jennifer needed this corrective understanding of her father. But now another thought crept stealthily into his mind. He knew this was not what Jennifer wanted from the session; and he saw the necessity of confronting that.

"Jennifer, the session started with you saying that you felt an emotional distance from your mother. Do you feel that way now?"

"I guess I do."

"Why is that?"

"Because we're fighting; it's a very familiar feeling."

"What would you like to say to your mother?"

"I don't want to talk about Dad," she said as she turned on the couch, away from Harry, toward her mother. "I want to talk about you and me. I always have the feeling that I can never get it right with you, that no matter what I say or do, you will find fault."

"You know I feel the same way about you. I thought I was getting better. I used to be so angry with you, but I don't feel that way now. I don't think I'm so bad any more. Even David tells me I'm getting better with you. David is my husband," she said to Harry.

"Yes, I know."

"I'll admit that you have improved, but you still tend to see the glass as half empty when it comes to me, Mom. Look at all the positive things I've done in my life. I was a very good student; I graduated from a wonderful college. I've got a fine career and a decent income. I have lovely friends, and I take good care of myself."

"You also work very hard to understand yourself," Harry added.

"Yes, and I've grown and matured. You know I have, Mother."

"You have. I'll be the first to admit that. And we get along better, don't you agree? That's why your complaint surprises me."

"Because what you focus on is what I haven't done, that I haven't found a husband, as though I'm an old maid at thirty. And have you ever wondered why I never talk about the men I date? It's because of your cynicism. You try to probe to find some fatal flaw in the man. Don't you think I know what you're implying, that if I'm with him there must be something wrong with him?"

"Hasn't that always been the case? The good ones don't stand a chance with you. Ask David; he's worried about you too."

"That may be, but he doesn't piss me off the way you do."

"Yes, because he's not your mother."

"No, it's because he's not as worried as you are. Do you know why? Because he has faith that I will eventually get it right."

"And why is that important to you?" Harry asked.

"It means a lot to me. If he has faith in me, it helps me to find faith in myself."

Harry glanced at Emily, who appeared to be suddenly deflated.

"What are you feeling, Emily?"

"That my daughter's right. I don't show confidence in her. I feel I've let Jennifer down. I guess I'm not so hot in the mom department," she said looking at Jennifer.

"Thank you, Mom," she said in a barely audible voice.

The three sat silently.

"Jennifer, what are you feeling?" Harry asked.

"It feels good. It feels like hey, my mom's listening to me."

"Emily?"

"Yes?"

"Would you like to respond to Jennifer?"

"I'm very glad that we're having this moment. I would like to be closer to you; in fact I long for it, Jen. But I'm so afraid of messing it up."

"Can you help her with that?" Harry asked, looking to Jennifer.

"Try to remember, Mom, that I'm an adult. I may be your child, but I'm not a child."

"I think I treat you like an adult."

"No, you absolutely do not. If you want to learn how, try this: stop bugging me about marriage. I'm not asking for your advice. Stop prying into my affairs, stop asking what I've been doing, and when, and with whom. It's none of your business. I'll tell you what I want you to know."

"Then what do we talk about?"

Harry and Jennifer laughed.

"I'm being serious," Emily said.

"We know you are. You may have to forge a new relationship," said Harry.

"You'll never tell me anything," Emily said to Jennifer.

"If you are more of a friend instead of the eternally vigilant mother, I will want to tell you more. Try it out, Mom."

"I'm not sure I know how to do that."

Harry was impressed with her honesty, and sympathetic with her confusion.

"It will take time, for sure," he said, "but this is a good beginning."

"Well, maybe you're right. My therapist says I'm over involved with Jennifer."

"Mom, you're in therapy?" Jennifer struck a high note of incredulity.

"Yes, it's been almost a year."

"Why didn't you tell me?" The incredulity remained in her voice.

"I don't know; I just never had a reason to."

"Emily, doesn't it seem incongruous to you that you want to know so much about your daughter's life, but you omit mentioning a consequential fact about your own?"

"It's a perfect paradigm," Jennifer commented. "Mommy needs to know what baby's doing, but baby doesn't need to know what Mommy's doing."

"Oh, you're exaggerating, Jennifer."

Despite Harry's efforts, Mrs. Slater never truly answered his question. It seemed to him that she was not ready to accept limitations on a parent's right to ask intrusive questions or to accept a child's right to privacy.

The back and forth between the two women continued, with an occasional clarifying interjection from Harry. All in all, Harry thought some progress had been made, but much remained to be accomplished. When it was time to terminate the session, Emily opened her purse, removed her checkbook, and opened it up.

"Are you planning to pay for this?" Harry asked.

"Yes, of course."

"No, Mom, you are not."

"Oh, please. I want to."

"No, Mom—my therapist, my session. I invited you. Put your checkbook away."

Emily looked at Harry, who smiled and shrugged.

"I'll pay you next week," Jennifer said.

CHAPTER 9

Changing Her Mind

That Jacques Giraud was a man of his word was soon confirmed for Jennifer Slater. Their first formal date was not a movie or dinner; it was on a tennis court. As Jennifer predicted, she soundly thrashed Jacques. The problem was in his service. Jennifer had a strong first serve and a second serve with good spin. She described her friend's serve as "artfully slow," and she was being extremely kind. Jacques's second serve was, as she mercilessly portrayed it, "pathetic." On those few occasions when he got past the serve and the play came down to the back and forth of volleying, he actually had a chance of winning some points. He had good ground strokes, particularly his forehand. Even his backhand was passable. He won no points with it, but he kept the ball in play. As the first set progressed, Jennifer noticed a growing frustration in her opponent. He tried to hit his serves with greater violence. Unfortunately, the result of this was far more double faults and no points gained. Once when they crossed paths changing sides she spoke to him. "Do you still have your balls?"

"One of them," he replied, his voice a barely audible high-pitched squeak.

Although his joke clearly indicated that he was taking his drubbing well, she began to regret the teasing. "Keep it up, girl," she said to herself, "and this relationship won't survive the match."

After she had won the first nine games, Jacques quit the competition.

"You're too good," he declared. "Suppose we just volley, no points scored."

Jennifer agreed and wondered whether she had played too competitively. After a few games she knew she could beat him, yet she poured it on. Easing off, she kept her volleys within his reach, avoiding winning shots. Once when he hit a sharply angled crosscourt shot that she could not reach, she stopped to applaud.

"You keep hitting like that and I'm cooked," she said.

"Okay, I'll go easy on you," he shouted back. "You do know I let you win, right?"

She laughed. Now they were really having fun. When they walked off the court twenty minutes later, Jacques lightly tapped the top of her head with the strings of his racket.

"You are such a confident player, I'll bet you've been playing a long time," he said.

"Since I was five—me and Dad against the world."

"You probably would have beaten me even then."

"You're too modest, Jacques. You would have taken advantage of my short arms and eked out a win."

"Thank you for your confidence, Jennifer. I so appreciate it."

She pushed him affectionately. "For being such a good sport I'm going to buy you lunch."

"Now that I do appreciate. Winner pays," he said.

They stopped for lunch at a small Mediterranean restaurant, where each ordered salad. In her experience men do not eat salad, she told him. Wouldn't he prefer a cheeseburger?

"Do I look like a typical guy, Jennifer, being a Jane Austen scholar and all that?"

"In some ways I'll bet you are a typical guy," she said to herself. To him she only smiled. The conversation that ensued over salads was mercifully light. For once he asked no personal questions. He inquired about her work, her relationships with the novelists she represented, while she asked about his students, in particular what they were like. They also talked about the usual things, movies and favorite TV shows (he watched only PBS), music and politics and sports. She surprised him with how much she knew about the latter subject, and he surprised her with how little he knew. *Not a typical guy after all*, she thought.

All in all, they had much in common, and Jennifer was pleased that the time she spent with him had been so pleasant. She had enjoyed herself. She looked across the table at him and noticed how good he looked. He was tan from the hours in the sun, a look that gave him a healthy glow. If only he would lose the Clark Kent glasses!

When it was time to leave, she did not invite him to her place. She had deliberately planned to meet Daryl for a movie late that afternoon. On the next day, Sunday, she had arranged to be busy too. On their next date the following weekend, the already arranged horseback riding, she would have to be clear with him about her feelings. She wanted friendship, nothing more. There would be no additional benefits.

They hugged in parting and assured each other that they had had a wonderful time. When he attempted to kiss her on the lips, she turned slightly so that the kiss landed on her cheek. She waved good-bye as she left. "That was stupid of me," she said aloud to herself in chastisement. "What was the harm of letting him kiss my lips?"

On horseback Jacques was a complete dud. For starters he chose the oldest, most decrepit-looking nag he could find. "I've seen better looking donkeys," Jennifer remarked. Together they moved at a pace befitting a nursing home squadron, which was perfectly fine with Jacques, whose nerves got the better of him whenever his nag threatened to canter.

"Whoa, whoa," he said.

"Don't let him go any faster than a turtle," Jennifer said in a light mocking tone.

"A turtle? That's too fast!" he rejoined. "What do you take me for, a daredevil?"

She liked that he could make fun of himself. *A self-effacing man is a rare man.*

At times Jennifer would ride far ahead and leave him to his dawdling, but she always came back. It wouldn't be fair to leave him alone; how could that be enjoyable for him? He encouraged her to ride ahead, however, because he worried she would have no fun moving at his snail's pace. At times she would offer words of encouragement, telling him he was doing much better, observing his quickening pace. She called his horse Lightning and worried whether it would be able to keep up with his demand for what she called speed.

"Yes, I might be too much for him," he said.

Nonetheless she noted that he still seemed a little tense, although much less so than at the beginning.

She brought her horse close to Lightning leaned over and kissed Jacques. He was clearly delighted by the unexpected display of affection. She wondered why she had done that and immediately regretted it. Perhaps she was grateful that he was doing this in order to be with her, to please her. She dashed off with her horse and stayed away a little bit longer. When the day ended, she invited him back to her apartment, although against her better judgment. She simply could not make up her mind about him. To contain the situation she told him that she had an early Monday morning meeting, so he could not stay long. She was clear in her own mind that this relationship would remain strictly platonic. Yes, she felt drawn to him, but only in a fraternal way.

After devouring a light lunch that she had prepared, they settled on the living room couch. A short conversation about trivial things was interrupted by a call on her iPhone. Her father was calling to say that he would not be coming into town the next day to see her. Her response was to reassure him that that was "fine" and that they would reschedule "soon." They talked for another minute.

"Sorry," she told Jacques. "I had a feeling he was calling to cancel."

"Is it fine?"

She did not understand the question.

"Is it 'fine' that he canceled? You looked disappointed, maybe even a little upset."

She agreed that she was disappointed; she had not seen her father in nearly three months.

"I think you feel abandoned by him."

"That's pretty harsh, Jacques. He didn't withdraw his love. It's just that his life changed and adjustments had to be made."

"You mean like when he left your mom?"

She observed that Jacques had a look of concern on his face, or was it sympathy? It encouraged her to talk. Feelings were begging to come out, if only they could. She agreed that momentous changes had occurred when her parents separated. At that time she'd entertained the hope that he would take her with him.

"And did he?"

"No, he couldn't."

"Why not?"

"He had to work."

"What about joint custody?"

"He just couldn't do it. He worked long hours."

"My dad was a hard worker, but he still managed to take care of me," Jacques said.

Jennifer experienced a sudden jolt of anger that she could not contain. It was acceptable for her to criticize her father; it was not acceptable for others to do so. Harry had learned that over time. Jacques was about to learn.

"Why are you comparing your father with mine? Were their situations exactly the same?"

Jennifer could see that the edge in her voice had startled him. He was not prepared for it. His eyes shifted away from her, and he appeared to be in deep thought. Then he looked directly at her and began to speak. "May I explain?"

She nodded assent.

"I can see that I offended you, and I'm sorry for that. For

me it's a personal thing, and that's why it touched a raw nerve. I love children and always wanted my own. I could never walk away from my kid. I would want full custody but of course would settle for joint. It would be a great struggle for me to end a marriage if there were children. So I reacted from a personal point of view, rushing to judgment, and that was wrong. Actually, my father's situation was different from yours. You were absolutely right about that. My mother died giving birth to me, so my dad didn't really have a choice. There was nobody else to take care of me."

That was the neatest *mea culpa* Jennifer had heard in her life. His explanation had been so obviously heartfelt that she found her own emotions in something of a jumble. *How does one stay angry with such a guy?* She was touched by his openness most of all. In a few words he had shed some light on the person he was. She had also learned something about him she had not known before, that he had been deprived of a mother. She felt a jolt of sympathy and a dollop of remorse that she had spoken so sharply to him. She reached out and touched his hand.

"I think I overreacted. I'm sorry about that," she told him.

"No need to apologize. I shouldn't be passing judgment on your father. So are we friends again?"

"Absolutely." *Hey, wait a minute. Is friendship all he wants?* "You know, Jacques, I didn't know you never had a mother. In fact, I don't really know much about you at all. It seems like I've been doing all the talking." Most guys in her experience *only* talked about themselves. She could turn to carrion before they asked a question about her. She began to sense that Jacques was an antiguy, whatever that actually meant, for better or worse.

"You haven't talked that much about yourself," he said.

"Bullshit!" she said vehemently. "How can you say that? I've been doing all the talking. I know zilch about you. I don't want to become like the guy my shrink once described. He goes out on a date, talks nonstop for a couple of hours, and then says, 'Enough about me. I want to hear about you. So what are your thoughts about me?' I don't want to be that guy."

"I had a hunch you were in therapy, "Jacques said.
"You're not?"

"I am. Would you like to hear my thoughts about you?"

"Absolutely not. I want to hear only about you."

"What would you like to know?"

"Well, let's start with what I do know. You had no mother, and your father went to work. So who took care of you?"

"Nannies and stepmothers."

She waited for him to say more. He said nothing.

"Is that it?" she asked, although she knew there was much more.

"I don't want to overload you with information," he said with a deadpan look on his face. She made a fist and pretended to sock him in the jaw.

"Okay, okay. I'll tell you more if you promise not to hit me again. We're from Paris, where I was born. I've gone from Paris to New Jersey. How's that for a downward trajectory?"

"I won't tell my Jersey friends what you just said."

"Thank you—that's a relief. I was three when my father remarried, a woman by the name of Marianne. I don't remember much about her because it was a brief marriage. Marrying Marianne was one of my father's least inspired decisions."

"Why is that?"

"Well, I have one memory of her that stands out. It's such a vague recollection that I used to think that I imagined the whole thing, that it wasn't a thing that happened in reality. But my dad later confirmed part of it—the part about the chimes—so now I believe that it really did happen. I seem to have a terrific memory for bad things."

"The part about the chimes?" Jennifer was intrigued.

"We used to have chimes hanging from a fixture in the ceiling, although I don't remember exactly. My dad and I played a game. He would lift me up and let me play with them. I loved the sound they made. I think I loved being able to make them chime. My father said I would giggle every time I made them chime. One day when my father was at work, Marianne picked me up and encouraged me to play with the chimes. When I did, she slapped me across the face. It must have been a very hard slap because those chimes scared me after that. This I know from my father."

Jennifer gasped.

"Attached to that is another memory; at least I think this actually happened. When he came home, Marianne suggested that he play the chimes game with me, but when he did I refused to play. He kept urging me to push the chimes, but I started to cry. I think he must have been really puzzled that I wouldn't do it. Those chimes never chimed again. So now you know my darkest secret. Can you match that?"

This last remark was said facetiously. Jacques was making light of the experience.

Jennifer did not buy into that. "My God, what a terrible woman! How awful for you!" Jennifer exclaimed loudly, holding in her mind the image of a terrified little boy unable to cope with so horrendous a caretaker. She could barely contain a strong urge to hug him.

"I think it must have been awful," Jacques said with a far-away look on his face, "but now it's like looking through a glass darkly. I somehow can't summon any feelings about it, it happened so long ago."

"But there's got to be some reason you remember it. I mean, you were traumatized so young. The feelings are there, I'm sure."

"I know. We've been looking for them."

"We?"

"My therapist and me. You know, beside my father and therapist, you're the only other person I've told. What do you think that means?"

"During lunch I slipped some truth serum into your drink." She thought she parried that dangerous question pretty neatly.

"I wondered why I couldn't lie."

"You said your father's marriage didn't last long. So what happened then?"

"We came to America when I was five. Dad hired a French-speaking nanny to take care of me. A year later he remarried. Then my sister came."

"You're a lot older than Annie, aren't you?"

"Almost seven years. So there were five of us. My father, Joanne—my stepmother—Annie, and Monique, our live-in French nanny."

"Things were better?"

"*Better* is a relative term. It wasn't exactly a happy time. My father was a hotel manager and worked long hours. Joanne managed a real estate office, was a really high-powered career woman; we didn't get to see much of her. Still don't. She wasn't the maternal type any way. And Monique spent most of her time taking care of Annie, who was a pretty sickly child."

"In other words, you were off on your own," Jennifer said, more a statement than a question.

"When I wasn't in school, I was alone in my room, reading or doing homework. In those days I was very shy and socially awkward, not like the masterful person you see before you today, so I didn't have any close friends. That's how I came to love novels. I started reading them when I was about ten."

"Yes," she said excitedly, "me too. When my parents started to quarrel, I would lock myself in my room, turn the TV on for white noise, and bury myself in a book. I read every Nancy Drew mystery in existence."

"I remember the first novel I ever read in the English language. It was *The Story of a Bad Boy* by Thomas Bailey Aldrich. It was written sometime around 1927. It really hooked me in. It was written in the first person, a kind of coming-of-age book. I totally identified with the narrator. After that, when I wasn't studying I was reading novels." Jacques shifted his position, stretching out with his feet touching the coffee table in front of the couch.

She looked at him. "You saw yourself as a bad boy?" She saw him as the opposite, as a very good boy, usually doing what was required of him perfectly, making his father proud, an always-staying-clear-of-trouble kind of kid. She could not have said how she knew, but *she knew*. Perhaps that was still his problem today.

"Well, bad in my thoughts, although I don't remember them now," he responded.

"I think compared to me, Jacques, you were an angel."

"How were you bad?"

"We're back to me, are we, still after my misdeeds? I was rebellious, contrary." She could have told him a lot more, but she was beginning to care enough to decide not to.

"It's true. I was a good little boy. I think I was too scared to be bad, but I had hopes."

"It's not too late, you know."

"It isn't? Then I could have gotten away with it; now I'd go straight to jail."

"It depends on how you define *bad*. I mean, I wouldn't recommend holding up a bank."

"I guess I'll have to drop that idea."

"What about your dad? Are you close to him?"

Jacques appeared to carefully consider the request. He gave a deep sigh. "You know, it's getting late," he said, glancing quickly at his watch, "and you said that you have to get up early tomorrow. Perhaps I should be off. We can talk more the next time."

What's this? Now he's talking about leaving? Guys don't leave voluntarily! Not the one's Jennifer knew. They had to be thrown out. She was startled.

"You're not leaving these premises until you've talked about your dad," she declared in her best autocratic voice. She grasped his hand in a gesture meant to resist his effort to leave. She knew she couldn't physically restrain him, but she trusted the gesture would suffice.

Jacques had begun to rise, but he hesitated and then returned to his place on the couch. She waited for him to speak.

"Yah, *mein führer*," he said, lightly mocking her peremptory tone. "It's hard to talk about, Jennifer. I thought I'd reserve that conversation for later. It will keep, won't it?"

"Uh uh. I'm intrigued, wondering why it's so hard. So now you have to tell me, please."

"My dad was pretty much all I really had," he said with a sigh, relenting to her entreaty. "I was never really close to my stepmother. I mean my second one, Joanne. She was okay. She was responsible and all that, but she wasn't a mother. I think even Annie was short-changed in that matter, although she got more attention, being Joanne's biological child. I always felt my dad would do anything for me, even put my needs before his own. He left Marianne because of me. He knew something was wrong, despite her efforts to hide it. His once jabbering, happy boy seemed depressed, too quiet, not himself. So he figured it out. He didn't tell me this until I was an adult."

Now that the floodgates were open, Jacques seemed to have a need to talk, so she nodded her encouragement and gave out an occasional "uh huh" to underscore her interest. *Thank you, Dr. Harry Salinger.*

"You know, in some ways we're very much alike."

"Uh huh."

"When you were talking before about how much fun you had with your dad, I felt envious. My dad worked so late every day that I didn't get to see him much. When we were together, our activities tended to be sedentary and cerebral. When I was younger, he read to me. When I was older, we played chess, talked about books, and things of that sort. The only fun I remember having with him is when he took me to the opera. He loved opera. Are you familiar with it?"

"I only went once, to *La Bohème*, which I really enjoyed. How are we similar?"

"I never felt I had enough of him; when your dad left home you had the same experience. In fact, it's clear to me you still don't get enough."

"Oh—uh huh." She knew he was right, and the pang she felt

confirmed it. He seemed to get her in a way not even her best friends had. And in so short a time!

"In therapy, I got to some feelings of anger. It was very difficult because I loved him so much, and it's hard to get angry with someone who—"

"Who—?"

"Who's gone. He was killed three years ago in a car accident." Jacques said it without a trace of emotion, as though he were talking about yesterday's weather.

"Oh, my God! How? What happened?" She was now sitting on the edge of the couch, leaning toward him, a shocked look on her face.

"He was on his way to Philadelphia to check out a hotel for his boss, who was thinking of buying it, when the driver of a big truck in the opposite lane fell asleep at the wheel. It was a head-on; they said he was killed instantly. When I talk about it, even now it seems unreal to me. Like, did it really happen? Am I talking about my father? We think we're in control of our lives but we're really not. It all comes down to luck. My dad was unlucky, and I suppose so was I." There was a little telltale catch in his voice when he uttered the last words, a little clue that helped her see beneath his placid façade.

She looked at this motherless man, now fatherless as well, and thought she saw a forlorn little boy, helpless and afraid. She noticed for the first time that there was something boyishly attractive about him. A lock of dark hair (almost as dark as hers) fell over his forehead. She thought she knew what he needed, and her heart went out to him. She put her arms around him and her cheek to his and held him that way as the seconds passed.

"It's okay, Jennifer. I'm all right. I've had three years to adjust." He put his hand on her back and stroked it. He was now comforting her. She broke off and looked at him, her face a mere inch or two from his. Their noses almost touched. He looked sad but was bravely attempting to conceal it with a forced smile. She felt a wave of sympathy for him. *How does one "adjust" to such a loss?*

"I didn't want to talk about this. It's still a very difficult subject for me. I don't want sympathy. It's life, and everyone has some pain. We were having fun—now look at us. I'm really sorry I put this on you. I need to grow up and move on."

"No, you don't. You need to have these feelings, and I'm your friend, so why shouldn't you expose them to me? I'm glad you told me."

"Thank you, I appreciate that. But I'm not feeling like mourning right now. Is it okay if we talk about something else?"

"Yes, of course. There is something that I would like to bring up, if I may."

"Sure, please feel free to say whatever you want."

"I really like you, I mean a lot." She said this because she felt it, even knowing that it might give him the wrong idea. At the moment she didn't care.

"I feel the same way about you," he replied, his sad eyes transitioning instantly to glad eyes. His entire face exuded happy surprise.

She closed the short distance between them on the couch and lightly kissed his lips. It was more a brush than a kiss, a promise of action rather than an action.

"You know what I think you need?" she asked, breaking off the kiss.

"No, what do I need?"

"For once in your life you need to be bad."

"Okay. And what do I have to do to be bad?"

"You need to be really, really mischievous. I mean a very bad, mischievous boy. I'll show you how."

Gently she pushed him backward until his head rested on the arm of the couch. She removed his glasses and placed them a few feet away. Without the glasses, she could see that his eyes were light blue. He had really nice eyes. Placing a hand on his hair, she kissed him on the lips, drew back and then kissed him again, this time more forcefully, her lips disappearing into his. It was an action born of sympathy, humanity, and identification. Once begun she had not the slightest intention of turning back.

The kissing continued. Jacques showed no sign of fatigue or any intention to advance to another level of eroticism. He said nothing more about leaving. She looked closely at him. His eyes were glazed, and he appeared temporarily immobilized, surprised, passively awaiting his fate. With his disheveled hair (she had run her fingers through it on the way to kiss number five) and his wrinkled shirt and tie, he looked well out of his familiar element.

Jennifer understood the power she held. He was infatuated, carried away, given over to her full command. There was no need to impress him, to work for his affection or arouse his desire. It was all there before her, an accomplished fact. She had acquired certitude. With Jacques she was a fortuneteller; their immediate sexual future lay plainly before her. She could not have explained exactly when she made the decision, or why. She told herself that nothing fundamental had changed. This was to be a mercy fuck and nothing more; nothing consequential was at stake here. He would be her friend, not her boyfriend. They would play tennis and other things, and if on a rare occasion she gave him a "benefit," that's all it would be. It would not interrupt the flow of their close friendship. For the truth was that she liked this sensitive giant of a man and felt empathy for him that she had not experienced for a long time. It was enough. It gave her justification. It was a pity that he wasn't really her type.

His shoes came off first—he wouldn't need them—and then the socks. His toes were long, the nails smooth and short. She loosened his tie and then slowly, deliberately, unbuttoned his shirt; she removed it, cast it to the floor. There was hair on his chest, but he was not particularly hairy. She was pleased to notice that his shoulders were solid and his arms well toned. He hadn't acquired them from teaching Jane Austen. She was a little surprised; she hadn't thought of him as strong. His muscularity exploded her prejudice that academics were invariably effete and flabby.

Jacques allowed everything to happen without lifting a

finger. Then, as though seized with a sudden desire, he attempted to begin removing her clothing.

"Not yet," she said as she gently pushed his hands away. "Don't worry, you'll have your turn. Just relax and let me do the driving for now," she offered in her sexiest, most seductive voice. He raised his eyebrows, murmured "Okay," and submissively laid back. Instinctively she knew he was not altogether comfortable with this arrangement, but she wanted to have her way. Jennifer went back to work, unhindered by any effort on Jacques's part to participate. She playfully ran her fingers through the hair on his chest. Moving efficiently and methodically, she opened his belt buckle and casually divested him of his pants. She noticed that he was having difficulty catching his breath, as if he'd recently engaged in strenuous exertions. In reality he hadn't moved a muscle, hadn't even twitched.

"Now may I?" he asked as he reached for her again, his patient passivity seemingly exhausted.

"Not *quite* yet," she answered as she turned him aside, "but soon. I promise," she added gently.

Only his shorts and tie remained. She smiled at what was obviously a barely hidden partial erection. With one fluid motion, her expert hands grasped the elastic band on the sides of his shorts; she pulled them down and over his feet. She held them for several seconds, dangling from her thumb and forefinger, her arm extended to its full length, an impish expression on her face, and she let them drop on the floor. Only a lonely tie remained to conceal a bare sliver of human geography; it hung down from his neck to a spot just due north of his genitals.

She looked at him. He looked back. The room was silent. Even the traffic outside appeared to stop and wait—no honking or screeching of brakes. The world was joining Jacques and holding its collective breath.

She touched him, a light, feathery touch, with fingers that moved slowly up his rapidly engorging shaft. When it reached what she surmised was its full dimension, she turned her gaze to his face. His eyes were shut.

"Jacques," she said in her oh-so-soft melodious voice, "*C'est formidable*." Thus encouraged, it grew still larger. She marveled at the power of a few French words. *What a language!* She took in the sight of his nudity and thought gratefully that he looked better without the formal academic garments than with them. For once, she was happy to observe, penile dimensions were commensurate with body size. She knew that was not always the case.

"You see, you *are* a very bad and mischievous boy," she said, continuing to slowly stroke his impressive member.

"I'm a bad boy? You're a bad girl!" he said in a choked voice.

"Oh, this is true—I am *so* bad," she said. She immediately incorporated him, enclosed and enveloped him, lips and tongue a superb substitute for tapering fingers. She heard him gasp and felt his shudder. His expression appeared locked in a shocked grimace. *Is this the look of ecstasy or something else,* Jennifer wondered.

His hips rolled slowly, pushing forward and then receding, beginning again. His gasps were frequent now, becoming more strident with each movement. He appeared to be on the brink of something grand when he stopped everything.

"*No!*" he suddenly exclaimed and gently guided her head away from him. He sat up and stared into her eyes. She knew for certain what he was silently asking.

"Come," she said as she extended her hand to him. It was precisely what she had said when she first led him to the apartment after the roof garden party. He dutifully took her hand, stood, and followed her to the master bedroom. Settled on the bed, Jacques finally asserted himself by removing her clothing. As she wore very little, he accomplished this quickly, his fumbling fingers meeting only token resistance from her bra. The sight of large firm breasts seemed to momentarily paralyze him. As he took in her full nudity his breathing became even shallower than before. Gently he pushed her back on the bed.

His hands roamed as he kissed her virtually everywhere. Now she was the passive one, allowing him freedom to explore wherever he sought to go. Things were transpiring at a rapid pace when Jennifer suddenly spoke. "Jacques, do you have a condom?"

He sat upright as though struck by a bolt of electricity. His right hand clutched his forehead in a gesture that seemed to say "shit! I knew I forgot something."

"A condom, a condom," he moaned, his face the mask of a shattered man who had lost something very dear to him.

"My kingdom for a condom!" he practically shouted in sheer frustration.

Jennifer could not contain a very girlish giggle. "Okay, Shakespeare—you might try the night table drawer."

He leaped off the bed in one ungraceful bound and began to frenetically rummage through the drawer. In short order he triumphantly produced the object of his desire. In the blink of an eye he bounced back on the bed.

"No one can save me now," Jennifer said in a bogus piteous voice, a pretend virgin about to be ravaged. Jacques was too engrossed in a necessary activity to pay heed to her words.

It began. She held him as he moved within her; she held him and noticed everything. He was a very noisy lover, grunting and groaning, occasionally issuing a sharp cry, as though encountering some painful stimulus. She noticed the beginning of a line of perspiration forming on his brow. She noticed that his eyes, barely discernible in the now dimming light, never left her eyes and never seemed to close. *Open-eyed sex, how unique!* She noticed that he was losing it, like a runaway train with its central braking mechanism out of commission. It felt to her like he was becoming wild and out of control. Experienced though she was, she had no model for this kind of lovemaking. The men she had known were too self-conscious to give themselves over to such sexual abandon. Even when they appeared to be losing control, she knew it wasn't really so. She knew it was a pretense, so to speak, a game of passion rather than the passion itself. Not so this time. She laughed at the way he was straining and pushing and heaving, at the way his eyes seemed to lose focus. Was he aware? Had he left his mind behind? She had an urge to soothe him, to slow him down. *You're taking this entirely too seriously, Jacques. It's just sex and it's unlikely to be the last time ever.* "Take your time, Jacques, don't rush," she actually did say, and she laughed again. It pleased her. It pleased her to be the object of such unrestrained lust.

Then it changed. She ceased to be a detached spectator. Perhaps that was initiated by his touching her with an insistent thumb in a very special place. Perhaps he was not as lost in it as she had supposed. There had to be some intelligence, some planning behind the strategic movements of that active thumb. It began with a slight feeling. She was like a swimmer observing a small ripple in the ocean far in the distance. In her experience the ripple sometimes flattened until it disappeared from sight, a disappointing mirage. Sometimes, like now, the opposite occurred. The ripple took on the shape of a wave moving closer to the lone swimmer. The closer it came, the larger it loomed. Would it overtake and overwhelm the swimmer? The closer it came the more inevitable its arrival appeared. Then it abruptly stopped, as if suspended in air. She wanted it now and moved her body as violently as she could. No more laughter came from her; it was too urgent a matter. She pushed herself into the body above her. She twisted and shook. No success. Such was not the case with him. His movements became frantic, frenzied; he began to cry out like a man possessed. His influence on her was infectious, profound. The wave moved rapidly again, overtook her, crashed through her and over her. Her cries were more ladylike than his and at a higher pitch but no less intense. More waves followed—would it ever end? She didn't want it to. She felt a warm tingling throughout her body that stretched even to her toes. She greeted the end of it with a vast sigh.

Jacques collapsed in a heap beside his companion. Between them, like a piece of flotsam brought in by an onrushing tide, lay Jacques's wrinkled tie, adorned with tranquil images of sailboats.

"Was that good for you?" she asked, a self-satisfied smirk on her face. They were lying side by side on their backs, a candle flickering nearby.

"Fairly good."

"I wonder what it's like for you when it's really good."

"We'll have to try again to see."

"Would you like a joint?" She left the bed to open that magical night table drawer from which all good things apparently issued and reached in.

"No, I don't think so."

"You don't indulge?"

"I did occasionally in college."

He probably never inhaled, Jennifer thought. *A good boy wouldn't.* She found what she was looking for.

"You know, it stimulates the sexual appetite."

"I don't think I need it," he said.

"On second thought I don't think you need it either. In fact, it might be a case of over stimulation." She returned the joint to the drawer and closed it.

"What are you staring at?"

"Nothing."

"You were staring at my ass," she said as she returned to bed.

"No I wasn't."

"The hell you weren't. You were thinking, *Wow, Jennifer has a really big ass!* Weren't you? Weren't you?" she said as she poked him repeatedly in the ribs.

He giggled and tried to push her hand away. Undeterred she kept it up.

"No, you're wrong. I was thinking, *Wow, Jennifer has a really beautiful ass!*"

"Okay—good recovery, Jacques. You think fast on your back. I'll let you live this time."

They quieted for a few moments. She was on her side facing him, while he remained on his back.

"You don't fuck like a professor."

"How is a professor supposed to fuck?"

"Daryl once had a boyfriend who was a professor of chemistry at Brooklyn College. She said his PhD stood for *Ph*enomenal *D*etumescence."

"Yeah, that's definitely true of chemistry professors. English professors are PhFs—Phenomenal Fuckers."

"I'll vouch for at least one of them," Jennifer said as she snuggled with him.

The next morning Jacques was the first to arise to teach an early class. Jennifer was awake, although her eyes were closed. She heard him banging around the apartment, showering quickly, leaving the bathroom whistling a vaguely familiar song. Where had she heard it before? "Oh my God!" she said to herself. "He's whistling 'Whistle While You Work' from *Snow White and the Seven Dwarfs!* How avant-garde!" She groaned. It was clear to her that he was very happy, light-hearted—high, in fact. When he stopped whistling, he hummed. She couldn't decipher the song. *Probably from the Civil War.* He came to her and tenderly kissed her good-bye.

"By the way, I thought you said you had to get up early?"

"I lied," she said.

"Under the circumstances, I'll forgive you. I'll call you tonight."

No game-playing there. She felt certain he would call.

After Jacques left, Jennifer began to experience buyer's remorse. How did it happen? Why had she changed her mind about him, and so fast? It was not common for her to engage in sex with a guy she had not been hitherto interested in. Did he put an aphrodisiac in her coffee? She had moved from wanting him to leave early to having sex with him three times throughout the night. It was one thing liking a guy, liking him like a buddy; it was another thing to engage in sex with him. The two didn't necessarily go together. Nor was it the mercy fuck she had planned. It turned out to be a lot more than that.

More what? More fun? It was a puzzle. She asked herself what she should do now. She experienced two simultaneous feelings that were diametrically opposite, like matter and antimatter. On the one hand, she wanted very much to see him again. On the other hand, she wanted to run away and not see him at all. Something about the situation made her nervous. She couldn't say why. Somehow she didn't feel like she was in command of herself. She'd acted so impulsively. Besides, he was so serious it felt like he was playing for keeps. She felt she was in unfamiliar, untrammeled territory. It was scary. Did she want this? Did she actually want him to fall in love with her? Was he the one she was looking for? Was she actually looking for anyone? She thought it would be a good thing to request that he go slower, entirely forgetting that she had been the decider and the initiator, the one to force the action.

She decided to inform him that the sex had been a mistake and that she had no wish to continue with that. Certainly that would make things easier for her. On the other hand, the sex had been awfully good. What harm would it do if it were kept to only an occasional thing? Or was she kidding herself? Sex wasn't something that was easy to control. It could lead to certain feelings, maybe unwanted ones. It was like sitting on a powder keg, never quite knowing when you might unwittingly set it off. *Once the genie escapes from the bottle—well, you know*, she mused. She should be strong and inform him that it was not to happen again. But what if she wanted it to?

When he called that evening, just as he said he would, she agreed to see him. She managed her dilemma by saying nothing. Somehow, when she heard his voice, her resolve fell sharply away. He was cute and witty. She could tell how much he liked her. How could she disappoint him? They went out, and he spent the night again, and it was by no means a platonic evening. Jacques was less frantic in bed, more playful, and took more time with those delightful preliminaries. He turned out to be a rather considerate and endearing lover. It was all so troublesome. If only he'd turned out to be an asshole, that would have solved her conflict.

On the positive side, Jennifer came to a firm decision about the man. She would bide her time. There were no deadlines here, no need to rush anything. Pleased with herself for having arrived at so sensible a decision, she put the matter temporarily out of her mind. In time the right path would open up, and she would find the courage to take it. She was sure of that.

CHAPTER 10
Friendly Advice

There may have been no reason to rush things, but that wasn't how Jacques felt. Having tasted the sweetness of first love, he wanted more. At least that was Jennifer's interpretation of his aggressive behavior. It seemed as if he wanted to see her all the time, a fact that compelled her to frequently say no. Yet each time they did meet they were intimate; her ability to say no did not extend to the erotic arena. That became a problem for her. For it was true that her bottom line concerning Jacques had not changed. She thought he was a wonderful man with many virtues—intelligence, sensitivity, openness, honesty—but something vital was missing. She wished she could name it, could nail the *je ne sais quoi* mystery. She wanted to enjoy him for she loved being with him, but she did not want to fall in love. Most of all she did not want him to fall in love with her. Yet how was that to be prevented? The last thing she wanted was to hurt this lovely guy.

She sought out her friends for friendly advice. Family would have to wait; she didn't trust them as much.

"Why did you have sex with him?" Hillary asked as they sat with Daryl in an Upper West Side Starbucks. Jennifer had chosen to sit at a table near a lone woman working on her laptop. There would be no conversation to compete with, and that person was obviously too engrossed in her machine to bother eavesdropping. Hillary's question annoyed Jennifer because of its hint of disapproval.

"I don't know. What difference does it make?"

"You shouldn't have done that. You can't know a man that soon."

That's Hillary for you, the moral police in action. Jennifer regretted telling her about the sex. She should have known better. She thought of defending herself; then she reconsidered, remembering past conversations with Hillary and the futility of arguing with her on an issue of values.

"You're right. I shouldn't have slept with him. That was bad of me. I should have consulted with you first. You would have brought me back to my moral center. I'm going to see what I can do to undo that. Hmm. Perhaps time travel would do the trick. Then I could go back to a time before we had sex and kick him out of the apartment instead."

Hillary looked frustrated. She attempted a different angle.

"Okay, then why are you still having sex with him, since you know he's not the one?"

"Because it's fun," Daryl interjected, coming to Jennifer's rescue. Daryl was all for fun. She was one of the nation's leading hedonists. Her *modus operandi* with men was to have sex first, followed by the relationship (sometimes).

It dawned on Jennifer that she was now receiving advice from both a moralist and a hedonist. Jennifer shook her head. *Hillary has a point,* she thought. If Jacques felt the same way she did, then having fun would be no problem. But Jacques was showing distinct signs of being love-addled, and that was spooking her out.

"He'd crawl up my ass if he could and decamp there permanently."

Having said that, she emphasized the point by taking a deep bite from her buttered croissant.

"How do you stay so slim when you eat like a demon?" Hillary noted. She had a regular coffee in front of her that she had only sipped twice.

"I have a lot of space to fill up, while you have only a little," Jennifer said in a reference to Hillary's diminutive size.

At that moment the woman at the laptop packed her things and rose from her place. Standing, she looked almost Jennifer's height, although much wider around. "That doesn't work for me," she said directly to Jennifer before putting on a jacket and sauntering out.

Jennifer smiled and nodded.

"Maybe you can fall in love with him, only you need more time," Hillary suggested.

"It doesn't feel that way."

"Why not?"

That was Hillary for you, asking unanswerable questions. It was a little like a physicist asking why there is something rather than nothing. *Who the fuck knows?* Jennifer tried as best as she could to give an approximate answer. She began by admitting that it was an area of great uncertainty. She could *say* what she was feeling but could not *explain* why she was feeling that way.

"When I first met Allan, I was so excited I couldn't wait for his phone call. I would have died if he hadn't called me. When he called, my heart jumped into my throat. There was no way I could say no to him. I was clay in his hands, to be molded any way he wanted. Well, I don't feel that way about Jacques. I don't get nervous when he walks in the door. I don't have fantasies about him. I don't even think about him when he's not around. Oddly enough, I like him better as a person than Allan, but the feeling is not there."

So what was the problem, both Hillary and Daryl wanted to know?

"Do I let this happen? Is it fair, especially since I'm not going there with him? It's nice to have a guy drooling over me, but don't I have some obligation? If he were some jerk, it wouldn't matter to me, but he's a really good guy." Jennifer demolished the remainder of the croissant, as if to push down a bad feeling with the croissant.

Hillary firmly declared that Jennifer was obliged to break

up with Jacques. It was the right thing to do. The longer she waited, the harder it would be for Jacques. It was wrong for Jennifer to put her desires before his interests. That was the moral point of view.

Daryl disagreed. Jennifer should do what was best for her. Jacques was responsible for himself. She didn't have a gun to his head, forcing him to stay with a girl who wasn't really into him. "The time will come when he realizes the score, and then he will decide for himself what to do," she asserted. It shouldn't be Jennifer's decision. That was the hedonist point of view. Jennifer preferred Daryl's view, but thought that Hillary had decency on her side.

At that moment two teenage girls sat at the table vacated by the laptop girl. "Isn't he hunky?" one said to the other, a comment that elicited a flood of stentorian giggles from both girls.

Jennifer frowned. "Hey, whatever happened to that guy— what's his name, Rothstein? You know, the one you met at Meg's engagement party. Did he ever call?"

"Yes, he called that night," Hillary said.

"And he's so shy, it's really sweet," one of the teenagers at the next table said.

"Cool."

"I feel so lucky that he likes me," the other said to her green-with-envy companion.

"Let's go—let's walk," Jennifer said.

As they stepped out on Broadway they began walking south toward the train station on Seventy-Ninth. Jennifer addressed Hillary.

"So Rothstein called the night of the engagement party. Didn't keep you waiting long, did he? Isn't that strange?"

"I don't think so. I thought it was nice."

"I'm not saying it was strange of *him*. If you recall, you were asking me what you should do if he didn't call at all, or if he waited a full month to call. Remember?"

"Oh, sure."

"And then he calls that same night."

Lightly dressed, all three girls huddled against a surprisingly strong wind.

"So?"

"Never mind," Jennifer said, deciding that it would be impractical to explain. It might take up too much time.

"So how did it go with Rothstein?"

"Doug. I like him."

"That's it? Boy, you don't give out much information." It was Jennifer's chronic complaint about Hillary, the close-mouthed girl.

"I've only seen him a few times."

"How many?"

"Five, I think."

"Five? Holy shit! You never said a word. Why didn't you tell me?"

"You never asked."

"She didn't tell me either," Daryl said.

Jennifer didn't ask because Hillary was a constant complainer about a lack of dates. Why bother to ask?

"Besides, what is there to tell? We're just getting to know one another."

The striking difference between Hillary and Jennifer began to assert itself. The difference between Hillary and Daryl was even more astounding. Jennifer wondered to herself why they were such good friends.

"It's not like we've been intimate or anything," Hillary further explained.

They reached the train station, where Hillary would depart. They remained standing to finish the conversation.

"Oh, of course not. Whoever heard of such a thing?"

"Now you're being sarcastic, Jen. He's fine with waiting; it's not like he's pressuring me."

Daryl looked at Hillary as though she were a creature from outer space.

"Okay, so he's like a typical guy, very, very patient. What do you like about him?" Jennifer began to shiver against the cold.

"He's sincere, and funny, and affectionate."

"Shit, I think we're dating the same guy. "

"It feels like winter's returned," Daryl said as she pulled up her collar against the wind. It was unseasonably chilly for an early summer's day. Daryl seemed impatient to leave.

"Look, I wish you luck with Rothstein. You deserve something good," Jennifer said.

"You too. Maybe you should just be friends with Jacques. If you really think you're going to end up hurting him, you know. It's not fair."

"Thanks, Hill. You take care."

They all kissed and lightly hugged before going separate ways. After Hillary entered the subway, Daryl encouraged Jennifer to have fun and not worry about the future. Jennifer answered that she was worried about hurting his feelings.

"Excuse me, Jennifer, that's what we do, we hurt one another. It's unavoidable. It's life. Is he fragile?"

"No, I don't think so. But he is very sensitive."

"Okay, but you can't predict the future. Maybe he'll dump you!"

Jennifer did not think that was even remotely possible. In fact, she entirely discounted it.

"Listen, Jen. I'm fucking jealous that you're having such a good time, and here you are agonizing about consequences that may never happen."

They parted moments later, one walking east, the other west. As Jennifer walked she thought about Daryl's advice. It was certainly true that she could never absolutely predict consequences. But in this particular case she was pretty sure what they would be. Her body shook as she walked. Was it from the cold, or was it from future dread?

Among all her friends, Jennifer valued Meg Simon's opinion the most. Meg took a different slant than the others. She was less interested in giving advice and more interested in understanding Jennifer's feelings toward Jacques as they related to her relationships with men in general.

"Maybe it's a good thing you're not falling in love with Jacques," Meg said to Jennifer as they walked north along West End Avenue toward Meg's apartment. Witnessing the puzzled look on Jennifer's face, she offered an explanation.

"If history is a proper guide, it indicates that when you fall in love your brain atrophies. You overlook monumental blemishes, excuse bad behavior, and hang on when the handwriting on the wall plainly says stay away from this guy! The process seems to be reversed with Jacques, so maybe you should hang on to him."

Jennifer found herself instantly annoyed. While Meg was her best friend, she was also the one most inclined to be dubious, to be suspicious of Jennifer's motives and intentions. Her other friends were as aware of her wrong turns and mistakes, but they were not so quick to draw conclusions. She loved Meg dearly and understood that she wanted the best for her, but increasingly Jennifer found herself in a defensive mode with Meg.

"That may be a good idea, Meg, but I'm in an unfortunate position. I seem to prefer to act on my feelings instead of yours. My apologies." Jennifer's sarcasm perfectly mirrored her inner feelings.

Meg explained that she was not as concerned about Jacques, and she was certainly not predicting that he was the guy for her. It was far too early to know. Her concern was about Jennifer and men; she gravitated toward Mr. Wrong, guys who looked good on the outside but were empty within. Meg fell back on the old metaphor of moth to flame and sighed at the end of her speech. Looking cautiously at the traffic as they crossed the street, she missed the slight smile at the corner of her friend's mouth.

"It's true, I really dig shallow guys."

"You joke about this, but it really isn't a joking matter," Meg said, continuing to strike a very serious tone. "Because the other side of the coin is ignoring the good ones. It's Mr. Wrong that you find so very exciting."

Jennifer couldn't deny it, not even to herself. She registered the truth of it, but dimly. She refused to retain it in her brain for more than a moment or two. And then she discarded it.

"You talk as though—" Jennifer was interrupted by the cacophony of an impatient driver's horn in the midst of one of those traffic blockages that drove people crazy. She looked scornfully at the perpetrator's vehicle, waiting for him to ease up on his horn before she continued to speak.

"You talk as though I'd better get this right immediately or I'll die a lonely old maid. I'm only thirty years old, and it so happens that I'm enjoying my life. Stop being such a mother hen, Meg. I already have a mother, thank you, and she's quite enough."

"Sure, and if she had done her job better you wouldn't be so wary about letting a little love into your life."

"Thank you again, Dr. Simon. I also have a therapist—no need for a second one. What I really need to figure out is what to do with Jacques. The guy's obviously settling down for a long-term stint. Do I continue to see him, and if so under what terms?"

Meg hesitated. "I haven't noticed that you've been taking my advice lately, so do you actually want it?"

"Will you give it freely, without a guarantee that I'll take it?"

Meg decided not to give advice after all. Instead she talked about her feelings. She expressed a wish that Jennifer would give her new friend a little more of a chance, not because she believed Jacques was Mr. Right. Rather, she thought he was "the type of man you should be with, a serious man with good character."

It sometimes amazed Jennifer how quickly Meg made such determinations about people. It would be fine if she were always right, but she wasn't. She wasn't initially so hot on Dan, Jennifer recalled. She decided to address this issue on the spot.

"How do you know this? Character is the most difficult

thing to read. People are complicated, and they don't readily reveal their true selves. You hardly know Jacques. How many times have you actually met him?"

"A couple of times before my party. Dan and I had dinner with Jacques and Annie. That's when I warmed up to him. I really liked the way he treated Annie. He was like a good parent, encouraging, proud of her, gently protective. Maybe that was because they lost their father. You know about that, don't you?"

Jennifer nodded.

"You could see they were close, that they really loved one another. That gave me a good feeling about him. Of course, I don't know him well, and he may look better than he really is. But I still hope you don't cut yourself off from the experience of him, however it eventually turns out."

Nothing Meg said was out of line. Jennifer understood that Meg was being honest with her, and she wanted her friend to speak her mind, to be direct and forthright. Nonetheless, she could not shake her pique, the edginess toward Meg that she had retained throughout their conversation. What was it? She continued to think about it until she thought she grasped it. She felt that Meg had been condescending, that the Fountain of Wisdom had been lecturing her as though she were in possession of some superior knowledge. Jennifer wondered whether it had to do with Meg's engagement and forthcoming marriage. That gave her a leg up on the "failed" Jennifer Slater. The word "failed" reverberated in her mind. She rejected it outright. She was thirty years old, and her life wasn't over. She had failed at nothing. In her anger she forgot everything that Meg had said to her, like rubbish to be thrown aside at the soonest opportunity.

Jennifer did not consult Dr. Harry Salinger. Her rule was never to discuss a man in the early stages of a relationship. She believed it trivialized the therapy session, which should be reserved for much more serious matters. Who knew how long she would be seeing Jacques? Why talk about him now?

So Harry remained unaware of the Jennifer-Jacques caper. However, the advice from her friends had the desired result. The three different opinions crystallized her way forward. She would be honest with Jacques, expressing her true feelings come what may. She hoped he would accept a strict friendship. Certainly there were men who could. But if not, so be it. There would be another man to come along. Jennifer had no difficulty acquiring men. When Jacques called, she intended to tell him that they needed to "talk."

When he did call, he asked whether she would like to see a hit Broadway show; he had access to two orchestra seats. Who would turn that down? And who, after a wonderful evening experience, including a fabulous dinner with excellent company, would bring up a matter that could possibly terminate their relationship? Not Jennifer!

CHAPTER 11

Jacques Talks

Jacques Giraud had no qualms about discussing Jennifer with Harry. He had in fact talked about her since their first meeting at Meg's engagement party. Now things had heated up dramatically. Rushing to Harry's office, still high from the last exhilarating experience, fully convinced that he was madly in love with a most exceptional and sensational woman, he was eager to deluge Harry with the story. He talked about nothing else. The tale unfolded in its broadest sweep. There was a lengthy litany of adjectives to describe this new love, such as "beautiful," "intelligent," "witty," "passionate," "perceptive," "introspective," "sensitive," "playful," and, most striking of all, "luminous." Jacques gave few details of the many hours he spent with this luminous person, and he'd entirely omitted the facts garnered about her life from the account. Swept away by irrepressible feelings, Jacques missed the trees for the forest. He refused to be deterred by humdrum details. He was lyrical and poetic. Figuratively speaking, his feet never touched the ground.

"I do worry about this going down too soon," he at last said, after he had stopped for a moment to collect new thoughts. He did not fail to notice that Harry had remained reticent and inscrutable while his rhapsodic account of this new woman unfolded.

"What's the worry?" Harry asked as he straightened up in his chair. He seemed suddenly activated.

Jacques expressed a small concern that he was falling in love too soon, that he was still in the process of getting to know the woman. But as soon as he'd mentioned it, he dismissed it. She had been pretty open talking about herself, and he had learned a great deal about her. Beside that, she was the one who had been slowing it down. He would have been happy to see her every night if she had been available. She was not. Jacques attributed that to a very active social life with many friends. He thought there was no need to worry about it. Why should she change her life just because she met a guy? He knew women who did that, and he didn't respect them very much. Then there was the fact that she never called him, but that might be because he frequently called her, which eliminated the need for her to call him. True, she was sometimes tardy in getting back to him, but so what; she was a busy girl. All in all, Jacques found nothing to complain about. They were now lovers, and her passion convinced him that she had developed strong feelings for him. He saw her frequently, as much as three times weekly and always Saturday night through Sunday night. Yes, it was all good. Perhaps worrying about a fabulous experience was irrational, a neurotic tamping down of his happiness.

Harry wanted Jacques to talk about his anxiety about falling in love too soon. What did that feel like?

Jacques thought it had to do with the fear of losing control, his worry that his emotions would overwhelm his intelligence—heart above head, so to speak. That was a scary feeling for him.

"Why is that scary?" Harry asked.

Jacques seemed stumped and pensive. "I don't know."

Silence descended on the room.

Jacques tried again. "I think it's become too important, too soon."

"Okay, so let's get to the scary part. What's the worse that could happen?"

"It could fall apart. That would be a huge disappointment. I can't remember ever feeling this way about a woman."

"So the problem is your fantasies; your fantasies about her have soared," Harry suggested.

"You are right on the money," Jacques declared. Of course that was it. His feelings had been oscillating wildly lately, from runaway enthusiasm to dark moments of doubt. Would his dream of love, of family renewed, fade? Would it all crumble into smoking ruins? He dared not share these reservations with Jennifer. They were too off-base, too premature. They'd had a few dates and a truly lovely time. That was all. It takes time to know someone. Why was he dreaming of everlasting love? How could he correct this?

Harry wasn't inclined to issue warnings. He had an entirely different read on the situation. "Enjoy yourself," Harry advised. "Calm down and have a wonderful time with this glowing woman. You have presented no serious evidence to cause hesitation. *Carpe diem*—seize the day and stop projecting into the future. Do you think you can do that?"

Jacques, bright-eyed, smiled. "Yes, sir, I copy that."

"It sounds like you're having the time of your life. Good for you. Good for you. You deserve it. In time we'll get a clearer picture of what you have here. And if it turns out that she's not for you, you'll move on. Sure you'll be disappointed; it'll be a real downer. But you're resilient—you'll recover."

Jacques appeared satisfied with that.

"By the way what's her name?"

"Jennifer."

Weeks passed, and with them a sizeable number of dates and sleepovers. Jacques found his feelings oscillating from paradisiacal tranquility to inexplicable worry. Nine times out of ten it was the former. The exception occurred when Jennifer underwent a mood swing. A hint of temper, a silly argument, a glimpse of contrariness, or a display of pique was enough to send him to the hedging side. Often he kept this to himself, at least at first, not mentioning it to Harry or to anyone else. Whatever incident occurred never seemed to rise to the level requiring disclosure. The good times would invariably roll in and the bad vibe would be eagerly buried, until the next mood swing. Overall Jacques continued to believe that he had met the love of his life.

Jacques sat with Jennifer in a movie theater, a large box of popcorn between them. The film that they were waiting to see was a popular one, and this being Manhattan, it was necessary to arrive very early to obtain good seats. The theater was dimly lit but not dark, the screen blank. Seats were rapidly filling up as people flowed into the theater from doors on each side.

"I had a great session with my therapist," Jacques said.

"What did you talk about?

"You," Jacques said. Jennifer nonchalantly reached over to scoop up a handful of popcorn from the container that Jacques held in his hand.

Jacques waited for a reaction.

"What did he think? No, wait. I bet I know." She reached for more popcorn.

"I doubt that. Would you like to hold this?" He proffered the popcorn.

"No, you hold it."

"So what do you think he said?"

"'Run, Jacques, run. Run for your life, Jacques!'"

"Exactly." He moved the popcorn to his left hand and put his right arm around her shoulder.

"So?"

"So."

"Why aren't you paying attention to that wise man?"

"I guess it's the rebel in me."

"You, a rebel? I can smell a bad-boy rebel a mile off. I'm sitting next to you, and I don't smell a damn thing! What's he like, your therapist?" she asked.

"What does he look like?"

"No, I don't care about that, Jacques. I mean, how does he work with you? Does he talk a lot, does he give his opinions?" She dipped her hand again in the container of popcorn.

"Yeah, he's pretty interpersonal. If I want his opinion about something, he'll give it. I wouldn't say he's laid back at all. What about yours? What's he like?"

The question elicited a renewed need for popcorn and a few moments of contemplative chewing.

"I'd say he's somewhat different. Not that he's reticent, but he's more into listening than talking. He's more likely to ask questions than to give opinions. He's a bit more talkative now than he used to be though. The first year of therapy he spoke very little." As she talked she ate more popcorn. Jacques looked into the box. Noticing it was already half empty and realizing that he hadn't eaten any yet, he took his arm from around Jennifer's shoulder and grabbed a handful for himself.

"Was that okay for you, his hardly talking?"

"Yes, it was what I wanted; I didn't want him to say anything."

"Really? How come?"

"Because at that time I was afraid that anything he said might be a criticism, and that's the last thing I wanted."

"And now?"

"Now it's fine when he talks. Now I'm the critic in the room. I sometimes give him a very hard time."

"Why?"

Jennifer looked contemplative. "Because I can."

"Better him than me." Jacques again threw his arm about Jennifer's shoulder. Turning his body and head toward her, he announced, "I'm going to kiss you."

"Why?" she asked softly, turning her head and lips toward him in a simple gesture of compliance.

"Act of defiance toward my shrink."

"Well, bravo," she said as they kissed.

The screen lit up, and the coming attractions, with the accompanying crescendo of noise, came on.

One hundred minutes later as they left the theater, Jennifer asked what he had talked about during the therapy session.

"I told him what an amazing girl you were, and he cheered my good fortune."

Jennifer fell silent.

That night, as they prepared for bed, Jennifer suggested not having sex. That had never happened before, and it stunned Jacques. It seemed to come out of the blue. To his question she replied that she believed things had advanced too quickly, practically at a "feverish pitch," she said.

"So?"

"So I'm not sure it's what I want." She explained that she liked him very much, that she certainly felt close to him, but was unsure they were "right" for one another. Perhaps they should be friends for now. Perhaps they would be better friends than boyfriend-girlfriend.

Jacques's heart sank. Jennifer seemed cold, having made the announcement without a trace of sentiment or emotion. He didn't understand and told her so. Everything had been wonderful between them. He had been having the time of his life and thought she had been too, so why this? He felt desperate for an answer, desperate to find some path toward reassurance.

She was unable to give him an answer. She was vague and evasive, giving Jacques a distinct impression that she was reluctant to be open with him. This was a Jennifer he had not experienced before. Finally she gave him something, although it was certainly not what he wanted to hear.

"I don't feel I'm falling in love with you. Please don't ask me why, because I don't know. Believe me, Jacques, I wish I could, but it's just not happening."

He suggested that maybe she needed more time and pulling back was not the answer. He felt rising anxiety as the conversation continued. She said she thought it was best for them to not have sex, a simple reiteration of what she had said before. He knew he needed a strong response to that. There was something he needed to know. He needed to know but was simultaneously afraid to know.

"So does this mean you'll be free to date other men?"

"We both will."

"And have sex?"

"It's not what I'm looking for at this time," she said quickly.

"But of course it could happen."

She didn't exactly deny it, although she said it was "unlikely." That hardly put his anxiety to rest. For the first time she seemed to show some uneasiness, some uncertainty. It gave him a slender hope, and he seized upon it.

"That's not acceptable to me. If you're with another guy, there's no way in hell that I can be your friend." That felt good. He would take a firm stand and mean it. It would drive him crazy to think of her sleeping with someone else. His jealousy would be unbounded. She backed off then, agreeing that they would not date others. For once he felt he had the upper hand with her, now that she had made a concession.

"Of course if that's really what you want, to date other guys that is, then that's what you should do, and we should break up."

She told him it was definitely not what she wanted, and she was so strong about it that he believed her. He then pointed out the inherent contradiction in her position. How was it possible to not have sex but also to not date or have sex with anyone else? He said it felt like "monastery living." She made no reply to that. Instead she sat still, a puzzled look on her face. He had taken most of his clothes off, but he began to dress.

"Where are you going?" she asked, looking surprised.

"I'm going home."

"You should stay. It's very late, and it's silly to go back to New Jersey at this hour."

"I don't feel like staying."

When he left, she seemed somewhat alarmed. That was good. He wanted her to feel that way. On the Path train Jacques experienced a mix of feelings. What he feared most had happened; he now believed he would lose her—it was just a matter of time. He would probably never know why, but did it really matter? At times he felt like crying, and some tears did form in his eyes. Occasionally he would slip into anger, and then he would contemplate retaliation. That led to a decision. He would not call her again. He would wait for her to call him. *Ha!* That had never happened before. On their next meeting he would tell her that he was not the least interested in a platonic arrangement; it had to be all or nothing at all. It was her choice. But what if she didn't call? Then it would be over, and he would never see her again. In his anger he was determined to let it play out that way. He would leave it up to her. And if she didn't call, it had been fun while it lasted. Jacques had a memory of something Harry had once told him. It's better to feel anger than to feel broken hearted.

CHAPTER 12

Dinner at Eight

Harry needed to think, for once not about his patients, or his supervisees, or his colleagues or friends. He needed to think about himself. In his life, filled with requests, obligations, and demands, that was not so easily accomplished. He was stupendously busy, and during that busyness Harry had little time for Harry. Something had changed. He knew it was something deep within. He knew he needed to get away from it all, to take a few days off and go to a place where there would be no distractions, where he could be alone to think. That place was his home away from home, a tranquil, bucolic residence in the country where he could lose himself in rounds of mindless chores. And while sweeping and cleaning, while changing the bedding, pruning the weeds in the garden, cutting wood in preparation for a winter that was far off but bound to arrive, and the necessary food shopping, he could immerse himself in that inner mental life that he had too long ignored. After all the years of his personal therapy and all the time treating patients, Harry realized that there were still aspects of himself that remained hidden.

Harry asked himself why, after eight years of working with Jennifer Slater, he was suddenly having sexual fantasies about her. And why, after four years, was he doing the same with Amanda Blake? The mystery was soon resolved. He was lonely and unhappy. He had lost the love of his life and was hungering for love again. Memories don't keep you warm at night. Living in the past doesn't make you happy. Harry once said to a friend, "We are creatures of the present; we err if we live in the past or the future." Now that message was coming home. He could no longer lie to himself that he was leading a fulfilling life. Having admitted that he was lonely and hungry for female companionship, he felt the absence all the more keenly. He wondered what he would do if he went to a party and met two unknown women: Jennifer, or someone like Jennifer, and Amanda. Who would he gravitate to? Would he choose Jennifer, twenty-eight years younger than him? She exuded sexuality. Amanda was more low-key, more sedate. He would have an amazing time with Jennifer; it would be sexual bliss, but how long would it last? The age difference would eventually undermine the relationship. It would be like building a dwelling directly above a major fault in the earth. Nothing could last on such a dangerous foundation. Yet perhaps short term was what he wanted. No entanglements, no situation from which he could not extricate himself without paying a terrible price.

With Amanda there was a better chance of something long term. Perhaps it wouldn't be amazing, only good enough. He had more in common with her too. The relationship would run deeper because of it. There was still a thirteen-year difference, but the generation gap was bridgeable, unlike the yawning gap with Jennifer. Realistically, he could not be with Jennifer. She was his patient, not a stranger. The professional risks would be enormous. His safety resided in keeping it all in the realm of fantasy, daydreams, or even night dreams. He also knew he would not be interested in anything short term. It was Amanda. With Amanda, whom he liked tremendously, there could be a possibility. The question was whether she wanted what he wanted. So what stopped him from going for it? Why had he dithered so long?

Harry was beginning to believe he'd lost his chance with Amanda Blake. He had passed up key opportunities, which might have left a woebegone impression. Perhaps she interpreted his passivity as indifference or, even worse, as the behavior of an irresolute wimp. He shuddered at the thought and felt a twinge of shame. During their last telephone conversation, she'd seemed so remote, and she had hurried to end the conversation, as though he were an unwanted burden, even an irritant. Had she given up, perceiving him as a lost cause? Perhaps she'd found someone else, someone less conflicted, not so locked in the past, someone who consistently and unhesitatingly pursued, which was no less than she deserved. Harry was sure that a woman of Amanda's caliber should have no difficulty finding men who would like nothing more than to be with her. It crossed his mind that such a person might actually have been with her when he called. She seemed suspiciously ill at ease speaking to Harry.

Nonetheless, she'd accepted his invitation to have dinner at his place, without much apparent enthusiasm, allowing him to cling to one last particle of hope that perhaps all was not lost. He tried not to read too much into her acceptance. She might have agreed to come out of simple politeness; after all, they were still friends. Harry knew for sure that this would be his last chance; he was running out of opportunities. To hold back now would surely clinch her doubts that he was unavailable for anything but friendship with her. And that would be his fault, his alone.

At least this time there would be less doubt for him to struggle with. He had resolved at long last to put away (or was it to put aside?) the ghost of his late wife and move ahead with Amanda, if she allowed it. He knew what he wanted; there would be no turning back. Now what he needed was to summon the courage to take the risk. Life was about risk, wasn't it? He took himself on a long bike ride down the road past his house. It was the first time he had ridden that bike in years, and he found it rejuvenating. When he returned home, he was glad he had made the trip. For three days he had spoken to no one but his children.

Cooking dinner for Amanda was a very good experience

for Harry, although that hint of melancholy—the unforgotten memories of what used to be—was never far from the surface of consciousness. It felt good to be cooking again, recovering the skills he had honed with food, and especially recovering the incentive for reengaging with it. It felt like something long dormant had come alive within him. Best of all it preoccupied his mind, temporarily removing his worries about what would transpire that evening.

He had decided upon a roast chicken because he knew Amanda loved chicken. The meal was important to him, so his preparations were elaborate. He salted the chicken two days in advance and took the trouble to insert herbs, thyme, and rosemary under the skin before refrigerating. His skills in the kitchen all came back to him as if it were yesterday, like riding a bike after long years away from it. Best of all, it completely absorbed him. It was a happy time that elicited largely good feelings. He had forgotten how much fun it was to cook, especially for some important other.

With the meal prepared there was nothing left to do but await his guest. That was when the unwelcome and dispiriting thoughts returned, accompanied by a little jangle of nerves and tightness in his stomach. He began to worry about his performance when she arrived. Would he experience the same on-edge tenseness as the last time he was alone with her in a situation that was fraught with sexual potential or failure? Harry had come to understand after much soul searching that he wanted Amanda badly; he feared her desires were different and that at the end of this adventure disheartening disappointment and loss waited. He would lose the fantasy of her, the golden hope of a future together, even the lesser wish of fulfilled passion, however short-lived it might prove to be. Yet he would be the first to admit that something had been gained through this sometimes agonizing process. He wanted to love again, to have a close companion throughout the remainder of his life. He wanted a final separation from his past life, from Sarah. That realization gave him pain, but perhaps it was a necessary pain, like the feeling when one leaves anything of great value behind.

But why this nervous feeling again, this dread of disaster? He knew his anxiety was an exaggeration. The upshot of failure would not be the dire result that his anxiety foretold. He would surely survive rejection; he was determined not to withdraw from life again. There would be another woman at some point, at some time. He felt suddenly angry with himself, angry at the anxiety. "You're too old for this," he admonished himself, as if age by itself should bring wisdom and inner tranquility. "Where's your self-confidence?" he scolded, as if he could restore it by decree. "You can *do* this," he said emphatically and out loud, and then he laughed at his feeble effort to bring relief, laughed because his bravado struck him as slightly ridiculous.

The laughter momentarily set him free and allowed his mind to wander. What would sex with Amanda be like? At first the question brought him pleasure. He imagined himself making love to her, missionary style, looking into those limpid blue eyes, witnessing their glazed ecstasy. Before long a stray, unbidden contraband thought crept in. *Perhaps that glazed ecstasy will never happen; perhaps Amanda will prove to be a fussy, stressed lover, the type of woman who troubled fornication.* She was brought up in the wealthiest part of Westchester County, in the village of Mamaroneck, the offspring of an old Presbyterian family, literally a Daughter of the American Revolution, whose forebears were the first to settle this country. At times she seemed to him overly proper and refined. She once described her parents as "straight-laced" and "anachronistic." They were strict with her, monitoring her comings and goings. The word *sex* was never uttered in the house. She was a virgin when she'd married, and she said her marriage had been pretty much a sexual desert. Perhaps some of that was her responsibility. How could Harry know? Could such a person cast aside inhibitions and have fun in bed?

Their backgrounds were so dissimilar—would she think him a coarse or boorish lover? His stock hailed from Eastern

Europe. His grandparents lived in a Russian shtetl and came to the States speaking Russian and Yiddish and not a word of English. So he and Amanda were East and West, upper and lower classes. Could these so different backgrounds be reconciled? Harry recognized that this was his anxiety talking to him again, but it seemed no less real for that

Amanda arrived one minute after eight, a vision in a flimsy yellow cotton dress. The steaming hot weather that summer day dictated the lightest raiment. She wore sandals that exposed polished pink toenails. Her arms and legs were bare, and Harry could not avoid noticing the absence of hair on her golden, smooth-skinned limbs. She greeted him with a radiant smile that instantly gave him hope.

"You look stunningly beautiful ... Amanda," he said, and his heart skipped a beat because he was about to say "Sarah." It wasn't dodging a bullet. Harry thought it was more like dodging a rocket-propelled grenade. It worried him. Was he sabotaging himself? Instantly he pushed the thought to the back of his mind. *Don't be in your head*, he cautioned himself. *Stay in the moment.*

"Chilled Sancerre," she announced as she handed him the bottle of wine. "It's wonderful, perfect for a sultry summer day, I thought." She showed no sign of nerves.

She's not worried about calling me by her former husband's name, he observed with a touch of self-contempt.

Busying himself in the kitchen again helped settle him down. The meal went over extremely well; she lavished praise, declaring that everything was delicious. She expressed surprise that he had such a cool hand in the kitchen. She had not known that he loved to cook. He could have told her how little he'd cooked meals since Sarah's death but elected not to.

"So you think that I can't function outside my office? 'Poor Harry, I wonder who ties his shoe laces now that his wife is gone?'"

"Something like that, yes. Men are so helpless. But you know, Harry, it has its sex appeal. We girls like to mother our boys."

"Well, now I'm sorry I didn't burn the chicken."

"You have sex appeal whether you burn the chicken or not." That felt good. That felt encouraging. He thanked her, felt an urge to kiss her, but couldn't quite break through the psychological barrier. Ah, but he felt he was so close! Instead he asked if she would like to hear some music, low and sweet.

She told him she would, gladly.

He played a CD of old, familiar standards and sat on the couch next to her, very close. She appeared to take it in stride. They listened to the songs and the singer with her husky, sexy voice.

"I love this one," he said before long. "I hadn't heard it for years, and then it played on my car radio. It was just a few weeks after I lost Sarah, so the words really resonated. I cried like a baby. Too bad this version is a piano instrumental." Should he be talking about Sarah now? He seemed not to be able to help himself.

"I know this. It's *Dancing in the Dark*, isn't it? I always enjoyed listening to it," she said.

"The lyrics are pure poetry," Harry said. "It says so much in just a few words. When you first hear it, it seems as if it's only about two people dancing in a darkened room. They continue dancing until the music stops. The next few lines alter that impression. You realize it's really a metaphor for life. When the music ends, so does life. It makes a point about the brevity of life, how it 'hurries by.' In the next few lines the lyricist presents a new idea, a thought about love and its meaning. Love is likened to a light that brightens our lives, another lovely metaphor, and helps us to 'face the music.' I think that signifies life's paradoxes and uncertainties, its travails and terrors, including the inevitability of death. It means confronting matters that we would prefer to avoid, even things within ourselves. The last line is 'we can face the music together, dancing in the dark.'"

"It is lovely," Amanda said, her face reflecting a deepening sensitivity to what Harry was saying. "But why in the dark; why the metaphor of dark, of night?"

"Life is a mystery. We don't know why we're here or what the future has in store for us. So we're all dancing in the dark."

"I think I understand now why the song has so much meaning for you. It reminds you of your life with Sarah."

"No, it doesn't, Amanda. It may have once upon a time, but now it reminds me of something else."

"Yes?"

"It reminds me of how much I miss being in love."

Amanda put her arm around Harry's shoulder. It was a gesture of sympathy and tenderness, Harry decided. For him it was also a powerful green light.

If Harry had a remaining doubt, Amanda's little gesture removed it entirely. He suddenly felt lightheaded and could have danced on a cloud. Kissing her forehead, he then turned to face her and kissed her lips. They kissed again and again, each time with greater intensity. Gently he pushed her back on the couch, fully in charge, at last the confident initiator. He was directly above her, kissing her face, her eyes, nose, neck, and cheeks. Her arms circled his neck. He could feel her trembling. When he momentarily stopped and raised himself above her, looking at her face, she stretched out her hands to pull him down to her again. Emboldened, his hands began to wander over her body. It seemed so easy; so easy that it rendered his obsessive worrying startlingly inane. All that mental energy wasted, an exercise in foolishness. She was so ardent, so responsive. Now he needed only to claim his prize. Unhindered by doubt his excitement grew.

"Let's lie on the rug, Harry, there's more room."

He practically lifted her off the couch and on to the floor.

They began to fumble with each other's clothing, clumsily but with a sense of deep urgency, as though time were running out and they would soon have to stop. Yet there was no way either would stop until there were no clothes left to remove. It happened rapidly. It ended when he removed her pink panties. The room was lit by a single lamp, and its warm golden light was amazingly becoming to her, giving her an angel's glow.

He was now full of instructions delivered quickly and silently to himself. *Take your time. Don't rush. It's going to happen now. It's a sure thing. She wants this as much as you do. Women like lots of foreplay, so go with that, don't rush it.* It was as if he were trying to remember how it was done, like a young man on a pair of skates unworn since childhood. Inspired by her lovely nakedness, restraining himself was a struggle, accomplished only by repeated caveats to slow down and reminders of the need for lengthy foreplay.

Very shortly she inserted him, while he was still working on foreplay. Evidently she was not a typical woman. Practically hurling her legs across his body, she clamped them tightly around him while elevating herself, beginning a steady stream of chatter. She would not keep still. Her arms encircled his neck just as before.

"Oh, Harry, Harry, Harry," she whispered. "Do you like this, Harry?"

Was she kidding?

"Uh huh," he said. That old *uh huh* again!

"Oh, Harry, you have a lovely cock," she whispered in his ear in a low, conspiratorial voice.

The noun surprised him. What kind of a Puritan was this?

"Faster, Harry, fuck me faster. Oh yes, yes! Grip my ass. Tighter, tighter, oh yes, like that!"

She rose and kissed him hard on the mouth and then settled back again.

"Do you like this, Harry?"

"Yes, yes."

"And this? Do you like this?"

"Yes, yes."

"Should I keep doing it?"

"Yes, yes." Harry did not have a no in him.

"Will you do it to me too?" she asked.

"If you like."

"Ah yes, please do. Ah! Yes, perfect, do that, do that. Do you like my pussy, dear?"

"Oh, God, yes. Love it!" It was Harry's most articulate sentence.

Amanda's uninhibited vocalizations continued for another two or three minutes and then abruptly stopped. She began to pant and grunt, softly and slowly at first, then louder and quicker with greater volume and quickness. Just as abruptly as she'd stopped speaking, she began again.

"Oh, my God! My pussy's on fire! Oh, oh, oh! Oh, yes, Harry, oh yes, here it … here it… here it is! Oh, Harry, Harry, Harry!" Her legs and buttocks shook as her arms and legs gripped Harry much tighter than before. *"Harree! Oh, Harree!"* And over she went.

Harry struggled to join her but could not. Although he'd had limited experience with women, he had never before encountered such flagrant directness during the act of lovemaking. This wanton display of lust excited him so much that he came perilously close to a premature ejaculation. With monumental effort he held back and successfully stymied it. His problem was that he could not now recover that moment of impending consummation.

After Amanda settled down, she spoke again. "Oh Harry, what a lovely fuck," she said in a soft, lovely voice.

Harry was happy for her and delighted that he was the responsible agent. But he also felt it was now incumbent upon him to reach a climax. Why was it taking him so long? It was all so very exciting that Harry could not figure it out. The longer it took, the harder he tried; the harder he tried, the longer it took. In his self-conscious awareness, he'd lost the immediacy of the moment. He apologized for his slowness.

"No need, Harry, there's no rush. Take your time. I love it."

Harry couldn't expect more support than that, if only he could believe her. Somehow he felt his prestige was on the line. He forged ahead, determined to succeed. He increased his speed and the forcefulness of his thrusts. It may not have helped him much, but it definitely helped her. After a few minutes he heard her calling out.

"Oh, oh, oh, oh, oh," she started. Beneath him, she writhed, rose up, and pushed into him. "Oh, oh, oh, oh, oh, oh, oh … Oh, oh, oh, *oh, oh, oh, oooohhh*," and off she went again.

"Oh, lord, I came again!" she exclaimed, quite unnecessarily, Harry thought. *At least someone is having fun.*

After calming down, she sensed Harry's frustration.

"Harry, why don't you let me come on top of you?" They switched positions, Amanda sitting up and athwart Harry, Harry on his back.

Having momentarily uncoupled, she immediately retrieved him, unerringly guiding him into her again.

"No, don't move, Harry, let me do the work. You just lie back and think very sexy thoughts."

At this point he was grateful that at the very least he had never lost his erection. It gave him hope. Amanda moved slowly, rhythmically, and reached back to gently stroke an erotic place.

He stirred.

He felt her tightening on him, tightening and releasing, a process that was repeated again and again.

"God, you're very strong down there," he croaked.

"I've had lots of practice," she explained seductively, with an abbreviated laugh.

For some mysterious reason those words proved magical to Harry, for in no time they summoned him to his supreme moment. After laboring so hard, it happened when he was doing no work at all. He held her closely as she lay on top of him.

Later, lying quietly next to Amanda, Harry wondered about what had just happened with him. Why had it taken him so long? The question plagued him because everything had worked out so well. She was eager and thrilling and everything he could have hoped for. So why was there a problem? Was he afraid somehow to allow himself the full pleasure of her? Was there some remaining secret guilt toward Sarah that motivated him to hold back? Or was it something else, something so deeply embedded in his unconscious that he remained clueless regarding it? It wasn't that things were perfect with Amanda. Things had happened that provoked his fear. He needed clarification. He was not the type of person who could sit on his anxiety and let things ride. He needed to know where matters stood.

"Are you sleeping?" he asked.

"No, I'm not."

"You're so quiet."

"I'm just enjoying the moment quietly," she said. "And you?"

"I was just thinking. You know, for a time I thought you were losing interest in me."

"Really? When?"

"The telephone conversation when I invited you to dinner. I felt you couldn't wait to get me off the phone."

"That's true," she said. "Was it so obvious?"

That answer left Harry in a quandary. He was developing a distinct sense that it was the most inappropriate time to discuss this. But he needed to know; he absolutely needed to know. Was it simply a temporary loss of interest, or was she entertaining another man? Harry believed he needed to be self-protective.

"So what was that about?"

"Are you sure you want to know?" she asked in a weighty voice.

Harry tensed as apprehension filled him. He was sure now. Her question and the manner in which it was made gave her away. She hadn't been alone. Amanda had another lover. This made all the difference in his feelings for her.

"Yes, I would like to know," he said in a tight voice.

"I had to pee. I mean it was urgent, and it seemed like you didn't want to get off the phone. I know I should have told you, but somehow I neglected to. I can be an awful prude sometimes."

"Really? I never would have guessed it tonight."

"Yeah, I was pretty slutty, wasn't I?"

"No, not at all; just experienced."

"I'm not that experienced, Harry. It's not like I've had many lovers since my divorce three years ago."

Harry wondered how many but was afraid to ask.

"But there's someone else you're seeing," Harry said. It was a question, although cloaked in the form of a declarative sentence. He held his breath and anticipated the worst.

"What gives you that idea?" she said in a calm, smooth voice.

"You pretty much gave it away when we were having sex."

She actually laughed.

He thought it strange. Was this a laughing matter?

"Really, I did? I'm dying to hear how you divined this."

"Remember when I told you that you were strong 'down there'?" Harry asked, unable to shake a downhearted feeling. "And you said you had 'lots of practice.' Well, what else could that mean?"

"Perhaps it meant exactly that. You know what Freud said: sometimes a cigar is just a cigar. No hidden meaning. The first man I went with after the divorce was a sex therapist. He taught me how to tighten myself, said it drove him crazy. I soon learned that he *was* crazy, although it had nothing to do with that. However, I never forgot the lesson. So I still practice."

"Nobody else?"

"Nobody else. The decks are clear."

Harry juggled two opposite thoughts. Number one was that he was very obtuse, particularly for a therapist. Number two was that he was very elated, but not because he was obtuse. It was because he had been wrong, and wrong, and wrong again. He wondered what was wrong with him.

"You've had trouble figuring me out, haven't you?" she asked.

"You bet."

"When I invited you over for dinner and you left without touching me, I had a thought. I thought maybe I should have answered the doorbell naked. Would that have locked it in for you, Harry?"

Harry thought that over very carefully.

"Probably ... not. I may have thought you were expecting someone else."

"Like the delivery boy?"

"Something like that."

"You reminded me of one of the old Peter Sellers's movies, when he plays Inspector Clouseau. He keeps getting clues that he completely disregards. I was beginning to despair. I thought of being blunt, you know, sort of suggesting that we adjourn to the bedroom."

"Why didn't you?"

"I didn't want to make it that easy for you. All kidding aside, Harry, what do you think that's all about?"

"I think I was worried that you thought I was too old for you."

"Never crossed my mind, dear."

"So, Amanda, how does it feel being with the biggest clown in Christendom?"

"Well, not so good. But if you fuck me again that might help to nullify the feeling."

CHAPTER 13

Jennifer Talks

When Jennifer arrived at Harry's office, she immediately brushed past him with barely a sidelong glance and hurled herself onto the couch. It was a gesture fraught with meaning; she rarely utilized the couch unless something serious was brewing. She knew instantly that broaching the subject of Jacques Giraud signified that he was *important*, a recognition that hitherto she had been loath to admit.

"I met this guy," Jennifer suddenly announced, and she launched into a lengthy soliloquy in a somewhat frantic effort to bring Harry up to date. She talked while lying in a supine position on the couch, her eyes turned to the ceiling. She could not see Harry, who was seated behind her. Jennifer revealed that she had met "this guy" at Meg's engagement party, had dated him "for a while" without ever considering him important enough to bring him up in therapy. Things had changed, however; her feelings had changed, "although not entirely," and now she found herself unable to make a decision regarding him. Her major problem was that she never felt completely "at home" with him. He was a wonderful guy in many respects, different "in a good sense" from previous boyfriends, yet "not exactly" what she was looking for. For one, he was not her physical type. She described him as a "nerdy intellectual with horn-rimmed glasses, square, a bit undernourished, very tall but slightly stoop-shouldered." He tended to dress very formally in shirt and tie and sport jacket, and his taste, especially in music, was ghastly, although she was okay with his love of opera, a love that perhaps unfortunately she didn't actually share. This was not to say that she in any way "disliked" opera. He was also not very good at picking up clues. She liked him and she was quite open in showing that to him, but his crystal-clear enthusiasm for her was off-putting.

Before Harry could reply she rushed to explain. The man called constantly, at least once a day, despite the fact that she never called him and occasionally said no to his invitations for dates. Nonetheless, she was anxious to let Harry know that he did take no for an answer, and there was nothing obnoxious or "stalker-ish" about him. He was perfectly warm, charming, and consistent; yet, strange to say, she felt he was "too good." What she meant by that, she hastened to say, was that he was too easy, too available, too adoring, and eager for more from her than she was ready to give. The bottom line was he didn't excite her. That was the one thing she had with Allan, despite all his faults, that was lacking with Jacques.

Throughout this speech Harry had remained a silent Buddha, sitting on his monarchical throne behind the couch. Now she at last lapsed into silence, waiting for Buddha to speak. She felt tense uncertain about Harry's response.

"So what's the problem?"

The sheer simplicity of the question momentarily stunned her. What indeed was the problem? She tried to put together a reasonable response, stammering some of the time, seeming unsure of herself. It was not very typical behavior for her. As things proceeded between them, she explained, the gap between their feelings for one another expanded. She believed he was in love with her, while she had not fallen in love with him. That singular fact preyed on her conscience. She liked him too much to let this continue.

"So perhaps you should stop seeing him?"

Yes, that was logical, but she liked him too much to stop.

"What do you like about him?" Harry asked.

Jennifer took a moment to organize her thoughts. "Well, two

things most of all. He seems to be very comfortable talking about his feelings. That's refreshing in a guy; it isn't typical. And second, he really gets me. He gets me because he wants to. He asks a lot of questions, and he really listens to my answers. How many guys are like that? If there are any, I haven't been meeting them. And he's honest—honest about his feelings, honest about everything."

Harry asked whether there was anything else. She said he was very intelligent, had a great sense of humor, and was very respectful of her feelings. She thought over what she had said. Feeling a little embarrassed, she added, "I know it seems like I *should* be falling in love with him. In fact, I wish I were—it would make things so much easier. And then, like I said before, there's the physical thing. I know I'm sounding shallow, Harry, but I can't help it."

"I don't think it's shallow. Chemistry is important. If there's no passion, what you have is friendship and nothing more."

Jennifer lapsed into silence. She finally broke that silence in a soft, low voice. "Actually there is passion."

"What?" Harry asked. Did he not hear her?

"I enjoy sex with him. I mean, he gets so excited it's like having sex with a hurricane. Once, though, I had a fantasy that he was Allan. That's significant, isn't it?"

Harry agreed that it did mean something, but it was not clear what that was.

She asked for an explanation.

"When you do that, you're creating distance between yourself and the man you're having sex with. It's not uncommon and not necessarily a bad thing, unless it happens very frequently."

Jennifer thought it would be appropriate to inform Harry of the latest development, that she had suggested a friendship without sex.

Harry wondered why, since she enjoyed sex with him.

She explained that she wanted to protect Jacques against future pain. If she continued with him, he would become even more attached to her.

"Are you sure you want to protect *him* from future pain? Perhaps you want to protect yourself."

"Is that it?"

"You said you liked him very much. Are you sure you'll never become emotionally involved with him? Your previous attachments with men didn't work out so well. It could be that you're afraid that he might hurt you."

"It doesn't feel that way to me," she told Harry.

"Then another possibility is that you're still hoping that Allan will return. If he does, it will be messy to have another boyfriend."

Jennifer vehemently denied this. She was through with Allan. Absolutely.

"So how did the gentleman react to your suggestion?"

"He said no. He said it was all or nothing. So what do I do with this guy?"

Harry refused to answer that question. It was her choice, not his.

That wasn't good enough for Jennifer. She needed something from Harry. Anything.

"When you boil it down, it's simple enough. You met a great guy who really likes you; you also like him, and you're not sure what you want to do. Walking away seems like a poor option; continuing makes you anxious. We need to come to grips with what that anxiety is all about."

Jennifer thought that over and remained quiet. *Why is everything so difficult?* She truly did not want to work on anything. She wanted an answer *now*. She needed to decide *now*. But she need not tell Harry *now*.

"Living with uncertainty is hard for everyone," Harry said, "but sometimes absolutely necessary."

Grasping those words of wisdom, Jennifer came up with a solution. She changed the subject. Something had come up with her father that she wanted to discuss.

At the end of the session Jennifer rose from the couch and strode toward the door.

"By the way," Harry said, "does your boyfriend have a name, or do you want him to remain anonymous?"

"He's not my boyfriend. He's a guy that I'm seeing."

"My mistake."

"Jacques," she said as she walked out the door.

Jacques. The word produced a shock wave through Harry, something like a thunderbolt. While it was true that Jacques had mentioned that he was falling in love with a certain Jennifer, there had to be at least twenty thousand young Jennifers bopping around the island of Manhattan. Besides, Jacques's lyrical apotheosis of *his* Jennifer bore not the slightest resemblance to the prickly character of *Harry's* Jennifer. How could they be one and the same? And since Harry's Jennifer had never mentioned a Jacques (until now), how was he to have put two and two together? It was all clear now; surely there were not two Jacques in the Big Apple with a girlfriend named Jennifer. Identifying the couple created a problem, a situation fraught with complications. Harry always assiduously avoided treating two people who were involved with each other. Once they knew the truth, would it set off a competition between the couple at the first sign of trouble? Would each vie for Harry's support? "Whose side are you on, Harry?"—that sort of thing?

And what expectations would there be? Would Jacques want to know Harry's opinion of Jennifer? And how easy would it be for Harry to remain faithfully neutral in his work with them? Was Jennifer the right woman for Jacques? She was already ambivalent, while Jacques definitely was not. The imbalance in their feelings for one another was pronounced. Was Jacques once again making a poor choice? And if Harry tipped him off, wouldn't that be a betrayal of Jennifer? On the other hand, maybe Jennifer wasn't such a bad choice. Clearly, she liked Jacques, maybe more than she was willing to admit.

How was Harry going to handle this? His head was spinning. Despite so many years of doing this work, the situation was utterly unique. Did he have a choice in this matter? He had been seeing both of them too long to refer one to another therapist.

There was yet another problem. Confidentiality was a

therapeutic rule of biblical proportion, somewhat tantamount to thou shalt not kill. He had to be careful not to carry what one said to the other unless explicitly permitted to do so. Similarly, he could not divulge to either of them that the other was in therapy with him. That would break the rule of confidentiality. But how could he remain quiet? And what would they think if they accidentally made the discovery? One of them might casually drop Harry's name and the other might pick up on it. Would they understand the necessity of his silence? Would they both feel betrayed? Would he be forfeiting their trust? He could hear Jennifer's voice already: "Harry, how could you keep this a secret from us? I feel you played us for fools!" For once in his professional life he was flummoxed. He needed advice. He needed to consult a shrink. "I'm fucked!" he said to himself.

When Jacques viewed the caller ID on his phone and saw that it was Jennifer, his heart jumped into his throat. Momentarily hope displaced despair. Three days had already passed without a phone call, and he was beginning to believe that it would never come. But the sound of her voice, so remote, edgy, cool (or was it cold?) immediately dispelled hope. She suggested that they get together "to talk." He agreed to meet her at her apartment the following night. Jacques visualized the ending, how she would act, how he would respond. He wondered whether she would be authentic, or would she say, "It's not you, it's me." He hoped not. No doubt she would tell him why she had elected to stop. Would it matter? It might only be what she believed the reason to be, not what it actually was. The years with Harry had taught him about the unconscious, that what resided below the level of awareness often held sway over what resided above. Jennifer might not actually know why Jacques wouldn't do for her. Then again, the thought passed through his mind that she might have met someone else. If that were the case, the mystery would be solved. He shuddered at the thought. If it were true, it was unlikely she would tell him. She would spare his feelings so that he would never know. He berated himself for even entertaining the possibility. It was masochistic of him to go there, of no benefit at all.

Jacques thought about the time spent with Jennifer: their first meeting at Meg's engagement party, the dates that followed, the tennis match, the horseback ride. He thought about their first lovemaking, how entranced he was, how sure he was that he had met the love of his life. His eyes welled with tears as the memories flowed seamlessly through his mind. Despite his effort to put them aside, they appeared to have a life of their own, insistent, unstoppable.

He was eager to see her, not because there was hope but rather to get it over with. He could not say for certain why he felt so darkly pessimistic. The evidence was hardly overwhelming. How much can you actually tell from the mere sound of a voice? He had an intuition, a presentiment of an approaching end, and it was impossible to shake. He found the feeling he had now, the waiting, unbearable. He barely slept that night and taught his classes the next day in a semistupor. He felt like he was living in a hazy dream, like nothing in his life was real. He traveled to New York from his home in New Jersey, arriving hours before the appointed time. He wandered the bustling streets, looking into the faces of passersby, noticing the ones who looked happy, feeling strangely out of place. He passed outdoor restaurants and cafes and looked at people sitting, eating, engaging in animated conversation. He felt no hunger, although he'd had nothing but coffee in the morning, and would not eat. He understood now what it felt like to be an outsider, unable to participate in the hurly burly of life, unable to feel alive, feeling only numb, deadened to his inner self, weirdly detached and uninvolved. But as the threatening hour approached, he began to feel something; he began to feel afraid. His hands were sweating; his mouth felt dry, as though he had burned through all his saliva and there was none left.

He rang Jennifer's doorbell and took a deep breath. When the door opened, Jacques Giraud's life changed. In a nanosecond he realized that he had been wrong. The anticipated calamity was not to be. The stress, the dread of the last twenty-four hours, instantly fell away. A wave of elation and renewed life and excitement swept over him. Pessimism and gloom vanished completely, replaced by the glow of runaway happiness. All of this happened at a glance. Jennifer Slater answered the doorbell stark naked!

She did not speak to him. She threw him a "fuck me" look that sent thrills up and down his spine. He could have spent a week just taking in the wonder of her lovely nakedness. If only he were a Leonardo da Vinci—how he would have painted her! She quickly took his hand and guided him into the living room, where a sheet and some pillows lay across the floor. She brought him down upon it, put her arms around him, and they became lovers again. When he recovered from insane sex, his hunger for food returned big time. It was as though his entire body, including his stomach, had woken up from a long slumber and suddenly come joyfully alive. Telling him that she was not dressed to go out, she decided they should order in.

"Honey, you're not dressed for ordering in either."

She threw on a pair of shorts and a top. They cuddled on the couch, waiting for their food to come. He wondered whether he should say anything. *Why not let it go? Sometimes it's best not to stir things up.* Since they were now kissing, why not just enjoy the moment?

Jennifer broke the silence. "You've got a crazy girlfriend. I hope you know that."

"It's my cross to bear," he answered lugubriously.

"Do you forgive me?"

Forgive her? If she told him she had recently committed a murder, he would have forgiven her. She was now irresistible to him, the most beautiful girl in the world.

"I'll think about it," he said.

His soul had been plucked out of Hades and sent crashing into Paradise. When the food arrived, she would not let him pay for it. "You're my guest," she said. She thought it laughable how quickly he demolished his meal. His appetite had returned.

CHAPTER 14

Harry and Izzy Confer

Harry once jotted down on a pad for his amusement the following description of his friend: "Dr. Israel Gross, redoubtable analyst, near octogenarian, bearded, crinkly-eyed, larger than life but diminutive in size, relentlessly voluble unless maddeningly silent, saltier-than-thou, renowned for his erudition and grandiose for that, yet curiously self-effacing, is the perfect paragon of paradox."

"Izzy" greeted him with a wave of his hand as Harry drove into the old man's driveway in Hastings-on-the-Hudson, Westchester County, New York. He lived with his wife in an eighty-year-old colonial house about thirty minutes by car from Harry's place in Manhattan. Upon arriving on a Saturday afternoon, Izzy ushered him into a large study lined with books of various kinds, mostly psychology but including history, biography, and fiction as well, all carefully sorted according to category within in-wall bookcases.

Izzy had heard of Jennifer before. Jacques was an entirely new subject. Upon learning about Harry's dilemma, he pronounced the situation "full of landmines." He agreed with Harry's conclusion that Jennifer and Jacques, whom he persistently referred to as "the Js," must eventually learn the truth about the remarkable coincidence. How this could happen was of course the issue at hand.

"Hmm. Very interesting. Of course, you can't tell them

directly—that would not do," Izzy said from his rather large, soft, plush black leather chair, which seemed to swallow him up, with the odd effect of making him appear even smaller than he actually was. "What about couple's therapy?"

"Couples therapy?"

"Yes. You invite them to come in at the same time."

Harry mulled it over. It didn't seem like a bad idea, and it was certainly original, the sort of thing he expected from his friend, who often thought outside the box. But Harry immediately felt resistant to it.

"I don't know. I think that could backfire. They might consider that deceptive and feel themselves tricked. Besides, they may not want a couple's session. It is rather early in their relationship after all."

Izzy stretched his legs out, crossing them at the ankles, a physical act that necessitated his sinking deeper into the chair. To Harry he looked extraordinarily relaxed. Izzy stroked his beard, a gesture that gave the impression of serious meditation.

"Looked at another way, perhaps it's not such a good idea for them to find out the truth, Harry. They might break up soon. Why would they ever have to know?"

"I have a feeling that's not going to happen, so I would prefer not to be passive about this."

"Yes, that's understandable, but you must be aware, my friend, that once they learn the truth your troubles will multiply."

Harry nodded acknowledgement. He knew there would be difficulties, but he blanched at the word *troubles*.

"The Js might be unduly concerned about the privacy of their sessions," Izzy warned.

"I know that, and I will make it clear that what they tell me will be held in absolute confidence. I will not tell one what the other said."

"And they might not absolutely believe you."

"Well, nothing can be done about that," Harry said, throwing up his hands in a gesture of helplessness. Izzy sat up and crossed his legs, an ankle on the top of other thigh. In a way it made him look younger.

"What are these two like?"

They seemed to be sliding from topic to topic, Harry noted, but he had a go at it nonetheless.

"I'd say she is somewhat flighty. She's a changeling. At times she's charming, witty, irresistible in her way, while at other times she can be a ball-buster. He's consistent—wears his heart on his sleeve and tends to be very idealistic. She has the capacity to be quarrelsome and a troublemaker, although she can also flip around and be apologetic and sweet. He's easygoing and eager to please. She's sometimes indecisive, while he can be too quick to make decisions. He wants the relationship and knows it; I think she wants the relationship, too, but doesn't know it."

"Oy vey!" Izzy shook his head.

"I think they make a pretty good couple," Harry said.

"No doubt it's true love. But let's get back to the main issue."

Which issue was that? Harry had forgotten.

"Remember I talked about a mine field? Let me give you a few illustrations of that. Suppose you ask Jacques a question, like do you trust her? Doesn't matter why you ask that—you ask it, and he thinks, *Does Harry know something that I don't? Is she cheating and Harry can't tell me because of that confidentiality thing? Is he warning me?*

She may be as pure as Snow White, but he's ready to go straight home to blast her. Maybe, like Othello, he's ready to strangle her."

"It could happen," Harry admitted, "but how is this helping me?"

"Forewarned is forearmed, Harry. What you can anticipate, you can prevent. Actually, when I think about it, it could be worse." Izzy uncrossed his legs, placed them firmly on the floor, leaned forward, and clapped his hands in a gesture that seemed to say "a great idea is forming." Harry sometimes wondered whether Izzy's sitting postures were a reflection of some ever-changing mood.

"He's on a roll," Harry muttered to himself.

Izzy began to speak. "Suppose she *is* cheating on him, and he's still goofy over her, totally smitten and in la-la land, thinks he's got the best thing since noodle pudding. You, on the other hand, know that she is fucking her brains out with the butcher down the block." Izzy looked positively gleeful.

"The butcher-in-the-bedroom syndrome. So?"

"So it's not going to affect your work with him? You're not going to suggest, however subtly, that maybe he shouldn't be so trusting?"

"And if I do?"

"Wouldn't that be a violation of confidentiality? You're taking what she's telling you in confidence and using it against her."

"Not a problem."

"Really? You'll have to prove that to me, Harry."

"If she's fucking the butcher, she won't tell me."

"Why not?"

"Because she won't trust me to keep her secret. Isn't that what you warned me about before, that they won't trust my assurances of absolute confidentiality? So it won't be a problem."

"Now, Harry, you're not being serious. She may very well tell you. Guilty people want to tell."

Harry held in his mind the image of a dueling match with an avuncular man with an undersized body and oversized brain.

"I think you're underestimating me, Izzy. What makes you think I couldn't handle this matter? Do you really imagine that I would allow myself to retreat into moralism, that I would relinquish my professional stance? If she were cheating, the work would be with her, not with Jacques. She would have to explore her reasons and what they signified about the relationship with Jacques."

Izzy nodded thoughtfully. He seemed impressed, although reluctant to give up his ground entirely. "But you have feelings toward Jacques, don't you? You like him, right?"

"Yes, I do. How is that relevant?"

"So you'll have feelings about her cheating—feelings of anger. Maybe even contempt for her; feelings of sympathy for him. It will be a predictably tough environment to maintain complete objectivity."

Harry instantly recognized the truth of this, but he also would not concede his ground.

"Why are we projecting a future that is not likely to occur? I've been with this girl for eight years. She's had several boyfriends and never cheated, even though they were pretty shitty relationships. Of all the worries I've had about her, that's not one of them."

Izzy had a surprised look on his face. He had picked up Harry's tone. Sitting further back in his chair, his back firmly lodged against its back, he laced his fingers together in front of him and spoke. "Ah! I see you're pissed off at me, Harry. Perhaps I deserve it. Forgive me, but I was only trying to investigate all eventualities. Cheating may never be the problem, but I think it is a sure thing that your emotions will be enlisted at some point in this saga. Should I drop the subject, or may I ask one final question?"

Harry's intuition told him to say no to that "final question," and he would have, if only curiosity hadn't gotten the better of him. He nodded his assent.

"How do you feel about the Js fornicating?"

Am I in treatment? Harry wondered. *Will I receive a bill after forty-five minutes? Will I get a professional discount?*

"I feel fine," Harry replied, a wee bit defiantly, "because now I will hear both sides of the equation, instead of just one. It will give me an opportunity to learn so much about them."

"An excellent point, Harry. I never considered that. However, I think you've neatly evaded the question, which was not the general one of what you felt about treating both of them, but the specific one regarding their fornicating."

Harry laughed. The old bastard had a point.

"Over the years you've mentioned this Jennifer a few times,

and you've always given me the impression that she's one hot number."

"I never said that."

"No, you didn't; you implied it."

"Yes, and?"

"Well I'm just wondering whether ..."

"Whether?"

"Recognizing of course that you are the complete professional with very firm boundaries, whether, nonetheless ..."

"Yes? Ask the question already, Izzy."

"Whether you've ever imagined what it would be like ..."

"Yes?"

"To be the recipient of this ... erotically charged woman's ... uh, favors?"

"Never."

"And having entertained this delightful image, no doubt more than once, whether you think of Jacques as, shall we say, a lucky dog?

"Nope, never considered it."

"Impossible," Izzy declared. "I want to fuck all my pretty patients, always have, always will."

Harry wondered whether Izzy could still get it up. "That's why you have a reputation as a lecher."

"True, but I'm also a normal man. Lechery is the natural state of the species. Ask any pornographer. We're only talking about fantasy, Harry—imagining, not acting. Stop pretending you don't have balls. You've wanted to fuck Jennifer, probably since the day she first wiggled into your office. And you want to fuck Amanda Blake too, but that's another story. The ethics are much less certain. The profession doesn't approve of our sleeping with a supervisee, but it's not illegal; you can fornicate without having to litigate."

This was a subject Harry very much wanted to avoid. "Amanda's no longer my supervisee, she's yours."

"As if that matters. Harry, the truth—are you shtupping

Amanda?" He asked this question while jabbing his forefinger directly at Harry.

Harry had to give an answer; not giving one would be equivalent to a confession. "Absolutely not."

Izzy observed his friend. "You know, there's an old Yiddish saying, Harry: when the penis goes into the air, the brains go into the ground. You should take my advice and stay away. You're an authority figure—it's Oedipal. You know. It's all too dicey. It will stain your splendid reputation."

Too late, you old fart.

"As I recall, I came here for advice regarding, uh, the Js. I think we've come pretty far afield."

"Oh, you want advice? Do nothing. Why do they have to know they're both seeing you? What good will it do them?"

Harry considered that, but somehow it didn't sit well. Keeping the knowledge a secret from them felt a little bit like cheating.

"Izzy, your shoes."

"Yes?"

"They don't match."

"That's true, they don't. Does this distress you?"

"Actually, it has no impact on me at all. I find it curious though," Harry said with a bright smile.

"You do?"

"That you are so observant in one way and so oblivious in another."

"Story of my life, Harry. I pay too much attention to the inside and not enough to the outside. So I walk into walls, put my pants on backward, and wear different shoes. But I can spot an obsessive compulsive personality at a hundred paces!"

At that moment the door to the study flew open, and a sweet-faced woman, no more than five feet tall, in her late sixties, poked her head in to invite them to lunch.

"Listen to this, Lizzie," Izzy said loudly to his wife, "I think you'll enjoy this. Harry has two patients who are fucking each other, and they don't know they're seeing the same therapist. How's that for coincidence?"

"Oh, Harry," Lizzie said in a voice full of feigned sympathy, "the gods are sporting with you."

"I can handle the gods, Lizzie, it's your husband I'm having a problem with."

"You take him too seriously, my dear."

"You don't?"

"Of course not, Harry. How do you think I stayed married to him for forty years?"

"That's been a mystery for many of us. Thanks for at last clearing it up."

"Maybe you can help, Lizzie," Izzy said. "Here's the problem: Harry can't enlighten his patients because that would violate confidentiality. But he thinks they should know the truth that he sees both of them. So what to do?"

"Which patient do you see next?" she asked Harry.

"That would be Jacques, on Monday."

"Why not ask him to find out who her therapist is? Make up some excuse," Lizzie suggested without a flicker of hesitation.

Harry and Izzy stared at one another, a look of stupefaction on both their faces.

"Why didn't we think of that?" Harry asked Izzy.

"We're best at solving the more complex problems," Izzy explained.

"If only that were true," Harry said.

So the game was afoot. Harry was happy that he was meeting with Jacques first, because he was more malleable than the other one. Casually, as if an afterthought, he suggested that Jacques request the name of Jennifer's therapist. When asked why, Harry merely said that it would be "a good thing" for him to know.

As it turned out it was a very easy sell. Jacques dutifully put the question to Jennifer.

"Why does he want to know?"

Jacques answered.

"What business is it of his?" she said with a touch of indignation. "Tell your shrink it's a private matter."

In her session with Harry she brought the "private matter" up. She thought it "weird" that Jacques's therapist wanted to know Harry's name and asked what Harry thought. The question put Harry on the spot. Lizzie's plan had obviously come a cropper. Harry should have guessed that Jennifer would be the weak link in the conspiracy. Could he rescue the plan, or should he consider it dead in the water?

"Yes, it's weird, very weird," he said for want of a better answer. He needed to stall so he could come up with a new plan.

"That's how I feel. But why is it weird?"

Harry had no immediate answer. "Well, figure it out, Jennifer. Why do *you* feel it's weird?"

"I really don't know; it's just a feeling. Why do you think it's weird?"

Harry reached in and pulled the answer out of his ass. "It's a violation of confidentiality. Why should you tell anyone the name of your therapist? As you yourself said, it's a private matter."

Harry was relieved. His answer almost made sense.

Jennifer loved it.

As if by magic Harry saw the way. "Hmm. That worries me, Jennifer, a therapist who ignores the cardinal rule of confidentiality. If it's who I think it is, Jacques—is that your boyfriend's name?—should not be seeing him. It could be a disaster."

"He's not my boyfriend."

"Hmm. I'm going to need his therapist's name. Forewarned is forearmed."

Jennifer consented. It wouldn't be good for her to be dating a guy who was in treatment with a quack. Never mind the contradiction of violating Jacques's right to confidentiality.

She put the question to Jacques.

"You're asking me? Whatever happened to 'it's a private matter'?"

"I changed my mind. Look, if you tell me yours, I'll tell you mine."

"I asked first," Jacques said.

Due to her mistrust of men and therefore fearing Jacques might not tell, Jennifer was reluctant to be the first to disclose the secret. She hit on the solution. They would each write the name of their therapist on a piece of paper, fold it, and hand it to the other. They would then open it at the exact same time.

Unfolded, they stared dumbly at the pieces of paper with their private information. A pregnant moment of silence ensued.

"How can this be? Your therapist is so different from mine. How can they be the same guy?" Jacques asked in a state of shock and confusion.

"It's not a they; it's a him. I think our therapist has multiple personalities," she said. "What worries me is—"

"What?"

"Is why the fuck he didn't tell us himself?"

CHAPTER 15

The Troubled Bikini

Jacques remained blissfully unaware of the depth of his girlfriend's ambivalence. Although inclined to avert his eyes from reality, he was not entirely blind to her defects. From time to time he would expose to Harry a grievance or two. It was through Jacques that Harry learned that Jennifer Slater was a woman who never met a light bulb she wanted to turn off, or a shower she wanted to end, or a checkbook she wanted to balance (a cause for bouncing a check she wrote to Jacques), or a telephone conversation with a girlfriend she wanted to end, or a rug she wanted to vacuum, or an insect she wanted to squash. Of course those were all small matters, annoying but easily tolerated. Of greater weight were her frequent somber moods and her quickness to anger. Little things set her off. When that happened she could be sharp-tongued and unpleasant. Coming from a reasonably tranquil family unit, he was unused to quarrelling. Disputes were settled with calm and rational discussion. He found these episodes confusing since they seemed to come from nowhere.

One incident he told to Harry concerned, of all things, toilet paper. Harry referred to it as "the toilet paper caper." Jacques explained to Jennifer that the leading edge of the paper should go *over* the roll. Jennifer had a habit of placing the lead *under* the roll. She asked what the difference was, and Jacques explained that it was easier to see and reach. As he further explained, his father, who worked as a hotel manager, always checked that the toilet paper was put into the spindles correctly in all the hotel bathrooms.

"That should have been the end to it, don't you think?" he asked Harry. "Well, it wasn't. She said something like, 'In my family we always put it under, and not a single mishap ever occurred. You see that I grew up okay, Jacques? My shoulder isn't malformed from having to stretch for the toilet paper. I like it under.' I swear that's what she said. So whenever I use the bathroom I switch it to the way it should be. That lasts until she uses it and switches it back. If that toilet paper were human, it would be schizophrenic by now! Until we come to an agreement, the toilet paper will never be safe. That's what she's like; she's always ready to pick a fight, even over the most trivial things."

Of greater weight was his sense that he was more into her than she was into him. He pondered the imbalance in their mutual affections and was disquieted. He persuaded himself that in time that would change for the better. He need only be patient and continue to love her. Thus, despite this daunting litany of complaints, the poor love-besotted man remained intractably benign. There was much good in their relationship, he reasoned, and Jennifer's loving qualities far outweighed the occasional misunderstanding. Jacques made sure that Harry heard about the good stuff. She was taking a cooking class because she wanted to be able to cook for him, and she tried out her new skills by preparing meals. She went out of her way for his recent birthday, taking him out to a wonderful dinner and topping it off by giving him a very expensive Bloomingdale sweater. Wasn't that love?

Yet there was no escaping the occasional issue. Just when things appeared to be going perfectly well, something irksome would occur. Even so, Jacques had developed the habit of letting things slide off his back. One past contretemps in particular underscored Jacques's invincible benevolence, even in the face of Jennifer's adolescent behavior. The event occurred on the last weekend before the Labor Day holiday. This was the story he gave to Harry: Jacques was engaged in the kitchen, while Jennifer was in her bedroom getting ready for the beach picnic planned with their friends. Suddenly Jacques heard an ear-piercing scream. Instantly dropping his activity, he "fearlessly" rushed toward the bedroom, quickly calculating with each step the potential hazards that might await him: a burglar under the bed—very unlikely. More likely some innocuous though hideous insect, a fat and ugly water bug or ghastly jumbo spider, or possibly even a spindly, terrified gray mouse cowering in a corner. To his surprise he found nothing more than a half-naked girlfriend with a pained expression on her face, standing in front of a full-length mirror. She was wearing only a bikini bottom.

"What's wrong?" he naturally asked.

"Look at me!" the distraught young woman gasped, her finger pointing to two narrow ridges of pubic hair peeking out along the edges of her bikini. "I can't go like this! This is gross," she cried.

Jacques admitted to Harry that he could have warned her about this. He waxed poetically metaphorical in his precise description of the problem at hand. Having paid close scholarly attention to every microscopic detail of Jennifer's private parts, he could have prophesied without the slightest fear of error that a skinny and inconsequential piece of cloth barely larger than a subatomic particle could never have efficiently concealed the entire warp and woof of his girlfriend's nether hair. In fact, he had long observed the intelligent design of Jennifer's pubic patch; how, like an advancing army sending forth its reconnoitering patrols, two thin rows of dark down departed from the thicker center as if to defend its perimeters. It was exactly these offending peripheral columns that created the source of the lovely woman's abundant distress. Jacques thought it sad for her and shed crocodile tears that she had neglected to embrace the quaint contemporary fad of shaved pudenda. As Jacques wryly exclaimed to Harry, "I could have predicted that this could lead to a future problem. In the face of evil, I remained silent!" He took full responsibility. Jacques warmed to the story the further he went into it.

"Can't you just shave it?" he asked Jennifer in a feeble effort to assuage her irascible mood.

"Shave it? What planet are you from?" she thundered.

"I guess she believed that abusing me provided the ultimate solution to her dilemma," he said.

"It'll leave those horrid red spots. No, thank you. Why the fuck didn't you remind me to take care of this sooner?" she asked aggressively.

Jacques reported to Harry that at that point he was beginning to form a premonition that he was being blamed.

"I'm not going," she said with an air of finality, folding her arms across her chest, an action that partially covered her bare breasts. Then, perhaps anticipating Jacques's protest, she petulantly stamped her foot, once more declaring imperiously, "I won't go. Call Meg and make up some excuse," as she virtually tore off the slender and hopelessly inadequate garment with one swift movement of her hands, eliminating the last meager shred of cover.

Jacques wondered why the task of lying to Meg fell upon him, though the courage to put forth that inquiry failed him. At that point, despite his stubborn reluctance to find serious fault in her, he began to dimly perceive that there might be something amiss in Jennifer's tantrum-like reaction. And he was actually looking forward to this outing at the beach. Racking his scholar's brain for a way out, he finally settled on the simplest plan:

"What about ... wearing a pair of shorts?" He held his breath, remembering how she'd responded to his last suggestion. Then he described in graphic sentences approximately what followed.

Without a word to acknowledge Jacques's superior wisdom, Jennifer turned about and began rummaging through her bureau. Silken, pretty underthings of kaleidoscopic variety were cast high in the air, flying willy-nilly everywhere. One struck a lamp shade, nearly toppling the lamp, which swayed one way and then the other before righting itself; a painting of the Madonna was rudely broadsided by a bra; one errant pair of lacy black panties landed squarely on Jacques's head as he stood, neither moving or removing it, mutely and calmly surveying the chaotic scene unfolding before his eyes. Finally, Jennifer found what she was looking for and triumphantly held a pair of very short cut-off jeans in the air. Voila! Problem solved. After hitching the jeans up, mercifully discovering that they were a perfect fit, she sheepishly looked at Jacques, who was standing at attention, the lace underpants still firmly crowning his head. She laughed, walked to him, and put her arms around him and her head on his chest.

"I'm sorry," she said. "Why do you put up with me?"

"May I now remove your undergarment?"

"No. It's a good look for you."

As Jacques described the bikini imbroglio to Harry, it seemed nothing more than a fond, embedded memory that he took much pleasure in telling. A tolerant and forgiving man in normal circumstances, Jacques could not bring himself to criticize Jennifer's puerile behavior. He could, however, poke fun at it. Still, there was a minor factoid that Jacques deemed too irrelevant to mention to his therapist. A month earlier Jennifer asked whether he would like her to remove all traces of what she possessed "down under," as she called it. He declined the offer. He declined because he was erotically stimulated by that dusky forest, with its shockingly stark contrast to the whiteness of the surrounding terrain. A patient need not tell everything to his therapist.

When Jacques left Harry's office, he felt a twinge of regret that perhaps he had revealed too much. If Jennifer had metamorphosed into a fly sitting on Harry's wall, she wouldn't have been very pleased. Jacques considered that he had been swept along by feelings of male camaraderie, a kind of frat-boy winking collusion with Harry. It was the old male conspiracy against women. Was Harry collusive? Jacques consulted his memory of how Harry took in the somewhat racy information. Harry had been unusually quiet while Jacques described the bikini calamity. Jacques recalled a slight look of amusement on his face. Jacques also remembered his therapist seeming to look a jot uncomfortable when Jacques's detailed description of Jennifer's hirsute horror unfolded. Yet Harry never stopped him. Regardless of what Harry may have thought, Jacques decided that it had been a breach of Jennifer's privacy. The more he thought about it, the more ashamed he felt. Surely he could have told his story without so much anatomical detail. He was tattling inappropriately on the woman he purportedly loved. He made a mental note never to repeat that mistake.

CHAPTER 16

A House in the Country

Harry owned a house in Ulster County in the Woodstock area, about three miles north of that village. He and Sarah always dreamed of having such a home as a weekend retreat, and they struggled in the early years of their marriage to save enough money for the down payment. The 110-year-old ramshackle farmhouse that looked its age wasn't anything much. They might have passed it by had they not recognized its redeeming features, the most salient of which was its affordability. It sat on ten acres, its borders partially surrounded by woods, and despite its dilapidated condition, it retained a certain rural charm. Its Greek Revival front entry and columned front porch, its narrow dormer windows and sheet-metal roof suggested to the couple that restoring the creaky old edifice might prove to be a rewarding project. For the next seven years they renovated the home. The southern-style front porch needed a new ceiling and floor. Inside, the crumbling plaster walls required immediate attention, and a second bathroom had to be constructed. They spent as much on the repairs as they had on the purchase. To save money, they painted the entire place themselves. Practically all their spare money and all their spare time went into the enterprise. It was, however, a labor of love, and it brought them even closer. It was their mutual dream and a source of pride for both of them.

It wasn't that the Salingers disliked living in New York

City, with all its cultural offerings, its myriad restaurants and entertainments. Rather, they both loved the tranquility and beauty of nature and immensely enjoyed hiking, the outdoors, rummaging through country antique shops, meandering in farmer's markets, and all the other pleasures associated with country living. In particular, Sarah took an interest in gardening and transformed herself into the family botanist. Harry's specialty was bird watching, and he could expertly identify any winged specimen that happened to swing by.

After Sarah's death Harry could not bring himself to sell the old home. There was too much of Sarah in it. He well understood that holding on to it was a way of clinging to the memory of his wife and to the life they had once forged together. The children wanted him to keep it as well. They had grown up in that country haven, and although they rarely visited it now (they had their own lives to lead, after all), it was comforting for them to know that they still could. Harry rarely returned to it, and when he did he was rarely alone. His recent short stay was an exception. He would invite his children or his brother and sister-in-law, and if they weren't available, he could usually entice a close friend or two. Izzy and his wife had visited a few times. It would not do for Harry to be always alone, to rattle around by himself in that house of bittersweet memories.

His neighbor, Sam Evans, looked after the place in Harry's absence and made sure there were no frozen pipes, or roof leaks, or anything that might prove damaging to the old structure. Sam was a retired veterinarian in his late seventies, still hearty, who lived about a half-mile down the road. He had been a friend to both Sarah and Harry for more than fifteen years.

Harry was a little sad to see the place these days. The garden, once so lovingly attended to by Sarah, had gone to weeds and dead bushes; initially he had hired someone to act as a garden caretaker, but when she moved out of the county he let it all go. Since he was so rarely there, why spend the money?

Now Harry was on his way back to the house, driving north on the New York State Thruway with Amanda Blake sitting next to him. He planned to meet his children there, introduce them to Amanda, and spend a day and night with them. Harry had been with Amanda for four months, and he thought it was an appropriate time for her to meet Katie and Brad. It was early in December, but the seriously cold, snowy weather had not yet arrived, and he looked forward to starting up the old brick fireplace and spending a cozy evening with the three most important people in his world.

Amanda had questioned how good an idea it was to meet the children in that particular venue, since it was so much a part of their lives with their mother. Wouldn't it be strange for them to see her there, taking their mother's place, so to speak? Harry considered that notion and then dismissed it. It was time for all of them to move on. They were adults now, kids no more. Brad was twenty-six, two years older than Katie, certainly old enough to accept the new reality. The venerable home that had come to symbolize the past might now be made to stand for the future, a renewal of life and joy and pleasure. How could Amanda argue with that? She gave her consent for the expedition to a changed reality.

Harry had a different kind of worry. "I'm concerned that you won't like the place," he told her. "It just doesn't compare to your palace in Bedford."

Harry was referring to Amanda's three-million-dollar-plus home, a rich woman's establishment full of glass, cathedral ceilings, skylights, state-of-the-art conveniences, very expensive furnishings—the ultimate in roomy comfort and luxury that in comparison made his place seem shabby and rough.

She turned to look at him. He felt her eyes focus on him, but he kept his glued to the road in front of him.

"Sure, and when you came to Bedford I worried that my half- acre would seem claustrophobic when compared to your ten acres." She placed a hand firmly on his thigh and leaned toward him, her eyes still on his face in profile.

"I'm sure I'll love it, sweetheart, and I'm looking forward to meeting your kids," she said reassuringly. He glanced quickly over at her and caught a glimpse of her radiant smile.

"I'm still not sure of that, although I appreciate your encouragement. It's pretty much gone to seed from lack of tender loving care. I have a house cleaner come in once a month, just to keep the spider webs from taking full control, and Evans keeps a watchful eye on it, but it hasn't really been lived in since Sarah's death."

"We can change that," she answered, and Harry felt a surge of good feeling.

"I would love that." He again turned his face to look at her, returning her smile with his own. More and more he was recognizing how supportive and sympathetic she was. She never frowned on anything he did. Even during those occasions, now becoming less frequent, when he felt the need to reminisce about Sarah, she listened patiently and demonstrated a heart-warming sensitivity. Signs of jealousy never appeared. Of course, he was careful not to draw comparisons between the two women, never to intimate to Amanda that she was falling short of the mark, lacking in something that the other possessed to the full.

Nevertheless, he knew in his heart that Sarah had set the standard of womanly beauty and virtue for him, that the angel of his memory could never be equaled, that all challengers were bound to fail. Despite his efforts at concealment, a suspicion may have evolved in Amanda's mind. She was a rather discerning woman. Not long ago she had observed to Harry that she sensed a caution in him, a holding back in his embrace of their new love. It felt to her like "an invisible wall," an impediment to his willingness to entirely give himself over to their relationship. She never brought up his lost love with Sarah as a possible source of his hesitations. Harry had been defensive in his reaction to Amanda's insight, partly denying it, partly attributing it to the newness of their love. He asked for her patience and indulgence, and she readily granted them to him.

As he pulled into the driveway Harry felt a rush of excitement. It was early Saturday afternoon, cold but sunny, with only a light breeze; the day stretched out before them. As the children had not arrived yet, there was time to show her around the place.

"I'm not quite ready to carry you over the threshold," he quipped.

"Could you if you were ready?"

"Sure, if there were an ambulance waiting nearby, with an orthopedic surgeon on call."

"I'll have to arrange it."

He gave her the tour of the house, each room eliciting a host of questions. Amanda appeared genuinely interested in everything—antiques, paintings on the walls, old photographs, an ancient rocking chair ("Where is this from? How long have you had it?"); even an odd knickknack or two evoked a question.

"Oh, Harry, it's perfectly charming. I love it!" she exclaimed. "Now all we need is a dog."

"What kind should we get?"

"A big shaggy country dog, a rough-and-tumble mutt from the local pound that we were born to rescue."

"While you're planning that, shall I make a fire?"

Harry went out to the side of the garage where he stored wood under a tarpaulin. He then built a pyramid of wood in the fireplace, and he heard her tinkering in the kitchen. He crumbled up a section of the *New York Times* and lit it with a match that he drew from a small wooden matchbox. Watching the very dry wood catch the flames he called after her. "What are you up to, love?"

"Making the salad we brought."

"You found the large salad bowl?"

"Uh huh."

Good, Harry told himself, *she's being domestic.* It was a familiar feeling to him, although one that he had become unaccustomed to. That they were already functioning like a team, cooperating with chores, brought him pleasure, a favorable harbinger of what was to come, or so he hoped.

"When you're finished, Amanda, would you wash the windows too?"

"You mean the way you did when you were at my place?"

Harry smiled. He enjoyed this back-and-forth teasing, a sure sign of how much like a couple they had become. The fire now blazing, he left to join her in the kitchen. They talked happily as they worked together to finish the salad. Later Amanda spotted the first car slowly rolling up the driveway.

"Someone's here," she called to Harry from her seat on the front porch. "I think it's Katie." Harry assumed it was, since typically Brad would be late. He rushed forward from the bedroom to participate in the greeting. Katie appeared, tall, slender, and light-haired, just like her mother. He'd always felt the likeness was uncanny. She was beautiful, too, just like her mother. It pleased him greatly to see the warmth on display as the two women embraced.

"Brad called, Dad; he said he's on his way and will be here in about thirty minutes. Oh, it's so good to be here again!"

"I can see why you love this place," Amanda said. "It's so beautiful here."

"Is Jonathan coming?" Harry asked Katie.

"Yes, I have to pick him up at the bus stop in an hour. He said we should eat without him. He had a bite before he left."

"Jonathan's the boyfriend," Harry explained to Amanda as they entered the house together.

Katie carried a small luggage bag with her. "The very serious boyfriend," Katie elaborated.

They settled on a couch and chairs in front of the now hotly blazing fire. Katie rubbed her hands together near the fireplace to warm them.

Amanda took the initiative by engaging Katie in conversation. Harry sat quietly, listening to the women chatting. He was glad they were getting on so well; Katie seemed to like her, or at least to feel very much at ease with Amanda.

When Brad arrived a short time later, his greeting to Amanda, a kiss on the cheek, was more restrained. Nevertheless, he was affable enough, and the tension that Harry contained in his body immediately subsided. Katie was the pussycat,

Brad the bulldog. As they walked into the house, the women leading the way, Brad turned to his father and made a gesture with his hand that could be interpreted as "Wow, she's hot!" In the evening, after a dinner of grilled chicken and squash, they sat around the fireplace. After Jonathan arrived, he and Brad gathered wood to keep the fire going. They all watched the flames rise in hypnotic concentration as if they had never viewed such a sight before. Katie and Jonathan snuggled on a love seat, her legs over his, his arms wrapped around her. Harry noticed Amanda looking over at the couple and fondly smiling. As he was sitting next to her on the couch, he felt a sudden urge to put his arm around her shoulders but felt constrained from doing so. It might be premature for the children to see that.

"Dad used to supervise you?" Brad asked Amanda from his chair near the fireplace.

"Yes, for four years."

"What was he like as a supervisor?" asked Katie.

"He was rather unusual. On some occasions harshly critical. In his somber moods, unreasonably demanding, frequently irrational, and volatile—sadistic, if you will. He was an excellent supervisor."

They all laughed, with one exception. Harry simply nodded vehemently.

"Hmm, that's curious; he was that kind of a father too," Katie added, to more laughter.

"My fan club," said Harry. "If I may switch to a pleasanter topic, do you know what I like most about winter in this house? No geese."

Katie and Brad nodded knowingly.

"They like to swim in our pond," Katie explained, referring to a small pond some thirty yards to the west of the driveway.

"That wasn't the problem," Brad added. "They had the habit of shitting on the driveway. Actually, for them it was more than a habit; it was a way of life."

"And it was good old Dad who had the task of sweeping it up," said Harry. "As you may have guessed," he said turning to

Amanda, "it wasn't exactly my favorite chore. Actually, I was aching to pass it on to Brad, since he loved the geese so much, but Sarah, ever Brad's champion, forbade it."

"That's because I was still a kid, and Mom had the wild notion that sweeping shit was a man's job."

"Yeah, she spoiled him," Harry countered.

Amanda followed this dialogue by looking first to the one and then to the other, the beginning of a smile at the corner of her lips.

Harry was unable to decipher that Mona Lisa smile.

"Once, we had two geese taking up what appeared to be permanent residence in our pond. There was just nothing I could do to get rid of them," Harry said.

"Dad would shout and bang pots; he would honk the car horn, but he couldn't scare them away," Katie said.

"They would just stare at me disdainfully," Harry said to Amanda.

"You poor guy," Amanda said, not really very sympathetically.

"Then one day we saw four tiny goslings swimming around with them. So then it became clear what it was all about. They were in our pond to give birth. But the kids were happy they stayed; something about how cute they were. They even gave names to them. That's why I thought they should clean up after them."

"But, as in so many other ways, Mom came to our rescue," Brad said.

"Oh, was your father that bad?" Amanda asked.

"Are you kidding, Amanda? Do you know what it's like having a shrink for a father? 'Well, what feeling does that stimulate in you, son?'" Brad said in a dramatic voice. "It felt like my feelings were his private reserve."

Harry looked at Brad but remained silent.

"What's wrong with that, Brad?" Amanda asked. "My children grew up with a father who never cared about their feelings. In fact, he showed very little interest in them."

"Yes, but they had a mom who was a shrink."

"No, I wasn't yet, not at that time. I wish I were, because I think I was blind to what it was like for them."

Harry again had to restrain himself from putting his arm around Amanda.

"Well, Dad wasn't that way at all," Katie spoke up. "He was always very interested in us. We were absolutely not neglected. Do you remember Arnold, Dad?"

"Arnold the pig," Harry said, grateful for the change in subject. "We used to walk over to a neighbor's farm so the kids could see the animals."

"The Giannoni farm," Katie said. "And Mrs. Giannoni made the most delicious jams, which she sold to us."

"So we walked over one day and discovered that the Giannonis weren't around."

"Apparently Arnold was minding the shop," Brad said.

"I think Arnold took a shine to the kids, because he followed us home. We tried to get him to go back, but he wouldn't hear of it. So Arnold temporarily became a member of the Salinger household," Harry said.

"Shall we tell Amanda what the real problem was, Katie?" Brad asked.

"If it's okay with Dad."

"Me? I don't have any secrets from Amanda."

"None?" Amanda said, her eyebrows arched at a most skeptical angle.

"Well, hardly any."

"Shall I, Dad?" asked Brad.

"I don't understand what the problem is. Am I supposed to be concerned about something?" Harry was truly perplexed about what Katie and Brad were driving at.

"Okay. We had to bring Arnold back, but Arnold had other ideas. Mom suggested that we drive him back. Big problem."

"Why was that a problem?" Amanda asked Brad. Harry had a sense that Amanda was intrigued.

"The problem was we had a new car, and Dad was envisioning Arnold crapping in it. You know that wonderful fragrance a new car has? Dad wanted to retain that for as long as possible. His terror was that it would be overridden by the odor of pig shit!"

"Goose shit, pig shit. Harry, I'm beginning to think you have a feces phobia," Amanda said. Even Harry laughed, although half-heartedly.

"Dad put his foot down," Brad continued. "He would not drive Arnold home. Mom said she would do it, but Dad wouldn't allow it. He was really alarmed; you might even say he was agitated. But Mom was the soul of common sense. We couldn't keep the pig. He wouldn't go back on his own or follow us back, so what else could be done? Katie, do you remember what Mom said?"

"No, actually I don't."

Harry didn't either. Nor had he remembered reacting so forcefully to the idea of driving Arnold home. Was Brad exaggerating?

"Mom said Dad was behaving irrationally and that they had no choice. Then she said—and I'll remember this as long as I live—'If Arnold makes in the car, you can always sue the Giannonis, Harry,' and I recall thinking that was the funniest thing I ever heard. Of course Dad had to finally relent. Mom was always the one to bring him down to earth. I was actually disappointed that Arnold behaved himself. I wanted to see Dad sue the Giannonis," Brad said with a hearty laugh.

Amanda turned toward Harry, and he felt her eyes on him. He wondered what she was thinking.

"Yeah, that's really funny, Brad," Harry said mirthlessly.

"Hell, Dad, I think Amanda should know about your dark side, don't you?"

"And what's your dark side?" Amanda said to Brad.

Brad shrugged his shoulders. "I'm a terrible teaser. And what's yours?"

"I think I expect too much from people, and then I feel terribly let down," she said. "I need to be more realistic, like I am with my patients."

"What's your dark side, sis?"

"I don't have a dark side, and that's a dreadful disadvantage. Nobody's afraid of me, even people who I wish were."

"I'm afraid of you," Harry said spontaneously and instantly knew that it was the truth.

"Oh, Dad," Katie said in a disbelieving voice. "What's your dark side, big guy?" she asked the hitherto quiet Jonathan as she poked a forefinger into his chest.

"I can't say no to you," Jonathan replied.

"That's a virtue," she said as she lightly pushed his arm.

"I understand that your ancestors came over on the *Mayflower*," Brad said to Amanda. "That's quite a lineage."

"Yes, but I'm not sure what to make of it," Amanda said with a slightly embarrassed laugh.

"Our ancestors came from the Bialystok stetl and arrived here on a cattle boat. They spoke Polish and Yiddish, and my great-grandmother was illiterate."

Harry looked at Amanda to see how she would react. He fidgeted in his seat, but she looked quite composed.

"Well, then, let's be glad that our ancestors never met," she said.

Harry laughed loudly. "I'll drink to that," he said.

Later Harry looked for an opportunity to spend a minute alone with Brad. He asked him to help bring more wood in from the pile near the garage.

"Are you angry with me about something?" he asked his son.

"I was just teasing you—don't take it seriously."

"Your teasing had an edge to it, so I think something's going on."

"Don't analyze me, Dad," Brad said tensely.

"Then don't be hostile to me. Do you have a problem with Amanda?"

"No, she's fine."

That evening Harry and Amanda decided to turn in early and said goodnight to his kids. She gave both a warm hug. She smiled at Brad, looking directly into his eyes. Harry observed that Brad quickly turned away. For once Harry possessed no desire to talk about the day's events. He was asleep and gently snoring only scant minutes after his head reached the pillow. Amanda told him she wanted to stay up to read and would sleep when she became drowsy.

The children left the next morning after a late breakfast.

"What was going on between you and Brad?" Amanda asked Harry as they sat, bundled up in scarves, hats, and sweaters, in rocking chairs on the front porch.

"When the kids were young, Sarah and I had a running dispute over childrearing. It was the one area of conflict between us. Sarah could not discipline them and never got angry with them. So I was left in the bad-cop role. Since Brad could be rambunctious, we had some rough patches. He looked to his mother as a buffer."

"You must have resented that."

"I did, but that only made things worse. But I thought we were over that. For the last ten years or so, Brad and I have been getting closer. That's why yesterday was such a surprise. It wasn't like him."

"Maybe it wasn't you then; maybe it was me. He may have been angry with you because you brought me here."

"But Brad has encouraged me to move on with my life, and he has never spoken one single word of disapproval regarding you."

"That's his head speaking. I wonder whether he knows his heart," Amanda said as she drew her wool scarf more tightly around her neck. The sun had disappeared behind a large gray cloud, and the wind picked up a bit. "This is not merely a home where he grew up. It is so full of memories and artifacts. It's like sacred ground, a memorial to his mother. Look, sweetheart, I don't blame him. It must be very hard for him to see me in the place his wonderful mother occupied for so long and so happily. We shouldn't fool ourselves. It will take time. It's cold; let's go inside."

Harry suddenly experienced a wave of gloom. The road

that he imagined stretching smoothly before him now looked quite different. There were pitfalls ahead, potholes and detours and warning signs. Nonetheless he wanted this. Something had happened in his life that he had not expected. He had fallen in love again, and it was too thrilling to turn away from it. The genie could not be pushed back into the bottle.

In the car on the way back to the city, he asked her about Katie.

"I think she made a sincere effort to be friendly and accepting," Amanda said, "but I'm not sure how she feels about me. Katie is hard to read."

Just then her cell phone rang, and Harry heard her address a man named Cy. Harry knew a Cy, a student of his at the Center. Was it the same man? He listened intently, without any particular concern at first.

"I can't talk to you right now, I'm with someone. I'll call you later."

Harry could not hear Cy's response.

"I'm sorry," she said to Harry as she closed her phone.

He thought no further of it. Cy could be anyone: a patient, a man she supervised, a student in her class at the Center. He trusted Amanda, so there was no cause for suspicion or alarm.

It stayed that way for two days, until he saw her with a man in a restaurant on Broadway. It was in the evening, and it happened as he was walking home from his office at the end of the day. He had casually looked into the restaurant window, when he was startled by the view. They seemed in serious conversation, although there was no actual physical connection, no touching or handholding. Harry felt an initial shock and confusion about what to do. He recognized the man immediately. It was Cy from the Center, once a student, now a therapist. Should he enter to say hello? Wouldn't that be embarrassing for Amanda? What would she say, and was he actually prepared to hear it? He told himself that he shouldn't read too much into what he saw. It might be nothing. She was in love with Harry. Everything about her behavior told him so.

In fact, she told him so. Then what was there to worry about? He continued walking, almost convinced that there was no cause for concern.

Then why not say hello? He turned around and started back toward the restaurant. As he approached, Harry discovered that he was beginning to have a bout of nerves; irrational, but there it was. He turned around again and headed for home. Once home he immediately turned on his TV set. He knew it was an insufficient distraction. It did not work. Two hours later he was still unable to stop thinking about Amanda and Cy. When the yellow-eyed dog Jealousy raised its hideous head, there was no ignoring it. *Amanda should be home by now—should I call her?* he wondered. Perhaps Cy was still with her. Did he want to know that? Sensing there would be no sleep for him unless he called, he went ahead. On the phone Amanda was as pleasant and as happy to hear from Harry as he could have wanted. He invited himself over to her apartment, which was close enough to walk to.

She greeted him with a kiss and a hug, and for a moment he considered dropping the matter. He was afraid of appearing ridiculous, suspicious of something that was almost certainly innocent. But the words forced their way out. He described what he had seen earlier in the evening.

"Why didn't you say hello?" she asked.

He explained that he thought he might be intruding. He asked what relationship she had with Cy.

"Someone I used to date."

"How long ago?"

"Earlier this year."

He expressed surprise; Cy was so much younger than she was, perhaps by as much as ten years. "I don't see the two of you together."

"The gap between our ages is less than the one between you and me. Are you saying that it's okay for an older man to be with a younger woman but not vice-versa?"

"Oops, you got me there. I guess my sexism is showing."

"I guess so," Amanda said a little peevishly.

"Actually, I never liked him, and I think that's why it's hard for me to think of you with him."

"Oh, really—you didn't like him? Why not?"

"I thought he was too aggressive to make a good therapist."

"Okay, but he wasn't my therapist; he was a guy I was dating."

"Why him?"

"I was feeling free. I was in an experimental period when I was dating a lot."

"How long did you see him?"

"A couple of months."

There was no way Harry could stop himself, even though he had a growing sense of losing control, of possibly slipping across the border into inappropriateness.

"Did you sleep with him?"

Amanda seemed to hesitate, and he was quick to apologize and to tell her she needn't answer. "It's none of my business," he reassured her.

"That's all right. I think I should be open with you. Yes, I did."

Harry absorbed her answer slowly. He knew she had sexual encounters, but he never imagined it might be with someone he knew, let alone someone from the Center. How would he feel meeting Cy, knowing that he was a former lover of his girlfriend? It bothered him.

"So he was more than a guy you were dating; he was your boyfriend."

"No, I never thought of him as a boyfriend."

"Why not?"

"I didn't see him that much, and I was dating other men."

"Just dating, or having sex with?"

Again she hesitated before answering. "I had sex with one other man."

"Who was that?" Harry recognized that he was becoming jealous and anxious. Was he also disappointed with her?

"His name was Justin, and I promise that you don't know him. I slept with him twice, and I decided it was enough."

"Why did you stop seeing Cy?"

"Because he wanted to see more of me and wanted me to stop seeing other men. I never saw him as a serious boyfriend; he was just someone to have fun with."

"And why are you seeing him now?"

"He wants to see me again."

"And will you?"

"Not a chance. Harry. I'm with you now, and I'm all for you. He needed to know that. That's what tonight was for. Any more questions?" she asked.

Harry shook his head. "You've been very honest," he said.

"I'm wondering what you're thinking about it. Are you feeling angry?"

"No, I think I understand." He also understood that understanding was not necessarily accepting.

"I had a stultifying, sexless marriage, and I wanted to break free. I slept with a few other men too; I felt it was good for me, and to be perfectly honest I haven't a single regret. Now I feel that being with you is good for me."

"And being with you is wonderful for me," Harry said.

It was true. It was also true that Harry had another feeling. He was uncomfortable with Amanda's freewheeling approach to sex. Sarah, a virgin when they met, had been strictly a one-man woman. Perhaps that was the problem; Amanda wasn't Sarah. He considered that he was being prudish and old-fashioned. Amanda had clearly slept with more men than he had women, but what of it? Whose fault was that?

The jealousy refused to dissipate. It kept insinuating itself into Harry's thoughts. He would have loved to know just how many men there had been. Too bad he was afraid to ask. Nevertheless, jealousy, that nasty emotion, failed to lessen his passion for her. He was never more passionate in bed. *Could it have increased it?* He wondered. Yet over the course of the weekend, something as yet undefined had changed.

CHAPTER 17

The Opposition Forms

Harry left a brief message on his son's cell phone requesting that they talk in person. He was angry with Brad but wished to avoid appearing that way during the conversation. Sensitized to criticism (particularly from Harry, but also from a former girlfriend), it was predictable that Brad would fall back into a fiercely defensive mode when pressed. Besides, was Harry's anger truly justified? Was it so peculiar for his son to resent the new woman in his life? Brad had been particularly close to his mother, perhaps in some way even closer than Katie had been. Katie had been Harry's girl, basking in his adoration and affection. Harry understood that Brad's anger was old, old anger that had attached itself to new anger.

To Harry's surprise, Brad, upon arriving at his father's apartment, immediately apologized for his words the previous weekend. Perhaps his expectations regarding Amanda had been unrealistically high, and his reaction to his disappointment resulted in his petulance. At least that was the theory he eagerly advanced.

"What were you disappointed about?" Harry asked, although he wasn't absolutely sure he wanted an answer.

Brad prefaced his assessment by calling Amanda a "nice" woman whom he actually "liked." Harry waited expectantly for the "but."

"But I think she's wrong for you, Dad. There's something

off-putting about her. I can't actually put my finger on it, but she seems too formal and stiff. I couldn't warm up to her. I have to say she's one handsome woman, and I keep remembering something you once said to me. You said I should be careful not to let beauty be too persuasive in my choice of a girl. I'm wondering now whether you're heeding your own advice."

"There's much more to her than good looks," Harry replied, keeping a careful lock on fully expressing his feelings. He wasn't happy about receiving advice from his twenty-six-year-old son.

"I know that, Dad, but she's so very different from us. She's old wealth, white bread Protestant, Westchester. And you are Lower East Side Jewish. Your father was a struggling salesman pounding the pavements of the city. She was brought up in a different world, and I don't see what you have in common, except that you're both therapists."

Harry laughed at the last comment.

"Believe it or not, Brad, being a therapist separates a person from the rest of the world, in a manner of speaking. It's an entirely different perspective. But in fact, Amanda and I have much more in common than that. We can talk for hours about a million things. Do you really think it's impossible to outgrow your origins? There was a much greater gulf between myself and my father than there is between Amanda and me."

Harry was growing impatient with Brad; he believed that his judgment was based on superficialities and prejudice. Needing to tread very carefully with his son, those were observations he was reluctant to say.

"You know, Dad, that I want you to be happy. And I've told you many times that you should meet someone. I can't feel comfortable with this one. She doesn't feel right to me. There's no spontaneity to her; she's too careful and calculating."

What was "calculating" for Brad was for Harry "judicious"; Brad's "no spontaneity" was Harry's "sensibly cautious."

"You said you want me to be happy? Well, she makes me happy," Harry said with more emphasis in his voice than he'd actually intended. He waited, a little uncertain, for Brad's response, feeling his body coiled like a spring.

"You have to please yourself, Dad."

"I think you want me to have a girlfriend in theory only," Harry said, coming as close as he could to an implied criticism, to a barely concealed show of pique.

"That feels like you're questioning my motives, Dad. I'm giving you my opinion; I'm not telling you what to do."

"First impressions can be off the mark," Harry rejoined. It was all he intended to say. The rest would have to wait for a later day.

While Harry would have preferred Brad's approval, did it really matter? Brad was still a kid in Harry's eyes, his character not fully realized. Harry knew his own mind and appreciated what Amanda had brought to his life, how she had renewed his spirit. Why then was he so bothered by their conversation? Having asked himself the question, he immediately summoned an answer. He longed for his children to accept and love Amanda, to have someone in their lives who might serve to at least dull the pain of loss that both had endured. Amanda could never replace Sarah, but she could become a positive maternal presence, filling an empty space left by their mother's premature death. Apparently it was not to be.

Katie also had reservations about Amanda. While she claimed to like Amanda, she found it difficult to "warm up" to her. She compared her to her mother, who was the kind of person who made everyone comfortable. She was so natural, so friendly and welcoming, that people took to Sarah immediately. She'd had friends everywhere, from all walks of life.

"Mom loved people, and they loved her too. Do you remember how many people were at the funeral? They came because they loved her. Everyone loved Mom. There is something stiff and formal about Amanda. I know she was making an effort to be especially nice, but I sensed she wasn't natural, she wasn't comfortable."

"I'm never going to find another woman like your

mother. She was one of a kind. So it's really unfair to make a comparison." Harry knew he could have done a better job of defending Amanda. Amanda had just met Brad and Katie, and that first encounter with the two most important people in Harry's life must have been stressful for her. What did they expect from her? But he refrained from saying anything because he was feeling angry, and he believed it wouldn't be helpful to express it. He'd wanted to hear their honest opinions even if he disagreed with them. Better that they came out rather than remain hidden. In time perhaps they would change their minds. He certainly hoped so.

Harry thought about his children and their unhappy reactions to Amanda. *There is a time when a child is ready to let go of a lost parent. Perhaps it comes down to age, or to the child's condition in life*, he thought. Harry believed his kids had not reached that time. They were not ready to lose their special mother. Their lives were in flux, their adulthood too new for them to be emotionally prepared. It was all too premature. That recognition filled him with sadness. Foolishly he had anticipated that they would welcome Amanda, that they would see how happy she made him. He had allowed himself to be guided by wishful thinking, a common human tendency. He knew life was more complicated than that. He rejected their views of Amanda. Given the situation, meeting them for the first time, how could she be anything other than tentative? Nevertheless, the children affected him. How could he be indifferent to their feelings?

At lunch with Izzy in a restaurant near his friend's home, Harry noticed that Izzy seemed uncharacteristically distracted. Twenty minutes had already passed since the moment they had entered the restaurant, and nothing Harry said, despite strenuous efforts, appeared to arouse much interest in the old wizard. Harry asked whether Izzy had something on his mind.

"Did you really think, Harry, that you and Amanda could keep your shenanigans a secret for very long?" Izzy asked.

Taken aback, Harry froze. Who had blown their cover? Coming so abruptly, Izzy's rebuke took Harry's breath away.

"What are you talking about?" Harry asked weakly, suddenly feeling cornered. Was Izzy bluffing? Did he really know something?

"Perhaps if the two of you were hermits, you could have kept the secret. Unfortunately you are not. You were seen holding hands while standing in a movie line. One person sees and soon the whole world knows. Gossip always has wings. I warned you about this, Harry. There are a lot of people who will use this against you, especially the ones who envy your success. They won't say anything to your face; they're too timid and afraid of you. You'll soon see your referral sources dry up."

"I'll manage," Harry said, slowly regaining his balance after Izzy's surprise announcement. "People who envy me seldom make referrals. What are they saying about me?"

"Do you need me to tell you? These are a bunch of sanctimonious sons of bitches who will jump at the chance to disparage your reputation. You know the line: senior analyst seduces young student whom he supervises."

"Oh, for God's sake, she's on the verge of graduating and becoming a former student. I'm not supervising her, and she's hardly a young, impressionable girl; she's forty-five-years old. I hardly think I took advantage of her."

"Tell it to the judge, Harry. I'm not the one you need to convince. If they caught you having an orgy with three students and two patients, I'd still be on your side. I'd find some excuse for you, although it would take some time to conjure one up. This is not about age; no one cares about that. She is still a student; she was your student for years, and that's the rub. This is about authority, the inequality between an authority figure and a subordinate. Bosses can't have sex with their employees, professors can't have sex with their students, and supervisors can't have sex with their supervisees. That's the long and the short of it. Please don't expect them to be fair, because fairness doesn't come into this. If you ask me, I think part of the problem is your choice of girlfriend. If you'd picked someone else, someone like Henrietta Kravitz, I think there'd be less of a problem. But then I'm a renowned cynic."

Harry felt confused by this. It was Izzy's habit to sometimes be deliberately obscure; he was a renowned obscurantist. Occasionally Harry found it amusing. Today he found his teasing annoying. The matter was too serious. He asked Izzy what he was driving at.

"They're jealous, you ninny! Every one of them would like to do to Amanda Blake exactly what you're doing. Nobody wants the other one. If you had shtupped Kravitz, they would laugh at your bad taste, think that you must be pathetically desperate to have sex with someone who looks like a monkey, grumble at your irresponsibility, delight in your loss of prestige, and walk away smugly satisfied. Unfortunately you picked the Blake girl—how dare you realize their fantasy?"

"Fuck them then; fuck them all!" Harry declaimed, and for the moment he felt fully justified by the affirmation.

"Easy for you to say. If you won't think of yourself, what about Amanda? Have you considered that this might hurt her reputation?"

That rocked Harry for a second; in fact he had not considered it. When he turned it over in his mind, he found a different feeling. "Why would it hurt her reputation? According to your way of thinking, she'll be considered the victim."

"Do victims have much respect at the Center?"

"Okay, but that's still a decision she has to make, not me," Harry countered, trying somehow to find an appropriate exit from the corner he felt painted into.

"You know how I feel about this, Harry. Of all the women in the world to choose from, why pick one you've been professionally engaged with? There's no equality between a teacher and pupil, even a former one."

"And, according to you, why pick one that other men covet, particularly when there are so many Henrietta Kravitzes out there?" Harry said heatedly. He felt his blood pressure rise. He knew Izzy was just being Izzy, bringing bad news. Nevertheless he felt like killing the messenger.

"Cynical but accurate. So what will you do, my friend?"

"Get a second opinion."

"Speak to the president of the Board then."

"The newly elected one or the old one?"

"Tom Haas."

"Have you spoken to him?"

"I have. He took a hard line. He said that if you persisted in this 'liaison'—his word, not mine—it will result in a complete alteration of your status at the Center. The plan would be to freeze you out of some functions, such as teaching and supervising students. Eventually there will be pressure on you to resign from the Center. They want to do this gradually to avoid the appearance of a scandal. If you break it off with Amanda, however, and there are no repercussions with her, then they would reconsider. My impression is that Haas would be happy not to take action. He's very much aware of how much you've given to the place. Please think about this, my friend. Don't throw it all away. Your entire professional life will be affected."

"Friend, do you know what it would do to me to throw Amanda away?"

For once Izzy was speechless. He nodded silently. His next words came low and sober. "I was hoping it hadn't gone that far."

At home in the sanctity of his apartment, Harry thought about it. Amanda would never discard the relationship, regardless of a threat to her reputation. Harry felt that in his bones. No, it was entirely up to him. He was the one who would have to decide. Deciding was far from easy though. There were so many things to consider. His future, her future, the kids' views, all weighed against the undeniable reality that his life had become so much better since she entered it. Was he so disoriented by the fog of love that he couldn't find his way to doing what was practical and necessary? Or should love conquer all? He felt the walls closing in on him. There was no safe place for him now. *I really do not want to decide. Can't I put it off for a while?* He sat motionless and uncomfortable in his most comfortable chair, his mind a blank, his heart tumbling over. Eventually he emerged from his trancelike state, picked up the phone, and dialed Amanda's number,

CHAPTER 18

The Return of Allan Serkin

In January, seven months into their relationship, Jacques all but moved in to Jennifer's apartment. He retained his apartment in New Jersey near Rutgers but was seldom there, and most of his belongings were stashed at Jennifer's. He had managed to concentrate his classes into two days, rendering his commute quite tolerable. Jennifer accepted this arrangement but partially resented it. She expressed the feeling to Harry, who surmised that it exemplified the degree to which she was locked into her ambivalence toward Jacques. Her resentment was somewhat mollified by Jacques's announced intention of finding an apartment in Manhattan.

One snowy Saturday afternoon while Jacques was out looking at apartments, Jennifer visited Meg. They sat in the living room of her apartment, and Meg asked how an associate professor of English at a state university could afford the rent for an apartment in Manhattan. "Will he have a roommate?" she asked. The answer to that was no, and the explanation was that he could afford an apartment. Jacques, along with his sister and stepmother, had received a major settlement from the trucking company involved in his father's death. The amount was multiplied by the truck driver's lack of a proper license, a circumstance that spurred his company to settle out of court. Jennifer was vague about the actual amount collected by Jacques, though she knew it was "in the millions."

Meg gulped hard, and her eyes opened wide when she heard that scintillating monetary figure. She instantly offered a suggestion:

"Don't encourage him to move out."

That didn't go over very well with Jennifer, who was quick to note that Meg had always been a fan of Jacques. "I'm not prepared to live with a man I've known for only seven months," she said.

"Why not? Hillary is engaged to Doug Rothstein, and they haven't been together any longer."

"What?" Jennifer looked stunned.

"You didn't know that? How could you not have known that? She's told everyone. I can't believe she didn't tell you."

"She probably tried," Jennifer groaned. "She's left several messages, and I've been so busy I haven't gotten back to her yet. The messages didn't seem all that urgent."

"Well, he popped the question last week."

"I can't believe it. Rothstein's her first real boyfriend. I knew she was nuts over him, but I never thought it would go this far. I didn't even think they were fucking!"

"No?" Meg said in surprise. "Where have you been? That's been going on for a long time. Hillary isn't as backward as you think."

"Mama mia, why am I always the last to know? The bitch never told me."

Walking back to her apartment, Jennifer dug her phone out of her coat pocket and called the bubbling Hillary to congratulate her. Hillary spoke effusively about her new fiancé. It was clear that she was exhilarated and happy; there was no trace of ambivalence in her excited voice. She so adored Doug that Jennifer felt envious. It seemed remarkable to Jennifer that there had been no hitches in their relationship or disillusioning quarrels, misunderstandings, or miscommunications. To hear Hillary tell it, it had been love, love, love, as though they were perfectly matched and meant to be together. Where they first met at that magical roof garden party, it was practically love at first sight. If only she could feel that way about Jacques instead of gnawing doubt, her undefeatable chronic worry about making a mistake. Hillary was delighted to hear that Jacques had "practically" moved in with Jennifer. She thought how wonderful it would be if they became pregnant at the same time. Jennifer almost laughed; the thought was quite inconceivable to her. Speaking to Hillary was depressing, although she concealed it entirely from her friend.

As soon as Jennifer ended her conversation with Hillary she called Daryl, the perfect antidote to Hillary's happy, sunny optimism. Daryl did not disappoint her. She expressed a concern that Jacques wasn't serious about finding an apartment. Jennifer experienced a jolt of agitation. What if he was dragging his feet? What could she do?

"Throw him out!" Daryl urged. "It's your apartment. He has no right to park his carcass there," she said indignantly, speaking as though Jacques, who as yet had not actually moved in, had already "parked his carcass" and was refusing to leave. That spirit of angry indignation infected Jennifer, who immediately entertained the fantasy of warning Jacques that she would not tolerate a prolonged stay. Later, in the calm of her own apartment, she discarded the idea, thinking that it would be tantamount to putting out an unwelcome sign.

Jennifer's mother, when informed that Jacques would be moving in, showed a distinct lack of enthusiasm. That is not to say that she disliked Jacques himself. They had met once, and they had gotten along perfectly well. Mrs. Slater was impressed by the young man's obvious good breeding and gentlemanly manners. She admired his intelligence and that he was a professor. What she didn't like was the fact that professors lived in "genteel poverty," as she put it. Money was crucial to Mrs. Slater, and she desperately wanted to convey its significance to her daughter. If she had known of Jacques's tragedy-based fortune, it would have influenced her thinking in a profound way. But for some obscure reason, Jennifer neglected to inform her about it. She never asked herself about her odd silence and never mentioned it to Harry; she didn't want to tell her, and that was that.

"You should give him a time limit," her mother said to Jennifer.

"No, he can take as long as he wants," Jennifer breezily replied, a message that was at great variance from the one she'd given Harry, Meg, Hillary, Daryl, and even herself.

Pops, Jennifer's stepfather, established an almost instantaneous rapport with Jacques. They talked about the stock market, the economy, baseball, and politics, pretty much in that order. Pops loved him and was totally encouraging about the relationship. "We need an intellectual in the family," he said. The implication that Jacques might become part of "the family" was jarring to Jennifer.

Harry, being Harry, had an entirely different approach to the matter. As they sat together in his office on a miserable winter's day, the wind and rain lashing the window, Harry made an ordinary inquiry. He asked Jennifer what the issue "really" was.

"I feel I'm not going to be able to get rid of him."

The window, rattling from the fury of the storm, momentarily interrupted the session as both stopped to look.

Harry disagreed—that wasn't what she was afraid of.

"Are you going to tell me, or will we be playing ten guesses again?" she asked with a heavy sigh.

"You're afraid you *won't* want to get rid of him."

That interpretation of her inner conflict rocked her. She struggled for a response. "I think the storm outside is like the storm inside," she at last said.

Harry nodded thoughtfully, as if in agreement.

"I feel torn inside. I want it. I don't want it. I love it. I hate it. It makes me happy; it makes me afraid. I want it to last forever; I want it to end tomorrow. Is it worth it? Sometimes I can't stand the conflict, and that makes me feel it isn't worth it. But when I consider drawing back, I feel even worse. Now I have to consider *his* feelings as well as mine; he's so in love with me, and I'm responsible because I led him on. I feel trapped, like I'm in a prison of the soul that I constructed myself."

When she left his office, she found little consolation that the problem had been defined when the solution remained so inaccessible.

When Jacques gave up his New Jersey apartment at the beginning of February, the transition turned out to be a smooth one. He had been spending so much time at the apartment that a couple of extra days didn't truly amount to much. That is, not at the beginning. But when three weeks passed without Jacques finding an apartment, Jennifer began to suffer the familiar buyer's remorse that she had had before, although she couldn't remember when. It seemed to her that he was too particular in his apartment hunt, narrowing the range of what was acceptable far too much; was he looking for a palace in Manhattan at a reasonable rent? And close by?

"You don't need to find an apartment around the block, Jacques," she dared to say one evening. "Any place near the number one train will get you here pretty quickly. A taxi will get you here even sooner." He'd acknowledged that, but was he being honest? She felt a low-grade anger toward him, an ineffable impatience that she wasn't able to shake. It wasn't easy to be angry with Jacques, because he was sweet-tempered and affectionate. And he was passionate, his ardor for her never having cooled. Sometimes Jennifer felt irritated with herself for allowing him to settle in. He could have stayed with his sister or a close friend who lived in Brooklyn. *What was I thinking?* she asked herself. She felt her space had been invaded; it was like an occupying alien had been quartered in her residence. She liked his company though. If only the alien wasn't so lovely. Then she could really be angry!

The first e-mail from Allan Serkin seemed innocuous enough. It was the "thinking about you, wondering how you're doing" genre. Jennifer responded in kind, making sure she indicated no sign of pleasure or excitement in her return message. Surprisingly (to her) she felt neither of those two emotions, only an irrepressible curiosity. What was he up to, nothing or everything? Not that it really mattered. She felt empowered that the feelings she'd once possessed for him had entirely faded away. Nevertheless, e-mails continued to arrive daily. Sometimes they would come at night, with Jacques in the same room, and she would send off a reply while keeping a careful watch on his movements, ready to shut her laptop if he meandered by. The activity left her with a residue of guilt; she sensed something distasteful in her behavior. The message Allan spun had been enticing. He had changed. It intrigued her enough to continue the electronic conversation.

She agreed finally, after much hedging and doubting, to meet him for lunch in the middle of the week. She did not tell Harry because she anticipated his question: "Why?" She did not tell Meg either because she was certain of her reaction: "Why?" Hillary, the moral police, was sure to disapprove, so she kept the news from her. Daryl, the one person she might have told, was vacationing in Jamaica. And Jacques—well, she dared not tell him. She felt no guilt. What was there to be guilty about? It was just lunch, and she had not the slightest intention of letting it advance any further. That it was a step beyond talking through computers, for which she did entertain guilt, never occurred to her. The truth was that she wanted to see him again, to hear what he had to say, to learn if in fact anything had changed, to discover why he wanted to see her. She had never cheated on a boyfriend before and had no intention of doing so now. It was not at all about that.

They met at a Greek restaurant not far from her office, and his appearance (on time for once) reminded her of how attractive she had always found him. Slightly under six feet, Allan affected a strikingly casual, scruffy look. He was hatless despite the cold, and his thick light brown hair had a wind-blown, disarrayed look. A few days growth of beard accompanied the threadbare, unbuttoned maroon sweater beneath his old short green down coat. Under the sweater Allan wore a white shirt, frayed at the collar, the top two buttons opened. A pair of tight fitting jeans, undoubtedly the most expensive item he wore, culminated in a pair of well-worn brown boots. Allan sported the appearance of a man who was quite indifferent to sartorial splendor. He grinned at her, gave her a gentle hug, and kissed her cheek. "God, you look fabulous," he said.

For the next hour Allan talked mostly about himself. He went on about how he had "grown up," how he had found a "great" job at a software company, and how he recently received a promotion and "big" salary increase. He had been on this job for sixteen months, something of a record for him. He talked also about how he was hoping to "settle down," although he left it to Jennifer to determine what that meant. Allan asked but one question about her.

"I hear you've got a boyfriend. Is it serious; is he the one?"

"How did you know that?" she asked, wondering who could have disseminated that information to him.

"Your nemesis, Felicia. I ran into her."

Felicia? Who told her? And then Jennifer realized that any of her friends could have done so, even Meg, since they all knew Felicia quite well.

"When did you talk to her?" she asked.

"Uh, just yesterday. You haven't answered my question about your boyfriend."

She had almost forgotten the question. "About whether he's the one? I'm not sure. It's much too soon to make that judgment. I'm a long way from it." Having said that, she wondered whether she had unwittingly given Allan encouragement.

"He's a great guy, and I like him a lot," she hastened to add.

Allan smiled and expressed gladness that she was happy and had found someone she liked so much. Before they departed he told her how much he enjoyed seeing her again, and how wonderful she looked. Seeing her made him sad that he had not been a better boyfriend to her.

"He's a lucky guy," Allan said referring to Jacques.

As she walked through crowded Manhattan streets to

return to work, Jennifer thought about the meeting. Allan was as insubstantial as ever. After all his talk of personal growth, he'd presented little evidence of it. What he did present was an interest in flattering her and being as nice as possible. Of course he wanted to get back with her; that was the purpose of it all. *I haven't heard the last of him*, she told herself.

She was proud of the way she handled the situation. In the past, when she'd wanted him, she would hang on his every word, be the supplicant, the needy one. Today she'd been quite different, calmly sitting back and coolly observing him as he talked. In fact, she thought he was a trifle nervous, talking nonstop, as though the thing he feared most was a moment of silence between them. *My, how the tables have turned!* Jennifer made a decision. She would not see him again. It was over, forever, and it felt good to say it.

He called her cell phone two days later, which she was monitoring by then, and she refused to respond.

Jacques thought he had found an apartment in the West Village, except someone took it before he could put down a deposit. Jennifer wondered whether he had sabotaged himself. *Why was he too late?* The longer he stayed, the greater her annoyance was with him; but the grievance remained only in her head. She was reluctant to speak her mind, to show him her cross feelings. What was this hold he had over her? Was it his fault or her own? She wished she knew whom to blame.

One night, in the intimacy of the bedroom, he put his arms around her and uttered three words. It should not have been a surprise; after all, she had no doubt it was true. But he had never said it before, and she had actually taken comfort in that fact. Sometimes she thought it would be a relief if *he* broke up with her. *Good luck with that!* Those three little words, so common yet so charged, clouded her mind and plunged her into confusion. Should she respond? Should she respond in kind, to avoid hurting him? Wouldn't that be dishonest, since she didn't feel it, at least not at the moment? Her fear and confusion converted to anger, an anger that, since its origin was unknown, only served to confuse and upset her more. She felt an urge to slam him, but how could she justify meanness to a man who confesses his love? "How dare you say that to me" simply wouldn't do. It was too crazy, too utterly irrational. Instinctively she found a partial solution. She said she had "strong feelings" for him, but he needed to give her "more time." He seemed to accept that response, at least as far as she could tell. She had difficulty falling asleep that night, and when she finally did she had a series of disturbing dreams. In one she had been kidnapped and locked in a cellar, from which there appeared to be no escape.

The next day at work she violated her previous decision; she picked up the phone and dialed Allan's number. No planning went into this act, no careful search of motive. If asked she would have explained that she felt like it and would have minimized its significance. Naturally no one asked because no one knew. She wanted to keep it that way. When a jaunty Allan suggested dinner rather than lunch, she hesitated, turned it over in her mind, and then accepted his invitation. She had dinner with so many men in her life who she did not sleep with; why would this be any different? She was with Jacques. She knew how to handle this.

No sooner were they settled in the corner of a small, romantic restaurant than Allan spoke words she never imagined she would hear.

"I love you, and I want you back, and I want this to be serious." This from Allan Serkin, the commitment-phobic, indirect, usually withholding, and impossible-to-pin-down guy. It seemed very sudden to her. Allan was typically a slow worker, a beat-around-the-bush sort of boyfriend.

"You really have changed," Jennifer said with a grin.

"I mean it, Jen; I'm ready to commit."

"Commit to what?" She was not about to fall into his arms because he spoke words she once longed to hear.

"Same old suspicious girl," he answered, but he then immediately admitted that her suspicions were "understandable."

He reached out and placed his hand over hers as it rested on the table. He looked rather handsome in the dim glow of the table lamp. If only Jacques looked like Allan, he would be the perfect man.

"Look, I know I let you down before. Lord knows you have plenty of reasons to doubt my sincerity. Just give me one chance to prove to you that I mean it."

For another hour Allan regaled Jennifer with tales of how much he had changed, although he never really defined what he meant by the word *commit*, only that he wanted a "serious" relationship. Jennifer was impressed that he'd admitted to having been wrong about things, having made mistakes, in particular by letting her go. He wanted to make amends. When they left the restaurant and stepped out into the wintry air, she noticed for the first time that it was snowing heavily. She had been so engrossed in his conversation that she never took the trouble to look out the window.

Allan stopped and turned toward her. With his coat completely open and the snow beginning to cluster and sparkle on his thick hair, he cut a remarkably romantic figure in Jennifer's eyes. She could not help feeling the old attraction.

"Come back to my place," he importuned as he leaned into her, his face barely inches from hers. The abrupt boldness took her by surprise, although the request was not entirely unexpected. Every instinct told her to decline. Her mind quickly shifted to other voices: Harry's, Meg's, Hillary's, her mother's (she hated Allan), all speaking as one: *"Don't do it!"* Sage advice, she knew. And Jacques—could she do this to him, sweet, loving Jacques? Before she could reply Allan took another small step forward, wrapped his arms around her, and kissed her emphatically on the lips.

CHAPTER 19

Facing Amanda

Harry worried about Amanda. A healer of wounds old and new all his professional life, he now faced the prospect of having to *open* one. To make matters much worse, the recipient would be someone he loved. It upset and sickened him. He knew she would be unprepared and bewildered. There had been no warning, no process of gradual disengagement. The terrible fact was that in no sense did she deserve this, for she had been a wonderful girlfriend, loving, sensitive, and generous. The causes of the breakup had nothing to do with her. It was entirely situational and resided outside of her control or responsibility. If only she had possessed some egregious character flaw or had committed some grave violation of trust, it would have lightened his task. He attempted to rehearse what he would say, how he would say it, and how he would respond to her anticipated reaction. He thought it best to adhere to a prepared script, like a politician, tediously and repetitively staying on message, or like an automaton holding to its well-programmed software. His greatest dilemma was that he could find no reasonable way to soften the blow. It would be kind to allow her to display all of her feelings rather than to protect himself by rushing away. That was just about all he could do for her, although it troubled him that it was so little.

How had he gotten himself into this dilemma? Why did he not anticipate that it would end this way? Did he not care about her feelings? Did he selfishly plunge ahead because it was what *he* wanted, to hell with the consequences? In his obsessive preoccupation with Amanda's putative feelings, Harry lost sight of *himself.* Perhaps that was deliberate.

When he arrived at her apartment and stood face to face with her, all his plans immediately fell apart. He stood mute, but the expression on his face telegraphed the turmoil hidden within.

"What is it?" she asked in alarm. "What's wrong?"

He thought she had to have known that something was in the wind; he had been so secretive when he called to ask to come over. Then he told her, haltingly, clearing his throat, stumbling over words, what he had learned from Izzy, that their affair had become common knowledge at the Center. He intended to be more direct, but upon his soul he couldn't manage it. It became necessary for him to slide slowly toward his goal.

Amanda barely reacted to the news. "We aren't committing a crime," she said, "and this is surely not the first time this sort of thing has happened between supervisor and supervised."

Taken aback by her matter-of-fact response, Harry struggled for a reply. It was clear she didn't get the import of his words.

"I know, but I'm not an ordinary supervisor. I have a reputation; I'm a figure of authority at the Center. Everybody knows who I am and what I've done. I can't hide behind a wall of anonymity. People will think I used my position to take advantage of you."

"We know that's not true."

"Others think it is, important others."

"And that matters to you?"

"I'd be a liar if I said it doesn't, particularly where it pertains to your reputation."

"My reputation? If I'm not concerned about that, you shouldn't be."

Harry was surprised by the forcefulness of her statement. This was turning out to be just as difficult as he thought it would. He fidgeted in the chair he was sitting in, thought of standing up, decided it would look foolish, crossed and quickly uncrossed his legs.

"You're right. I shouldn't be taking cover behind a concern for your reputation. But you have to understand that your situation is different from mine. You have no concern for your livelihood. You're not dependent on your work the way I am." Harry looked at her, sitting only a few feet from him. He witnessed the swift change in the expression on her face as the full implication of his words reached her. This was a wretched business, and he was beginning to recognize how bad he was at it. He spoke again:

"Amanda, uh ... ah ... I've come under some ... uh ... pressure, I mean a lot of pressure, to end this ... uh, between us."

"By whom?" she asked.

"By the board of directors at the Center; there have been implied threats."

"What kind of threats?" she asked in a voice now only slightly above a whisper. Harry wondered what world of awful feelings lay just beneath the smooth surface of that voice. He felt the anxiety in his gut slowly rise to his throat, which he, for the first time, recognized was parched dry. He told her what he knew, that he might have to leave the Center. He tried to control his voice, but his dry mouth impeded an easy delivery.

"I see," she said.

There followed a prolonged silence between them, neither looking at the other.

"Doesn't speak very well for our colleagues, does it?" she said with a sudden display of feeling.

"You're blaming them?" He had expected to receive the brunt of the blame.

"Yes, I blame them—for making assumptions about you and me without having spoken to either of us. I blame them for being so judgmental, and for basing their judgments on doctrinaire, unexamined beliefs. I blame them for their busybody interference in our lives. We're not children, you know. Most of all, I blame them for ruining things for us."

These last words were spoken as tears filled her eyes, and she glanced very briefly at him. She first tried to wipe away those tears with a hand, and then she found a tissue in a pocketbook that was on a chair nearby.

"Amanda. I ... I ... I'm so sorry." Harry practically stuttered, as if he were trying to force the words from his mouth. He felt his eyes moisten too. "Do I get any of the blame?" He could have ducked that question but felt that would have been ignoble.

"I'm disappointed, but it's not fair to expect you to give it all up," she said, keeping her voice very low.

"Sure you can. You can expect me to behave gallantly and bravely. And you can be angry with me that I'm not."

"Perhaps it would help you for me to be angry, but I'm not sure it will help me. Perhaps I am angry with you, and in time I'll allow myself to feel it. I do feel very let down by you. I just don't know quite what to do with it. For now I'm reserving my anger for those shits at the Center. I used to think that the analytic world was a special place, peopled by the cream of humanity, by profound men and women who understood themselves and their fellows. What unmitigated bullshit!" Tears flowed freely; she fought a losing battle to stem them with the already soiled tissue. She crumpled it, throwing it onto the floor. "Excuse me," she said as she briefly left the room, to return with a full box of tissues.

"Don't you feel angry with them?"

"Yes, of course," Harry replied, noticing that he didn't actually *feel* angry.

"The problem is I have so many feelings that interfere with anger, feelings toward you, I mean," she said.

Harry looked into her eyes, waiting for an explanation.

"You've given me so much, Harry. Because of you I've experienced many feelings for the first time. My God, what have I been doing all my life? I've loved and felt loved by you. You're the only man who truly wanted to know me, to understand me.

I've felt appreciated by you. Even the sex we've had has been a revelation; sex that was so connected, feeling of true intimacy— all new feelings for me. I see now that I've lived a life of both privilege and deprivation. Sounds like a paradox, doesn't it?"

"No; not at all. I understand," Harry said with a new note in his voice. It was the sound of a deep sadness. It was the worse thing Amanda could have said to him. He wanted anger, not praise.

"I've lost you, but I haven't lost the feelings," she said. "I don't want to live any more without them. I have to find them again somehow. It's now the most important thing in life. You've done that for me, love, you've warmed up and opened my once inert heart, and I want it to stay that way."

I did that, and now I'm abandoning her, Harry thought miserably.

"You should go," she said in a tremulous voice, "while I'm still in control."

Harry rose, half wanting to run out, half wanting to stay. As they stood awkwardly facing each other, Harry leaned over and kissed the cheek she turned toward him. There was a last, tear-infused glance between them, and then Harry left.

On the street, his face suddenly struck by a fierce wind, an undesirable thought appeared in his mind. *How will I be without her?*

CHAPTER 20

Paradise Lost

Jacques Giraud was very comfortable in Jennifer Slater's apartment. He found her mattress quite suitable for sleeping and other activities, and a spare bedroom served perfectly well as a convenient storage facility for his books and papers. All it required for perfection was a decent desk. At this time, he dared not suggest it. He had not the slightest desire for space or the least inclination for time alone. That is not to say that he gave up the pursuit for an apartment of his own. He searched diligently, but given the extraordinary comforts of the place where he dwelled, along with its frequent erotic splendors, he discovered that locating a space equally commodious was a bit like finding a needle in a haystack. He knew that Jennifer wanted him to leave—she hinted as much —but he also divined that she was not seriously intent on his doing so quickly. Indeed, she sent mixed signals, and he was shrewd enough to discern them and pay more attention to the positive than the negative.

So he lingered, and as he did he grew comfortable putting to use things that belonged to Jennifer. When his old laptop crashed, he borrowed hers, particularly for the task of transmitting e-mails. She generously gave him permission to do so. Home from the university on a Friday afternoon, cheerfully engaged on his girlfriend's computer, he saw an instant message appear on the screen.

Jen. I'm so sorry I pushed things last night. I think that had I been patient things may have turned out better. The intimacies we shared tell me that you still care. I felt it. Please give me another chance to prove that I've changed.

Jacques responded "Have to go" and closed the machine down. It was unsigned, although there was no doubt about the sender. She'd told him about Allan Serkin. The user name was "allserk." The unexpected and shocking message turned things topsy-turvy for Jacques Giraud. His high spirits evaporated, to be replaced by the darkest brooding. What did this portend? How should he understand it? What actually happened? What could he properly determine from this brief message, as suggestive as it obviously was of significant meaning? He sternly instructed himself to remain calm, to approach this like a scientist, distinguishing fact from conjecture, proceeding in an orderly, methodical fashion until sense could be made out of five measly sentences.

One thing was clear: they were together last night. That meant she'd lied when she said she was meeting an old friend, Gail, for dinner. He never heard of this person. Did she actually exist? Why did Jennifer lie? Clearly she didn't want him to know about what she was up to. That couldn't be good. One hides only when one is guilty. Guilty of what though? Of simply meeting Allan or much worse? Was he being naïve? Should he assume that she was preparing to leave him to return to Allan? She said she would never do that. She promised she was through with Allan forever. So what? *Promises, promises. People don't always mean what they say, and even if they do they don't always follow through. There's a great gap between words and deeds.*

He was getting ahead of himself here, lapsing into conjecture when he should be sticking to the facts. He scolded himself and returned to that brief text. Allan said that he "pushed things." What else besides sex could that mean? Nothing. It was about sex. He also indicated that he thought he had gone too far, that "things may have turned out better" had he restrained himself. That too must be about sex. Could he then safely conclude then that they didn't fuck? Jacques desperately wanted to believe that, but was it a fact or only a guess? Could the message have referred to other sexual activities, short of intercourse? Or could it be that Allan wasn't making reference to sex at all? There was another way of looking at it. Perhaps they did have sex, and Allan's "pushing things" was a reference to wanting her to break up with Jacques. Perhaps she wasn't ready for that.

Allan did make reference to "intimacies." What else could that mean but sex? The idea that Jennifer, the woman he so adored, had gone to bed with another man sickened him. He walked to the bathroom and tried to vomit in the toilet, the image of her fornicating with Allan stubbornly lodged in his mind. He failed at the effort; nothing would come up. *I shouldn't jump to conclusions*, he told himself. The only true fact was that she had lied—she was with Allan last night. Another thought struck him. She was home reasonably early, not much after ten. If they slept together, wouldn't she have come home later, at two or three in the morning? No, not necessarily. How would she explain that to him, having dinner with a friend and staying out so late? She could have had sex and immediately left. On the other hand, she seemed unusually affectionate and lusty last night, and *they* had sex. Didn't that negate the possibility that she had sex only an hour or two before? Jacques felt instant relief; his mood perceptively lifted—until a new thought raised its ugly head. What if her affection was induced by guilt, a reaction to having fucked another man?

Jacques could not quiet his brain. He was tormented by doubt, fear, and uncontrollable jealousy. He paced the floor, his thoughts turning over and over, becoming repetitive, exhausting. Eventually he circled back to his original questions, rendering the identical tentative, inconclusive answers. Then a subtle shift occurred. *Why, why, why?* he asked himself. She seemed so happy. They got along so well. The passion was unflagging, on her side as well as his. Yes, they had their occasional spats, but what couple doesn't? They didn't really amount to a hill of beans. She expressed no dissatisfaction with him.

Why did she do this? How could she do this to him? Whatever happened between Jennifer and Allan, it was shitty behavior. He had been so good to her, so honorable and loyal. He had treated her like a princess, had given her his best. Did he deserve this, this disloyalty, this betrayal of trust? He began to feel aggrieved. This feeling, and the thoughts that led up to it, smashed through the dreary circle of his thinking and opened up an entirely new trajectory for his emotions. He became angrier and angrier. *That lying, deceiving bitch!* He thought of calling her at work. *No, I mustn't.* She would be home soon, and he needed to confront her face to face.

He continued pacing, his mental footsteps tracing a firmer, more determined arc. In time he became eager for her appearance, wanting to expose her as a liar and a cheat, to throw it in her face. Now he desired to believe the worst. *Of course they fucked!* How disingenuous of him to even contemplate otherwise. He wondered how long it had been going on. How stupid of him to think it was just one night! It could have lasted for weeks or longer. He ransacked his memory for other times when she came home late.

Harry must have known. It's hardly likely she would have kept something so consequential a secret from him too. The thought disturbed him. Harry couldn't have said anything; all that stuff about confidentiality must have tied his hands. But couldn't he have issued an innuendo, a cautionary word that skirted the issue of confidentiality—something? Jacques thought about his last few sessions. Was there something he missed? Was Harry trying to tell him? No, there was nothing, no change in Harry's demeanor, no mood shift of any kind that might have set off an alarm that might have been a catalyst for the emergence of even a single doubt. To have witnessed Jacques's cuckolding while intimating nothing—wasn't that being collusive with Jennifer in some way? Harry once promised to warn him if he thought Jacques was pursuing the wrong woman. What about that promise? Except for his sister, Jennifer and Harry were the two people he trusted most in the world. He felt wronged, betrayed. As his thoughts layered one upon the other and accumulated, a steady progression of feelings escalated, from upset to anger to angrier, to …

He heard a key turn the lock. As the door opened and Jennifer stepped in with a bright, breezy hello, Jacques Giraud had reached the pinnacle of his anger.

Jennifer did not remain bright and breezy for long. Recognizing his ominous mood, she immediately asked what was wrong. He showed her the damning e-mail. If Jacques expected a shocked reaction, or a look of shame, he was quickly disabused of that thought. She sat down on a living room chair and said simply, "Okay."

"Okay? Is that all you have to say?" he asked, his voice shaking with emotion.

"I know I should have told you the truth. I guess I just wanted to avoid a fight."

"Uh huh. So what does this mean, Jennifer—are you breaking up with me?" he asked. He felt his heart chill waiting for her response.

She stared at him, a look of surprise crossing her face.

"Of course not. You're making too much of this. We had dinner, that's all."

"Uh uh. I know it was a lot more than that. The e-mail is the evidence."

"Maybe a lot more on his side, but not on mine. I never intended it to be more than that."

"Come on, Jennifer, you're playing games. Whatever you intended, there certainly was much more." Jacques, who was standing, now took a chair opposite Jennifer.

"No, there wasn't." She was as cool as a cucumber.

"Okay, then explain what he meant by 'intimacies'—that is hardly a reference to holding hands."

"Jacques, I swear the word surprises me. I don't have a clue what he meant. It couldn't have been a reference to anything physical."

Jacques was feeling frustrated, convinced as he was that she was lying. He wanted to pin her down. He needed to.

"Jennifer, look at me. I wasn't born yesterday. Please be truthful. Are you saying that nothing physical happened, that you didn't even touch? I won't believe you if you say no."

"When we left the restaurant, he kissed me. That was it."

"Really? That was it? So what kind of a kiss was it?"

Jennifer grimaced. What was the emotion that it concealed now that she was being challenged?

"I think I should explain. We had just left the restaurant, and he asked me to come home with him. I had no intention of doing it. Then he grabbed me and kissed me. That was completely unexpected and unwanted. I guess he meant it to convince me."

"He kissed you where, how?"

"On the lips, where else? I had no time to react. I swear, Jacques, I didn't want it or like it."

"So then?"

"Then I pushed him away, turned around, and walked away. About halfway down the block I saw a taxi, jumped in, and returned home."

"Did he follow you? Did he say anything?"

"No, nothing. Nothing until this e-mail."

So that was her story. How could he refute it? It was plausible enough, except he didn't believe a word of it. He was quiet for a minute, thinking of a response.

"You know I want to believe you," he lied, "but your story just doesn't jibe with his e-mail. He said that he 'felt' that you still cared. You must have given him some indication of that."

"No, I didn't. I was polite and interested in what he had to say, but never more than that. If he thought there was more, it was entirely his imagination, not from me."

"And what did he have to say?"

"It was pretty much a long apology for past behavior."

"Which was just what you wanted to hear."

"It was what I expected to hear, not what I wanted."

Oh, she's so cagey! "And what did you want from him?"

She sighed deeply. "I'm not really sure, Jacques, probably to hear him grovel, to have him beg, and then to reject him. Sweet revenge."

"Really? Seems to me you haven't finished with him then."

"Yes, I have," she said firmly. "I have no intention of ever seeing him again."

"Now that you've been caught."

"No. You have to believe this. There was something about the experience that freed me from him. When he was rejecting me, I stuck to him like glue. Last night he wasn't rejecting me. When I walked away, I knew it was forever."

"Uh huh. Was last night the only time you saw him?"

"I had lunch with him last week."

"That's it?"

"That's it," she said, making a gesture with her hand indicating finality.

Jacques was irritated by her composure, her certitude, and the sheer lack of any sign of guilt. Riding the feeling he spoke his mind. "Why should I believe you?"

"Why shouldn't you?"

"Because people lie about sex. Because you lied to me already when you told me you were having dinner with Gail. By the way, who is Gail?"

"An old friend; I haven't seen her in nearly a year."

"I see. You chose her because you knew I didn't know her. That way, if you decided to fuck Allan and stayed out late, I wouldn't be able to call her when I was worried."

"Holy shit, Jacques!" she declared, for the first time showing emotion. "I'm not that devious, I'm not that calculating. If I said I was having dinner with Meg, I would've had to clear it with her first, and that would have been a pain because she loves you and hates Allan. Hillary wouldn't have agreed, and Daryl is out of town. And I've told you, sleeping with Allan was never an option."

"I don't believe you. I think you went back to his place and had sex with him." There, he finally said it. It was waiting to come out all this time, and at last it did.

"Jesus! How could I have pulled that off? Just think, Jacques. I met him around eight; we left the restaurant a little before ten. Allan lives in Brooklyn. That's about a thirty-five-minute train ride, and I was home about ten thirty. It would have been the quickest fuck in history, and I would have had to take a helicopter home."

Jacques shook his head. "I don't believe your time table. You could have left work early and met him before six. And maybe you didn't tarry long at dinner, left before seven. That would have given you plenty of time. You've already proven yourself to be a skilled liar, you even lied when you said nothing physical happened. You later admitted you had kissed him."

"I didn't kiss him, he kissed me."

"And you may be lying right now."

"I can prove I left work late. We have to log out. It's in the log."

"No doubt you can arrange to alter the time," Jacques answered with implacable skepticism.

"Oh, God. Look at me, Jacques, look at me. I swear nothing happened." She said it with such utter conviction that for a moment Jacques hesitated. Then he rallied.

"He said there were 'intimacies.' That's plural, so there had to be more than one kiss. So what else? Did he remove your clothes? Did you jerk him off? Did you take his cock in your mouth?"

Jennifer looked dumbstruck. "I can't do this any more, Jacques. You're crazed. I can't talk to you. I think I hardly know you."

"I thought I knew you, but I was wrong. I seem to make bad choices with women."

"Okay, okay," she said after another big sigh. "I can't prove a negative. I can only tell you that you can trust that it's the truth when I say nothing happened. Look at me, Jacques—nothing happened. I will admit that I fucked up by keeping this from you. I'm sorry. I really am. I didn't tell you about meeting him because I knew it would upset you. I had a moment of weakness. He's a guy I once thought I loved, and I guess I had to work something out for myself. But I'm telling you the truth about what happened. You're just making much more out of this than there really was."

"Am I? Tell me, Jen, how am I supposed to trust you now? You tell me you fucked up as a way of explaining your behavior. Do you think that's an adequate explanation? What's to stop you from fucking up again, if not with Allan then with someone else?" For the first time he noted tears in her eyes. Finally his relentless pursuit had gotten through to her.

"I don't know what more I can say. What do you expect from me?"

"I don't know. Maybe that's been my problem all along, wanting and expecting too much from you," he answered, his voice softening noticeably. "Obviously there's a great difference in our feelings for one another. I could never have done what you did."

"You're better than I am."

"It could be. Or it could be I was just more committed."

"So what now?"

"I don't think it's a good idea for me to stay here. I'll move in with Annie until I find another apartment."

"You're going to throw it all away because of this?"

"I didn't throw it away, you did." He thought that sounded rather firm and definite. "I'm going to go out for a while."

"No, I did not throw it away," she said in a steady, firm voice. "It's you, it's you, you jealous, paranoid jerk."

Jacques had wondered when her anger would appear.

He left the apartment moments later, believing that he had acquitted himself well, feeling justified.

CHAPTER 21
Jennifer Faces the Music

Jennifer's urgent request for an immediate emergency session was the last thing Harry wanted to hear. Whatever it was, it sounded heavy, and Harry was only interested in light. His grim depression dictated that patients should arrive, take their assorted positions, and talk about what Harry sometimes humorously referred to as "bubkis," which loosely translated to "nothing much at all." It was pleasant for him that Jennifer parked on the couch. He could close his eyes, slump in his chair, and look as miserable as he wanted, without having to worry about a pair of eyes looking intently at him and evaluating his every expression. If he wanted to drift off for a few seconds (because depression loves sleep), who would be the wiser? Then he could rouse himself again to listen somnolently to the drone of her words. He was soon shaken from his lethargy as Jennifer related her sorrowful tale.

At first she assumed a swift pace, gliding effortlessly (and nebulously) over the subject of how it started with Allan. She seemed in great haste to rush through the lunch and dinner with Allan. When she reached the confrontation with Jacques, the picture her words summoned took on a sharper, more distinct shape. She recalled that fateful conversation, if it could be called that, in great detail, as though it were important that Harry miss nothing of what had occurred. She ended the soliloquy with an expression of bitterness and frustration that

Jacques refused to believe she had not gone to bed with Allan. She vehemently maintained that nothing had happened.

"Something did happen," Harry corrected. "You lied to Jacques and secretly met with Allan."

"Okay, okay," she quickly retorted, "but it wasn't sex. It wasn't anything but talk." She seemed impatient and annoyed. Her tone had an edge.

"How do you define sex?" Harry was undaunted by her attitude.

"Vaginal sex, anal sex, oral sex, manual sex. That's what I mean. How would you define it?" she asked petulantly as if Harry were deliberately dumbing down.

Intuitively Harry sensed he was at a crossroad. He sat quietly thinking. There were so many different ways to go. Why did she decide to reconnect with Allan? What did she actually want from him? What did it reveal about her feelings for Jacques? Why did she keep this from Harry, and what did this demonstrate about her relationship with him? And what should Harry feel about this? He knew there was no correct way to proceed; there was only his intuition about how to most efficiently arrive at the heart of the matter. Harry was flying by the seat of his pants, and he knew it was important to get it right. The good thing about it for Harry, the silver lining so to speak, was that it immediately lifted him out of his numbing emotional fog, mercifully putting a distance between him and his misery.

"You seem to be anguished," he suggested, awaiting her response. In return he received an avalanche of words indicative of turbulent emotions, frustration, anger, and perhaps carefully hidden guilt. There were a few "if only"s; if only Allan hadn't sent that incriminating e-mail; if only Jacques hadn't read it.

"How ironic," she moaned, "that at the very moment I decided I really did want Jacques, Jacques decided he didn't want me." Implicit in these emotions was the notion that it was unfair, a matter of undeserved bad luck.

"He's breaking up with you?"

"Well, he's moving out."

"I see. That is a shock."

"I can't believe it either. He seemed so in love with me, and in the blink of an eye it feels like he hates me."

"Yes, that's quite a range of feeling."

"It seems so ... so needless."

Harry considered changing the subject. What advantage was there to continue along this line? Another approach was needed.

"What are your feelings toward Allan?"

"Allan? I have no feelings for him. Indifference, that's my feeling."

Could Harry believe that?

"Will you see him again?"

"Never. Even if Jacques doesn't come back, I'm through with Allan. I've never felt so cold toward him."

That surprised Harry, and he told her so. He inquired about it. He pressed her to reveal what happened between them.

"He was completely seductive, told me he now wanted me and realized how much he missed me, and how sorry he was to let me go. He said he had 'grown'; that was his word."

That sounded like the words she'd longed to hear from him. "So what was wrong with that?"

"What was wrong was I didn't believe a word of it. He even lied to me about something. He knew about Jacques, and when I asked him how and when, he said he heard it from Felicia the day before."

"How do you know that was a lie?"

"Because I found out that Hillary bumped into him two weeks earlier and told him. So I thought, why lie about something like that? And then it hit me. He reconnected with me just after he learned that Jacques had moved in, and he didn't want me to know that, because that's what it was all about. It was the challenge; could he take me away from my boyfriend?"

"I see, the oedipal thing." Harry was smiling.

"Whatever. So much for his growth thesis. He was the same old lying shit."

"Why did you agree to see him in the first place?" Harry thought he knew the answer to this, but did she? He leaned forward in his chair, as if he were afraid to miss even a single word of her reply.

"That's a good question. I think that it was just curiosity at first. Once I knew what he wanted, revenge was my motive. I wanted to hear him beg me to come back and then reject him. And to tell you the truth, it did feel good to tell him not to contact me anymore. That was in a telephone conversation. He tried to get me to change my mind, and I was kind of nasty to him. It was just this morning. He got all the frustration and anger I was feeling toward Jacques."

Anger toward Jacques? This struck Harry as incongruous, and he asked why she was angry.

"Because he's being such a hardass. Because he just won't listen to me. Because he left me."

Harry saw his opening and decided to pounce. "Really? Are you sure you didn't want him to leave?"

"What do you mean? Of course not." She seemed quite taken aback.

"Isn't that why you were playing with fire?"

"What the fuck are you talking about, Harry? You're talking in riddles again."

"Excuse me, but I'm a little suspicious. For months you've been enumerating all of Jacques's faults, and it was clear to me that you had a fit of anxiety when he moved in. Then you begin surreptitiously to see Allan. Is there a connection?"

"I'm still not clear about what you're saying."

Harry moved in. "Did you *want* Jacques to find out?"

"God, no!"

"Really? Then why did you behave so recklessly? Allan was communicating by e-mail. Jacques was using your computer to check his e-mails, with your permission. Didn't that seem dangerous? Didn't you consider that Jacques might stumble upon one of Allan's communications? You could easily have precluded that by warning Allan not to use e-mails. Text messages would have done equally well and would have been quite safe, unless of course you let Jacques borrow your cell phone as well."

In the absence of a response from the couch Harry continued. "I don't think seeing Allan was about Allan. I'm sure he's no big deal for you now. It was about Jacques." There, he had said it! It was what he intended to say all along.

"About Jacques?" she asked in a small tentative voice.

"About Jacques!" Harry said emphatically. "About sabotaging your relationship with Jacques. About arranging to destroy it without seeming to have that intention."

Harry realized for the first time that he was angry with her, very angry. He waited for her to speak, perhaps to deny everything, but there was no response. Her hand went to her eyes and covered them, but no words were forthcoming.

"My mouth is so dry," she said. "Do you have any water?"

Harry stood up and went over to the side of his desk, where he stashed bottled water. When she turned to take it, he caught a quick glimpse of her face. It appeared drained of blood and had a grave, weary look.

He waited until she drank and had composed herself, and then he spoke. "What I really want to know is why you have so little trust in me."

"I feel you're toying with me, Harry. I don't know what you mean, and I think you're being deliberately obscure," she said in an untypical shaky voice.

"Why would I do that?" he asked.

"Because you get off on torturing me."

"Well, then you're proving my point—you don't trust me."

"I didn't say that."

"Here you are, miserable and depressed, and I'm so callous that I'm toying with your feelings. What's wrong with me?" He felt in complete command. He knew now where he had to go.

"You have your idiosyncrasies," she said after a period of reflection, "but that doesn't mean I don't trust you."

"Come on, Jennifer," he said sharply, "if you trusted me, how come I'm the last one to find out you've been seeing Allan? I only get the news after the catastrophe strikes, and I'm left to pick up the pieces. What should I feel about that?"

"I was afraid to tell you," she said defensively. "I was afraid of the consequences."

"The consequences? You were afraid I would reveal your secret to Jacques? You were afraid that I would violate confidentiality, even after I pledged that I would never do that? Is that it?"

"No, that's not it. I was afraid you'd be angry with me."

"Why would I be?"

"Because Jacques is your favorite."

Was Jacques his favorite? It gave Harry pause. What to answer? It was almost funny. He had been fantasizing about fucking Jennifer for a year, and she believed that Jacques was his favorite!

Fortunately for him, he didn't have to answer because she continued.

"And I thought you would lose respect for me, that you would think I was fucked up for having anything to do with Allan. Then I couldn't see him."

"You'd stop to please me?"

"To avoid your contempt."

"When have I ever voiced contempt for you?" Harry asked, full of surprise from what she was saying. After so many years with her, he was astounded that he could still be surprised about anything she said.

"There's always a first time."

"I would have felt concern, but never contempt," he said in an effort to be reassuring. "Were you feeling contempt for yourself?"

She began to cry and reached for a box of tissues on the side of the couch. She dabbed her eyes.

"Oh, I've made such a mess of things; what's going to become of me? I'm such a loser. Maybe I'm beyond help."

"Great—attacking yourself after so many years of therapy. Maybe I've failed as your therapist." For the first time in the session he felt sympathy for her. She appeared deeply gloomy and full of angst, not unlike the way Harry had been feeling.

"I'm the failure," she insisted. "I fucked up."

"It was my job to help you not be a failure."

"Then help me get Jacques back."

"You're sure he's gone?"

"Yes, he's so gone. I just can't believe it. It all happened so fast. He won't talk to me. He doesn't answer my calls. I told him I have no intention of ever seeing Allan again."

"What does he say?"

"He says he'll never be able to trust me again."

Harry raised his eyebrows. Slumping in his great chair at the beginning of the session, he was now sitting as straight as a soldier at attention.

"Is he wrong?" he asked.

"Absolutely. He's being such a hardass. I told him that— why can't he give me another chance? I never dreamed he'd be so moralistic, so ... so ... judgmental."

Harry recognized that he was growing angry again. He restrained himself, knowing it was important to control it.

"Let me bring Jacques in with me, please," she implored.

"What good will that do?"

"Maybe then he'll listen to me; I want him back."

Harry was unconvinced. "You do your damndest to fuck things up and now you want him back? Which Jennifer should I believe?"

"I didn't realize how I felt until I lost him. Are you on his side, Harry?"

"Meaning what?" Was he on Jacques's side? If there was a wronged party, it was Jacques. Jennifer seemed insensitive to that, and there was no denying the anger Harry felt toward her.

"Maybe you don't feel I'm good enough for Jacques. Maybe you don't want to help me get him back."

"Do you think you're good enough?"

"You're evading my question."

"This is not about me, it's about you. Maybe you not feeling good enough has been the problem all along."

"Will you or will you not persuade Jacques to have a session with me?"

Harry heard the strengthening determination in her voice. She was less concerned about looking within than with fixing things.

"For you to say what? That he should stop being a hardass? I hardly think that will work. What else do you intend to say that you haven't already said? Or perhaps you think that with my backing you can get him to change his mind? I won't do that."

Jennifer jumped up from the couch; sitting on the edge of it she confronted him. "So I was right. You don't think I'm good enough for him."

This was hazardous ground, as Harry well knew, and he needed to be at his best.

"It has nothing to do with that. My job is to help the two of you make the wisest decision for your happiness, whatever that may be. You say you want him back, and I understand that. Jacques is a wonderful guy, probably the best guy you've ever gone with, and it will be painful to lose him. But what about that part of you that doesn't want him? She's receded from view right now, but I suspect she'll eventually reappear. Should we ignore her? Besides that, have you considered Jacques's feelings?"

"I know what he's feeling; he's pissed off."

"That's only what he shows. Is there anything more?"

"Like what?"

"Like hurt, like disappointment, disillusion; like a colossal loss of trust, like the feeling one gets when someone very important lets you down. Have you asked him about that?" Harry's voice had a sharp edge to it.

Jennifer leaned over to pull out another tissue from the box. She used it to absorb tears that had begun to flow freely. She looked unflinchingly into Harry's eyes.

"Tell me the truth, Harry. I've been with you faithfully for nearly nine years. What should I do? What would be best, in your opinion?"

"How about telling the truth? A little honesty won't hurt."

"I've been honest with Jacques."

"Have you? I don't think you've been honest with yourself. You tolerated the most outrageous behavior from Allan, while not giving a pass to the most trivial of Jacques's misdeeds. Have you ever thought why that was so? You've been up and down with Jacques, close one day, the next day pushing him away. Why? What is it you fear from Jacques? Jennifer, what is your fear all about?"

Harry said this with such deliberate emphasis that she could not avoid paying rapt attention. Jennifer remained seated on the edge of the couch, her head lowered so that Harry was unable to see her face. She was silent.

"Do you understand?" he asked in a suddenly softened voice. He wondered whether she had heard anything he said.

She nodded slowly, her head still lowered. "I just don't know the answer. If you know, please tell me," she virtually whispered.

He suddenly felt a surge of tenderness toward her, a feeling he had not encountered before. He struggled with what to tell her. What was she ready to hear?

"You defend against your loving feelings, as though they were a fearful threat." He waited for her to respond, to perhaps ask for further elucidation, but she simply nodded. He would have liked more.

"Do you have any feelings about what I said?"

"I suppose you're right."

"That's not exactly a feeling."

"I'm feeling lost."

"What does that feel like?"

"Confused, uncertain, full of doubt, not knowing where I am or what I'm suppose to do. Can we move on from this, at least for now? If Jacques is going to break up with me, I need some closure. I need to tell him how I feel."

"I will talk to Jacques about a couple's session." He would give her that, feeling more benign toward her as he was. "I think it's the right thing. The three of us need to talk. Let me caution you to not be defensive, Jennifer, and to listen to his feelings. And please think about what I've said; you can't be honest with him unless you know yourself. Okay?"

She nodded again.

Did she understand? Did she get it?

She lay back on the couch and was silent for what to Harry seemed like an interminably long time. Coming from the most garrulous of women, the silence rather spooked Harry. He had never seen her like this. Was he somehow at fault?

Later, with the session all but ended, Jennifer had some parting words.

"I may have made a huge mess of things," she began as she stood up and faced him, a look of defiance on her face, "but there's something you seem to ignore. When Allan and I left the restaurant, he propositioned me. I could have gone home with him and spent the night. That would have finished things with Jacques. I didn't do that. I listened to my better angel, and when I walked away I knew I was through with Allan. I went home. It was Jacques I made love to that night. Don't I get some credit for that?"

"Yes you do. And if I'm able to convince Jacques to have a couple's session, I suggest you continue to listen to your better angel."

As Jennifer departed, Harry stood at the window and watched her, a tall figure bundled in a long down coat hunched against a brisk wind on that glacial midwinter day, disappear from sight. He began pacing in his office, unable to forestall a growing inner agitation. Had he been too hard on her? As she admitted, she had taken a step toward the precipice, but then she'd turned back. Why then had he been so angry? And what if she had plunged over that precipice and wrecked the relationship with Jacques? As a patient, wasn't she allowed to screw up? There was nothing he'd said to her that he cared to call back. He believed it needed to be said. It was *the manner in which he said it*, the tone, the timber of his voice, that sharpness that betokened a barely controlled anger.

These consecutive thoughts led Harry to question his own motives. Did he have a vested interest in the success of their relationship? Was he overidentified with Jacques, knowing how much he loved Jennifer? Could that explain his anger toward her? Or was it simply an ego thing? How many times over the course of their years together had Harry instructed Jennifer to talk before acting? She had completely ignored that advice and muddled things up. Is that what got under his skin? If so, he was out of line. Patients would be patients after all and must have room to do their thing. He considered a third possibility. He had once promised Jacques that he would warn him if he witnessed him making another poor girlfriend choice. Had Harry failed to see that Jennifer was just such a poor choice? Did her behavior now prove that? Had he failed Jacques? Was that why he was so angry with her? These questions circled about in his brain without finding a definite answer. He knew that a therapist's job was to be objective and neutral. He was there to help the patient explore her inner being, not to champion a cause or a particular outcome. It was his obligation to create a warm environment for the patient in which she felt secure and protected, understood and accepted, a safe place brought about by the absence of criticism and judgment. Had he, Harry, accomplished that today? He feared he had not.

He worried that he had performed like an inquisitor accusing his prisoner of apostasy. Or was he being too harsh with himself? After all, he had relinquished his anger in the last part of the session and treated her kindly. Still, her final words had startled him, jarred him out of his complacency. These thoughts left him with a seemingly insoluble conundrum: why had he been so angry with Jennifer? What was at the bottom of it? None of his tentative answers, which perhaps provided partial explanations, seemed exactly right.

CHAPTER 22

Triad

Jacques Giraud, inconsolable and irate, surprised Harry by readily agreeing to join Jennifer in a session. Neither cajolery nor friendly persuasion was necessary. Despite Jacques's agreeableness, Harry worried. When feelings were hot, it was sometimes preferable to allow them to cool off before a face-to-face confrontation. He was also worried about Jennifer, wondering what more she could unwittingly do to sever the last bond that might still exist between her and Jacques. He realized his sympathies were with Jacques and knew he had to tightly control that. *Stay neutral and balanced*, he told himself.

They entered his office a silent and grim-looking pair, sitting on opposite ends of the couch as if expecting someone to sit between them. A light snow fell outside, melting as soon as the flakes struck the warm ground. There was an unnerving silence in the room, so much so that Harry imagined a penny falling to the floor would make a noise like thunder. An occasional distant sound of an auto horn broke through the gloom and silence of the room. Looking at Jennifer's haggard face, he wondered whether he should recommend an antidepressant medication. Perhaps he needed one himself. Looking at Jacques, Harry believed he could perceive a malevolent countenance. The mild-mannered, easygoing man he had worked with was nowhere in sight. This was a transformed Jacques, and Harry was not the least bit confident he would enjoy this new persona.

His reticent patients shifted uncomfortably on the couch until Jacques spoke.

"I have no idea why I'm here."

"What are you feeling?" Harry inquired.

"Like this is a waste of time."

"That's a thought, not a feeling."

"I feel impatient and angry."

Jennifer spoke up. "You're here because I need to say something to you, and I wasn't able to say it anywhere else."

"So now you have a captive audience, so talk," Jacques responded aggressively as he gestured dismissively with his hand. Harry felt a sense of foreboding. Jennifer sat for a while without saying a word, her eyes cast to the floor. Then she looked into Jacques's eyes and began to speak in a very soft, halting voice.

"I know how much I ... hurt you," she began, "and you didn't deserve it, not in any way. You've been wonderful to me. I really couldn't expect more. I just want to say ... how very sorry I am ... really I am. I'm sorry I lied to you. I'm sorry I saw Allan without telling you. Actually, I'm sorry I saw him at all."

Jacques stared back at her and shrugged. "Fine," he said and left it at that.

"Is that all you have to say, Jacques?" Harry asked.

"Sorry doesn't cut it for me; the damage has been done, and this doesn't make it any better."

"So what would you like from Jennifer?"

Jacques shifted his body to face Jennifer.

"Okay, I get that you fell out of love with me. So why didn't you just end it? Why did you have to sneak around behind my back?"

"I didn't fall out of love with you." It was the first time she had used the L-word with him. "If anything I was feeling closer, closer but more nervous."

"That doesn't make any sense to me," Jacques said with obvious impatience. "You're feeling closer to me, so you make a date with Allan, tell me a straight-faced lie, and spend the evening with him. So tell me why. Explain it to me, please. What were you planning? What was the purpose of it? And don't tell me it was innocent. You wouldn't have had to lie if it was innocent."

"I've been trying to make sense out of it myself. I can only figure out that the more important you became, the more I wanted to run away, all the time not understanding my feelings. Harry thinks I wanted to ruin our relationship as a way out of my dilemma."

"Well, you were successful," Jacques said. "How come you never talked about this? How come you never admitted to me that you were scared?"

"It was my secret. I kept it from Harry; I kept it from my friends; I kept it from myself. It was a well-kept secret."

"Why did you want to run away?" Harry asked.

"I don't know; I think I was afraid of losing control."

"Control of what?"

"Of my feelings—of becoming too attached."

"What's wrong with becoming attached?" Harry asked, wondering how far she could go with this.

"I don't know."

"Try. If you let yourself love, what happens?"

"I would become dependent."

"And then?"

"And then he would leave me." Her eyes began to glisten.

"That's ridiculous," Jacques burst out belligerently. "I was crazy about you. I adored you. You must have known that. How could you believe there was any risk of my leaving you?"

For a moment Harry felt like telling Jacques to leave the room. Of course he couldn't do that.

"I didn't think I was good enough for you."

"I don't believe any of this shit! You just wanted to get it on with Allan."

"That's not true," she cried. "Allan doesn't mean anything to me, and I have no intention of seeing him again. I've told you that, and I've told Harry too. If anything, meeting Allan helped clarify for me the difference between the two of you. You're emotionally honest and he's full of shit. I'm not so crazy that I would prefer him over you."

"Okay, maybe that's true, but if it is, your behavior doesn't make sense, and I don't get it. Can you clear it up, Harry—does it make sense to you?"

"I think I can. May I have your permission, Jennifer?"

Jennifer looked hopeless but nodded her assent.

Harry considered what he needed to say, what to put in, what to leave out. He would be talking not just to Jacques but to Jennifer as well. He needed to keep it simple and to the point.

"Jennifer's dad also adored her, Jacques; adored her, loved her, made her feel special. Then he left her mother and, in effect, left Jennifer too, dropped her cold. So why should she trust you? Or any man, for that matter? She blamed herself for her father's leaving, figured she wasn't good enough, must have let him down in some nameless way. That's why she doesn't think she's good enough for you." He looked at Jacques, trying to divine the impact of his words.

"Okay, so I wish I knew this sooner. I never would have allowed myself to fall in love. Once again I'm with the wrong woman. I should go."

Harry shook his head. *Unintended consequence.*

"Don't go," Jennifer said, a note of urgency rising in her voice. "I went this far with you. I can go further."

"No, you can't. Harry said it."

She looked pleadingly at Harry.

"Why do you think she's here, Jacques? If she hasn't given up on herself, why have you?"

Jacques shrugged. He looked at Harry, ignoring Jennifer's eyes.

"Why should I put myself in jeopardy? Why should I take a chance that this will happen again, if not with Allan, maybe with someone else? Here's the story I'm getting: she's afraid of being close. Only she doesn't realize it. So she has a few dates with Allan. She says there were only two, but who knows?

She's proven herself to be a pretty adept liar. Probably she was planning on fucking him, but she doesn't know that either because she's a pretty confused girl. Okay, maybe she doesn't have sex with him, but the intent was there. And now I'm asked to forgive and forget. I should take her back, forget that anything happened, and trust her." This was said to Harry as if Jennifer wasn't in the room.

"I'm not asking you to forget anything, and I'm not asking you to trust me. I'm asking you to give me a chance to work things out with you, and to work things out with myself. Why do you think I'm here talking to you this way, if I don't care for you? No, that's not good enough. I was beginning to think of you as someone to spend my life with. I never felt that way before, and I think it spooked me. That was another one of my secrets."

"You know, Jen, at one time that would have meant so much to me. I longed to hear those words. Now it doesn't mean a thing. I want to be with someone who's not afraid to be close; I want to be with someone who's normal."

For the first time Harry allowed himself to feel angry with Jacques. "What makes you think that you're not afraid to be close?"

Jacques looked confused. "I let myself be close to Jennifer."

"Only because you sensed she had some walls up. Now that she wants you, and she clearly does want you—that's why she's opening her heart to you—you're the one who's running away!" That was Harry's best shot.

"I don't get that." Jacques was being most stubborn. Harry once thought that was Jennifer's skill.

"Give me a chance to set things right," Jennifer said. "I can change myself."

"You can't be someone else, like you can just step out of character. You have to be yourself."

"Oh, really? Which self is that? Is it the self that lost self-respect, or the self that brought me here with you today, feeling worse than I've ever felt before? Or is it the self that kept me in therapy for nine years so I can finally choose the self I truly want to be?"

Harry turned his head slightly to look at Jacques. His face seemed immobile.

Jacques heaved a sigh. Was it a feeling of resignation that it expressed? Or was it frustration, impatience, or even indifference?

"Here's what it comes down to," Jacques began. "I put you on a pedestal. I thought you were my magical princess."

"I know. I never wanted you to do that. I knew I could never live up to that standard. I knew I would fail."

"You didn't live up to even a reasonable standard. I think I've heard enough. Harry, I'm going to be leaving therapy. I don't think it's helping me anymore."

Patients will always surprise you, as Harry well knew. This was the mother of all surprises.

"What help do you want that I'm not giving to you?"

Jacques was quiet.

"Should I have warned you about Jennifer?"

"I can't *believe* you're leaving Harry," Jennifer said, her drawn face etched in disbelief. She was sitting on the edge of the couch.

"Is this your business? Was I talking to you?"

"Wow. When you fall off a pedestal, you fall a long way."

Harry was unsure whether she was referring to herself or to him.

"I'll keep my appointment next week, and that will be my last session."

"Jesus, Jacques, I never knew what a complete asshole you could be," Jennifer said with more animation than Harry had heard before.

"That's it, I'm leaving," the glowering Jacques said. And with those parting words, Jacques scooped up his coat and walked out.

When the door closed, Harry and Jennifer sat quietly looking at each other.

"I don't know whether to laugh or cry," she said. "I don't think he understood a thing. How could he be so dense?"

"He's not my favorite patient," Harry said. That made her laugh.

"I hardly think I am either."

"You were pretty great today."

"I was?"

"Honest, genuine, real. Yes, you were. You've done a lot of work since I saw you last week."

She began to cry again and grabbed a tissue and dabbed at her eyes.

"Do you think he'll come back, Harry?"

"If he doesn't, he's not good enough for you."

"Really? You mean that? You're not just being nice?"

"I'm not as nice as you think," Harry said, thinking of Amanda. "And I most definitely mean it." For a moment he wished he were young again and Jennifer was his girlfriend. He wished he could rescue her from her unhappiness. She was looking beautiful to him again. And then he realized he still had a thing for her. So what? He probably always would.

"And you were dead-on right, Jennifer; he was being an unmitigated asshole."

"But it seemed so out of character, like Dr. Jekyll became Mr. Hyde."

"He's been massively disappointed by women before, by bad mothers and girlfriends. That's his problem." It was about as full an explanation as he could then muster.

"I feel very close to you right now," she said. She had never said that before, not in nine years.

"Me too. Does it feel okay?"

"Oh yes. It feels like … even if he doesn't come back, I'll still have you, so it won't be so bad."

"Absolutely you'll still have me. I'm not going anywhere."

CHAPTER 23

Harry and Izzy Revisited

At Harry's request, Izzy met him at a café near the Psychoanalytic Center. Harry had deliberately chosen the restaurant for its reasonable noise level. It was midafternoon, when there were fewer patrons and conversation was actually possible. The fact that Izzy was hard of hearing made the choice particularly significant. Harry listened patiently as Izzy pontificated about "the Js," Jennifer and Jacques. Lamenting in typical Izzian style over the trouble his friend was having with the troublesome pair, he offered a ray of hope. "I think," he said, "they will not break up." They had already broken up, so it seemed to Harry that the old man was going out on a limb, or so he suggested to his colleague.

"It is not a done deal," Izzy insisted. "You think because he's disappointed in his fallen queen he will not come back? All he's ever known from women is disappointment. He's right at home. When she stops disappointing him, that's when the trouble will start on his end. Then you'll have your hands full." And with that Izzy clapped his hands, as if he were enjoying the future difficulties he was foretelling. He wasn't through.

"As for the fallen queen, the mere threat of him leaving links him to her father, and he becomes much more valuable and challenging for her."

"A romantic you are not," Harry ventured.

"Phooey on romance! That's illusion, and this is life, this

is reality. The Js aren't freaks. They're like you and me and everyone else. And by the way, you say Jacques was a big jerk in the session. He did himself some good by being that way. Let her sweat to get him back. Why should he go back like a lamb? 'Oh, poor baby, are you crying? Papa will come back, don't you fret. See? All is forgiven.' Yuck. He stood up for himself. He was a man! In the end she'll respect him more for it."

"Well, I don't. He was an insensitive clod."

"Don't you know, Harry? Women adore men who are occasional assholes. Sweet guys finish last."

"Well, then, Amanda must be worshipping me."

Harry had been listening to Izzy with half an ear. He wasn't much interested in his views of the Js. Here was an opportunity to broach a new subject for their conversation, one that would be more of the essence for him.

"Talking about Amanda, there is something I need to bring up. When Jennifer first told me that she was seeing Allan, I was very angry. Initially my reaction didn't compute for me because I rarely get that angry in a session. At the time I reasoned that it was due to her acting out destructively without processing it with me. But hell, patients do that; why was it such a big deal? Then I thought I was overidentifying with Jacques. He was crazy about her. He had been wonderful to her. So how unfair was this?"

"And don't forget your fondness for that young man," Izzy added.

"Yes, that too. But that wasn't it either. How many love stories end this way? I've been around too long to believe I can protect my patients from heartbreak. So there was something else. It took me a few dream-filled nights to finally figure it out. One of those dreams tipped me off. It was *Jennifer* I was overidentifying with. Jennifer behaved with Jacques in the same way that I behaved with Amanda; only her sin was more indirect and less flagrant than mine. She took the subterranean route to scuttle her relationship. I used direct frontal assault. I was ashamed of myself, and that's why I was so angry with her. We were both miscreants when it came to loving. But that brings me to my main point. For weeks now I've been feeling pissed off at you also. I'm not going to sit on it any longer."

Izzy raised his eyebrows. He placed his fork, which was in midair, back on his plate. He looked unsmilingly at Harry and was about to speak when Harry raised his hand to form a stop sign.

"There's a time for everything," Harry said. "Now is the time for you to stop talking and listen. Just listen. If I have one regret in my life, it's breaking up with Amanda. So this is what I have to say about that: fuck our colleagues for interfering, fuck the Psychoanalytic Center, fuck my kids for being selfish brats, and most of all fuck you for being such a pompous know-it-all! My feelings for Amanda, like her feelings for me, were genuine. It wasn't about power or authority or foolish fantasy; it was about two mature people who grew close, two people who were happy together, who could talk the day long and not grow bored or tired of one another. It was about making love and losing ourselves in it. Do you understand that, Izzy? I never should have allowed anything or anyone to get between us. But I was too cowardly to protect it."

As Harry talked the fire within him grew, stoked by his words and the emotions they generated. His hands were in constant motion, gesturing broadly, as if to orchestrate the expression of those emotions. There was anger and there was anguish.

"Losing my standing at the Center, losing all my privileges, teaching and supervisory functions; losing referrals from friends and colleagues, and even losing your friendship would be nothing compared to what I *have* lost. I spent four years mourning Sarah, four years dying a little every day, watching life spin past me, a dormant, bereft, and lonely man at a loss for finding any way out. And then I found it—that is, I found her. Work is not enough, Izzy; it's just not enough. I feel sorry for people who think it is. I needed an emotional connection. I had it and then I let it go. And you haven't been a good friend to me at all."

Izzy listened in rapt attention, nodding on occasion, looking quite sad.

"Finished?"

"Yes. Now you can talk." Harry waited for the counterpoint, sure of himself and of the authenticity of his feelings. If it meant the sundering of their friendship, so be it.

"First of all you haven't lost her; you can retrieve her, and I think you should."

"Changing your position?" Harry asked, more than a little surprised by Izzy's about-face. How many times did he warn Harry to stay away from Amanda?

"Absolutely. I've changed my mind."

Now? After it's too late and all is lost? Izzy's change of heart didn't calm Harry; it unsettled him further.

"The last time I saw Amanda for supervision, we had an unusual session," Izzy began by way of explanation. "About five minutes into talking about her patient group, she broke down. I had to make a rapid switch from supervisor to emergency therapist. That's when I learned how important you were to her. Oh, my friend! Would you believe that I felt angry with you?"

Harry didn't know whether to laugh or punch Izzy in the nose. He opted for the former. "Angry with me?" he asked through his laughter.

"Yes, of course. Here was this beautiful, sensational woman with a broken heart coming unglued before my eyes. What a schmuck you were for breaking up with her, for listening to me! In my defense, my attitude soon changed. I began to examine my role in this. Admittedly, it was an ignominious one."

"No argument there," Harry said, thinking that Izzy's chosen word, *ignominious*, was perfectly fitting.

"Wait. There's more to come. You don't know yet what a scumbag I am."

Scumbag. Harry could not remember the last time he had heard that expression. Izzy had piqued his curiosity. *Just how bad is a scumbag?*

"I'm ashamed to say this, Harry, but it needs saying. I was

motivated by a base emotion; jealousy guided my advice to you. I was jealous of you and Amanda. I wanted to be you. I wanted to be the one who was fucking her."

Harry was speechless. If Izzy had looked carefully at Harry, he might have distinguished astonishment in his eyes.

"Oh, you wouldn't be thinking that I'm too old for that sort of thing, would you? Since when does the desire to fuck a pretty woman age out? Look at me, Harry. Do you think I'm not aware that I have no chance with the likes of Amanda Blake? Look at this sunken face, this scrawny, arthritic, doddering old man. There is not even a memory of a muscle here. Nor would I cheat on Lizzie, even if by some miracle, some miraculous clouding of Amanda's eyes, the opportunity arose. Frankly, I'd be afraid of having a cardiac arrest. No, I'm not talking about action; I'm talking about wishes, longings, dreams. I'm talking about wanting to be young again. Not even young like your son; young like you. That will do fine. I always tell my patients 'the mind is free, give yourself that freedom. Fantasy is unbounded by conventions or by reality. It's absolutely healthy as long as you don't confuse thought with action.' So why wouldn't I allow myself the same freedom? So I envied you. Thinking about you fucking Amanda frankly pissed me off. The problem was I didn't know it. What man wants to know what a stupid old fool he is? So I labeled that rotten jealous feeling 'concern for your professional standing.' In a flash I was no longer a stupid old fool. I was transformed into an altruistic friend. It's interesting. If you remember, I attributed jealousy, that shittiest of emotions, to our colleagues at the Center. I projected my denied feelings onto them. If only we therapists could develop immunity to the neurotic mental processes that afflict our patients! I hope you'll be able to forgive this pathetic, ridiculous bastard."

Could Harry forgive him? It was a complicated question. Sometimes the best defense is no defense at all, he knew, and Izzy had put up no defense for his obnoxious behavior. His *mea culpa* managed to defuse Harry's anger. Harry recognized that it wasn't easy for an egotist to allow a major flaw to be exposed.

Then again, Harry understood that he alone was responsible for his behavior. His was the exclusive culpability. In his heart of hearts he knew he was exaggerating the extent of Izzy's influence, or for that matter the influence of his colleagues and his children. No, it came down to character. That's what he had to come to grips with. Blaming others was a lie.

"I'll forgive you if you help me get her back."

"Strange. That's the only way I'll forgive myself. How can I help?"

"She refuses to meet with me. I suggested that we just talk, but she's opposed to it. She says it will only open the wound further. I said it might heal the wound, but she wasn't buying it. So now I don't know what to do. I've thought of telling her that I changed my mind about breaking up, but I'm afraid she'll turn me down flat."

"First of all, my friend, can you get it through your thick skull that the woman is in love with you? For God's sake, man, she's been a wreck since you dumped her. Her chin has taken up residence in her navel. How much persuading do you think she needs?"

Perhaps, or perhaps out of his guilt Izzy needs to believe it will all turn out well. Why should Harry believe that?

"If that's so, Izzy, then why is she being so difficult?"

"Because she's afraid of being hurt again, you imbecile!"

Why didn't Harry know that? If a patient had asked him that question, he would have given him the same answer that Izzy gave, save the "imbecile" part. Locked in this emotional whirlwind, he had lost perspective.

"So where does that leave me?"

"It leaves you to convince her that you love her and will never do that to her again."

Harry picked up a look in Izzy's eyes that he interpreted as an "I'm talking to a child here" look. "How do I do that when she refuses to see me?"

"Hmm. That is a good question. You don't want to do this over the telephone or, even worse, the computer."

Harry waited while Izzy cogitated. "I wish Lizzy were here," Izzy said. *Say, so do I,* Harry thought. "Okay, let me think what she would say. You know, I've been married to the woman so long I can dive into her mind whenever I want to. Okay, here's what she would say: pick a time of day when Amanda's sure to be home. Let's say Saturday or Sunday morning, not too late, not too early. Call her and tell her you're coming over at that time and you expect her to be there. Tell her you have to talk to her—it's not an elective, it's a requirement. Don't take no for an answer. Be immovably stubborn and impossibly difficult if necessary. Remember, there's a lot at stake here, like both of your futures. And if you're feeling fainthearted because she's putting up a wall of resistance, try to recollect that she still loves you—you can work with that. Bottom line: if she continues to refuse, you tell her that you're coming over anyway, and you'll be quite disturbed if she's not there. Use those words, 'quite disturbed,' and throw in that she owes you that much. Knowing how to induce guilt is always a formidable weapon."

How could Harry not forgive his impossible friend, that decrepit, flawed wizard? Wasn't it better to know one's friends' defects, so as to take their advice with a grain of salt? Harry still needed his friendship. Sometimes, given the twenty-year difference in age, he worried about eventually losing him. Life would be so much duller without the presence of Dr. Israel Gross. *Live long Izzy. Live long my friend!*

CHAPTER 24

Jennifer and Jacques Revisited

When Jacques called to say he needed to come by, Jennifer could not contain her feelings. She was alarmed, tense, uncertain, and excited. True, he had left a few things in her apartment, and she imagined that he was only coming to pick them up. There was no sign from him of a change of heart, not even the mere hint of an interest in reconciliation. She imagined that he would arrive, pick up his things, and leave; she had no guarantee that he would speak even a word.

While she waited for Jacques to arrive she couldn't sit still. She walked from room to room, staring blankly at the paintings on the wall. She let her mind wander back to recent days, when she'd told her friends about what had happened between her and Jacques. Their various reactions took her completely by surprise. She expected Meg, who absolutely adored Jacques, to be critical of her, to accuse her of rank self-destructive stupidity. Instead she was supportive.

"I'm really disappointed in him," Meg said.

"You are? Why?"

"So you lied and had dinner with Allan. What's the big deal? Do you break up with someone you love over that? What's the matter with him? If he can't get over that, then he's a baby and fuck him. Good riddance."

From Hillary, who was enmeshed in the wedding preparations dance, she expected apathy. Jennifer would understand Hillary's indifference if she were too self-involved and in love to care about anyone else. Instead Hillary began to cry.

"What's the matter, Hill? What? Talk to me."

"I so wanted the two of you to be together. I dreamed of our having babies and of putting them on swings in the park, of becoming total bores who talk about nothing else but our babies," she sniffled.

Ah so! A dream had died. It wasn't all that tantalizing to Jennifer anyway. "I guess I haven't found my Rothstein yet."

From Daryl she expected support. She found impatience instead.

"Why are you giving up so easily? Do you realize how many duds there are out there? Do whatever you need to do to get him back."

"Come on, Daryl. I have some pride, you know. There's got to be someone else for me out there."

"Sure there is, but what makes you think you're going to find him? If I found someone like Jacques, I would stick to him like glue."

That was a shocker. Daryl, who went through men like they were nothing more than pairs of socks with holes in them, talking like this? Jennifer put forth a tentative inquiry regarding her friend's sea change.

"I don't know; I made a decision. I want a man. One man."

When the shock wore off, depression set in. Daryl was superb at unwittingly stirring up bad feelings. "Okay, so I'll be single the rest of my life," Jennifer said to herself. She called Meg to help undo the damage Daryl had done.

"Stay with your anger," Meg advised. "In the final analysis Jacques is the betrayer, the abandoner of the relationship, not you. He's the coward for running away."

She expected her mother to be critical of her, of course. Jennifer gave her mother none of the details of the breakup, in keeping with an old strategy to keep her as uninformed as possible, operating on a need-to-know basis. What did Mom need to know? She needed to know that they broke up and nothing more. The session she'd had with her mother and Harry was insufficient to induce Jennifer to change her approach. Unexpectedly her mother appeared indifferent. "If you think it's best, dear," she said simply. That stunning nonreaction left Jennifer to speculate about the reason. Could it be that Mrs. Slater was operating under the misapprehension that Jacques was a relatively impoverished professor? If so, let her stay in the dark. If she knew the truth, she would be critical of Jennifer for blowing it.

Now she was left to face Jacques alone. If only she could have her friends with her—and Harry being there wouldn't be so bad either. Memories of their recent conversations and Jacques's anger and hard-heartedness swirled in her mind. Now she would stand her ground. She had committed no crime; this was more about his shortcomings than hers. But for all her bravado, she recognized the propensity to bite her nails while waiting for his appearance. Should she call Meg, or possibly even Harry? No, that was giving in to panic, a very bad idea. What was she so nervous about? It was over, and if she allowed herself to hope otherwise she was paving the way for a crash. She had not received one shred of evidence to suggest that he had softened. There was only the one telephone call saying he needed to come over. If she tried to build a hope around that she was a fool. *Meg was right—fuck him. Fuck him, fuck him, fuck him!*

She heard the doorbell and immediately checked herself out in a mirror before answering it. It wouldn't do any harm to at least look good.

"Hi," he said, barely looking at her. "I'll only be a minute."

Despite the pep talk she had given herself, her heart sank. He walked past her into the room where his things were stored. Not wanting to look foolish by standing around, she walked into the living room and sat on a chair. There was nothing for her to do now but wait for him to leave. An odd calm settled over her. The waiting and suspense were over; they were done. She wasn't even certain he would say good-bye on his way out the door. Jacques emerged from the room holding a jacket and a book. He walked directly to the door, looked at her from across the room; he hesitated, and her heart stood still. He seemed to slightly wave good-bye and muttered words that she could not decipher. And then he was gone.

She sat quietly for a while and then spoke one word aloud. "Shit!" Despite herself she had retained a hope through it all. How else to explain this extraordinary feeling of letdown, of sheer disappointment? *Hope.* Hope, that old enemy of hers, had done her in once again. Men seemed to be masters at dashing hope. Hope was to be avoided like a deadly disease. She must remember that for the future. *Hope for nothing, expect nothing; that's the way to go. Maybe the lesbians have it right. Women are so much more reliable than men. Women are better. If only some could grow penises, say about half of them, that would be the solution.* She found these thoughts strangely consoling.

Sitting alone in that room, a memory flashed through her brain. It was the image of Jacques sitting on the couch just after Meg's engagement party. God, that seemed ages ago. And to think how dubious she'd been toward him! Perhaps she would have been better off if she had left off with him then. What a strange and wonderful evening that was, the night they were first together, and then the dates afterward, and when they first had sex. "Come," she had said to him as she took his hand and guided him to her bedroom. How had they come to this place of emptiness? She felt burdened by the memories.

The doorbell rang again. *It must be Meg*, she thought as she rushed to the door. It wasn't Meg. It was Jacques.

"May I come in?"

They stood in the small foyer facing one another. *What now?* A small ray of hope, stealthy and unbidden, crept in. There it was, hope again.

"I don't think it was fair calling me an asshole."

"You were behaving like one."

"I was in a pissy mood. That didn't rise to the level of asshole."

"You're right, Jacques, it didn't rise to that level, it sunk to that level."

"I didn't lie to you; I didn't sneak around to see an old girlfriend. So what level did that sink to?"

Jennifer remembered Harry's advice to be guided by her "better angels." After all, he had returned. He was talking. Wasn't that a favorable thing? *There you go again, Jen, hoping.*

"You're right, that behavior was contemptible. That was me at my worst. You can't imagine how much I regret it. I was awful."

"It seems to me it took you a long time to admit it."

"You were so furious. You were attacking, so I felt I had to defend myself. You didn't give me room to look at what I had done. And as bad as it was, it was no way near as bad as you saw it."

"Yeah, but I had no way of knowing that for sure, because you're such an accomplished liar."

Why is he doing this again? What does he want? "Did you come back to insult me, is that what this is about?"

Jacques shrugged. Momentarily he was at a loss.

"I lied to you once. How does that make me an accomplished liar?"

"If you hadn't been found out, there would have been more."

It was his new theme. He assumed the worst of her. She had a notion to tell him to go fuck himself, but remembering Harry's words she calmed herself down. She remained angry nonetheless.

"No, you are absolutely wrong. When I walked away from Allan, it was forever. Do you remember what I did when I came home? I know I told you this once before, but I think it bears repeating. Do you remember how I practically tore your clothes off? Why do you think I did that?"

"You were feeling guilty."

Enough. She was not able to hold back. "No, you fucking

idiot. It was because I was happy. I finally knew that I wanted to be with you and no other. It was because I realized that Allan was at long last out of my system. And do you know why?"

She waited for him to answer. He didn't.

"It was because of you, you jerk!"

She was feeling open and strong and sad too. He understood her so poorly. If he left her now it would be all *his* fault.

"Do you think you can ever forgive my high crime and misdemeanor?"

He was quiet for a bit. What was he pondering? Then he blurted out, "You said you didn't fall out of love with me."

"Yes, I did. I stand by it."

"I came back because I didn't really want to leave."

That remark registered with her in a rather significant way. She looked at him standing awkwardly in the foyer, his jacket and book still in hand, looking sheepish and shy, just like he had when they first met. He really was an adorable-looking guy.

"I wanted to stay," he said.

"Then why didn't you?"

"You made me nervous. Why didn't you ask me to stay?"

"You made me nervous!" She laughed nervously. "In fact, I think that may have been my problem all along."

"I missed you," he said, looking sadly at her.

"I had trouble sleeping."

"We're having a really honest conversation."

"I know," she said, "it feels good."

"We used to talk this way."

"Yes, that's true. I don't know why we stopped. We've got to get back to that."

"Yes, we do, absolutely. So as long as we're being honest, I have something else to say to you."

Jennifer felt a knot form in her stomach. She braced herself.

"You're right. I was being an asshole. Can you forgive me?"

"Uh huh." She almost laughed she was feeling so giddy.

Jacques looked at her and seemed to hesitate. There had to be something important on his mind.

"Well, can I?"

"What?"

"Stay?"

"Sure, but there are conditions," she said, now feeling on top of the world.

"Conditions?"

"Yes, conditions. Two, actually. First, you have to come with me again to see Harry. Every week."

"Every week?"

"Once a week. But I don't want you to think this is all about me. I'm not the designated fucked-up one. You have problems too."

"Me? Like what?" he asked, sounding a little too innocent.

Was he kidding? "Do you remember what Harry said, that you had a problem being close?"

"I don't remember that. He didn't say that."

"You have a selective memory. We'll have to ask Harry."

"What's the reason for seeing Harry together?"

"Learning to trust."

"How long do you think that will take?"

The question plunged Jennifer into deep thought. "Uh … twelve to fifteen years."

"Seems reasonable," he said with a slight laugh. "And the second condition?"

"You have to stay in treatment with Harry."

"Did he put you up to this?"

She looked at him to see whether he was serious.

He laughed again. "I agree to your conditions. Can we make love now?"

Make love. How lovely! She hadn't heard that euphemistic expression for such a long time, certainly not from a man. It was such unfamiliar language that hearing it startled her. "Fucking" was more to the point, genital-to-genital connection, casual and emotion-free. Jennifer realized she was in the mood for "making love." She extended her hand to him. That seductive look that she knew he could never resist suddenly appeared in her eyes. He carelessly dropped his jacket and book to the floor, as though they were irrelevant and forgotten objects now. *Kerplunk* went the book when it hit the floor. She took his hand in hers.

"Come," she said.

CHAPTER 25

Harry Faces the Music

Harry found the message on his answering machine heartening. "We unbroke up," Jennifer sparingly and ungrammatically announced. Harry waited for amplification but heard only the click that revealed there would be none. Jacques provided more than enough amplification when he appeared in person. Jacques seemed as wildly happy as he had when he first announced Jennifer's existence to Harry. Of course, this time Harry knew who that Jennifer was.

"She loves me!" Jacques triumphantly declared. He also announced that he was canceling his next Monday session because he and Jennifer made a last-minute decision to spend five days in Paris. Jacques added that he would schedule a makeup session when he returned. There was one more surprise. Jennifer had suggested that Jacques move his things back into her apartment as part of a *permanent* arrangement. Harry nearly fell out of his big leather chair. But there was more. Jacques had actually *set a condition for his return*!

"I told her I would do it provided she gave control over the toilet paper to me. The lead of the paper has to go *over* the roll, not *under*, and that has to be *permanent*."

"And she agreed to that?"

"Well, not at first. She said she wanted to negotiate, but I stood my ground."

"And she caved?"

"She caved."

"Mazel tov," Harry said.

"Meaning?"

"It's a form of congratulations."

It was a very pleasant session for Harry, far better than the previous one with Jacques. In a small way, it lifted Harry's mood. If Jennifer and Jacques could reconcile, why couldn't he and Amanda follow suit? It provided that little push that he needed to call his erstwhile girlfriend.

The call to Amanda was excruciatingly difficult, just as he'd worried it would be. She gave no ground, despite his promptings. She was not the least bit interested in seeing him. Believing he had no choice, he fell back upon Izzy's strategy. He was coming Sunday morning at ten, and he expected her to be there. He made sure she understood that he would interpret noncompliance as a villainous act, comparable to Pontius Pilate ordering the crucifixion of Jesus. Despite the overkill, he wasn't certain she would be there.

On the appointed day and time he walked on rubbery legs to her apartment. At that time of the morning people were beginning to appear in the streets, out to buy the newspaper, or pick up the car, or head to their favorite café for breakfast. Harry noticed none of them. Lost in the world of his own thoughts, he kept his head down as he plodded quickly to her residence.

She was there. Harry instantly felt a sense of déjà vu. It was not only that he had been in this place with this woman before—of course he had, many times—but that he had once suffered from the very same roller coaster of emotions: hope and fear, the same noxious self-doubt. He had been wrong, devious, and false; he had much to atone for. Had he forfeited her trust and therefore her willingness to open her heart again to him? Izzy insisted that she loved him. *Will love be enough? Am I entitled to her sympathy, her understanding, or anything?*

Amanda's aloof demeanor as she ushered him into her apartment made matters worse for Harry. She seemed cold and distant, so unlike the woman he knew. She brought him into the kitchen, where a small table with two chairs accommodated them. *Why the kitchen instead of the living room? What does it signify?* Sitting in the straight-backed wooden chair felt so much less comfortable than the couch or soft, plush living room seats. Was it the typical seating for a short visit? She offered him neither food nor drink. He noticed that she was dressed more casually than ever before in ordinary brown corduroy slacks and a simple, loose-fitting white blouse. He imagined she was sending him a message that this was no special occasion at all. She sat opposite him and remained stone quiet, obviously waiting for him to begin.

Harry had prepared a speech, which he now decided to discard. He would speak spontaneously. Whatever came up came up. He would exercise no censorship. She deserved no less.

"It's confession time," he said after he had settled down.

He waited for her to speak. She merely nodded.

"I told myself a lie and then I repeated it to you."

She nodded again.

"I convinced myself that I cared about the opinion of others. You know, about my reputation."

"You don't?"

"Not really. When I told you that we had to break up, do you remember what you felt?"

"Of course I do," she replied, looking at him as though he were a schizophrenic. "I felt devastated."

"No. I mean, how angry you felt at our colleagues at the Center. You even asked me whether I was angry, and I said I was. Well, I wasn't. I thought about that. How could I not be when they were ruining our lives? What I finally figured out was that they had nothing to do with my breaking up with you."

He looked at her for some spark of a response. He saw none.

"I don't need them anymore. I'm burnt out at the Center. As a practitioner I'm pretty independent. My confession is this: they only provided an excuse for breaking up with you. It wasn't the real reason."

"I'm not surprised."

"You're not?"

"No, I'm not," she said. "I was worried all along that you would walk away from me. It came as no surprise."

"Well then, you knew something about me that I didn't know."

"Oh, Harry, it's so obvious. You even told me yourself. Do you remember you once said that attaching to someone new was like losing Sarah all over again?"

Harry recollected the scene in the restaurant. It was his first inkling that Amanda might want more than friendship with him. What a dilemma it provided! How far they had come. And now this.

"I knew I was in trouble with you then, but I told myself I needed to give you a chance. I thought that perhaps in time you would come around," she said.

"Actually, it's more complicated than that, Amanda. There's something I've never told you. My mother died of cancer when I was sixteen. It happened forty-two-years ago, and somehow I got it into my head that it didn't matter any longer. Well, I was wrong. It still matters. I was very attached to my mom. She was a fabulous woman, absolutely devoted to my brother and me. I never really dealt with the feelings her death left me with. I just kept on going. I distracted myself with studies and sports and pretended there were no such things as feelings. I didn't know from feelings in those days. I probably went into therapy in search of them, but that was many years later. So I left a part of myself behind. When Sarah died, also of cancer, I think I fell into mourning for both of them. Sarah's death reactivated the unfinished grief from my mother's death. I'm only realizing now why my grieving has been so prolonged. I lost the two women I loved before I was ready to deal with the losses. Then you came along, and I fell in love with you. Instead of initiating all the wonderful feelings that one is supposed to feel, it triggered fear and eventually flight. The prospect of losing you too was more than I could bear."

"I'm much younger than you."

"Is that some kind of a guarantee? My mother died young, and so did Sarah. Those deaths traumatized me. Why are you crying, Amanda?"

"Because you're not. Someone has to do it."

He looked at her and felt touched. How often in a life do you come across a woman like that?

"Mind you, all of this came to me since I last saw you. The loss of you merged with the others, and that set off this train of thought. I finally spent some time trying to understand myself. I haven't been in therapy for many years, and I guess the self-examination stopped with it. I tried very hard not to fall in love with you. I actually compared you to Sarah in order to find fault with you."

"That's a standard I can never measure up to," she said ruefully.

"Actually, that's not true. In some ways you compare favorably."

Amanda's eyebrows shot up. "This I've got to hear."

"In bed, for example."

"Oh, my God, really?"

"I swear!" Harry said with the brightest smile, leaving no room for doubt.

Amanda's face changed color and appeared to open up. "How else?"

"You're more introspective. Sarah wasn't a therapist, and it wasn't always easy to get her to talk about her feelings."

"Well, I appreciate your telling me this."

"Would you like to hear more?"

"There's more?"

He nodded.

"Would you like some coffee? I just need to heat it up."

For the first time Harry noticed that the carafe was half-filled, as though she had prepared enough for two. He told her he would love some.

"In fact," she said with her back to him as she prepared

the coffee, "I would like you to talk more about yourself." She turned back, took a few steps, and sat again in the chair across the table from him. "I like your honesty, Harry, but it still leaves a question. What is it that you want from me?"

Here was the crux of the issue.

"I've thought a lot about it. Love comes with risk, doesn't it? Do you remember Jennifer, a patient of mine? I talked about her a while ago."

"The difficult one?"

He nodded, although he felt like defending her. Another time perhaps.

"She did the same thing I did, with her boyfriend, that is. She tried to push him away. She came to the edge of the precipice, recognized that was a fall she didn't want to take, and drew back. I wasn't as smart. I plunged over, and now I'm begging you to forgive me. We're not as different from our patients as we think we are. It all comes down to figuring out what truly matters and what doesn't. I'm adopting that view as my philosophy of life. You really matter to me, dear. You're worth dancing in the dark with, come what may."

"Do you think you can cope with your fear?"

"Better than I can cope with the alternative."

"Which is?"

"Losing you."

Amanda didn't respond. Instead she rose to prepare the coffee, placing cups and saucers on the table, bringing milk and sugar over, pouring the coffee. Harry watched every move.

"I've been thinking about things myself lately," she said as she sat back into her chair. She drank from her cup as she considered her next words. Harry refrained from drinking; he began to feel some nerves. He was afraid his hand would shake.

"I recognized that I've been angry with you. I mean angry with you before we broke up. It began with the trip to your country house, with all those fond memories of life with Sarah. I was particularly angry with Brad."

"Yes, he was insensitive."

"So were you. Didn't you realize how uncomfortable it made me? I felt entirely left out. And it was your fault, Harry, not Brad's or your daughter's. I felt powerless. What could I say? I couldn't very well request a change of subject. That was up to you. You didn't protect me, Harry. I didn't need to spend a weekend hearing about life with Sarah."

Harry was about to say something in his defense, but he changed his mind and accepted responsibility. "Why didn't you tell me you were angry?"

"That's a problem I have. I'm too understanding and forgiving, and then I don't take care of myself. So I put the whole blame on the house. It was the house that brought back the memories. Perfectly understandable, no person was to blame."

Harry apologized again.

"I can't go back there, Harry. It has nothing to do with the house itself. It's a perfectly charming place, and I could have been quite comfortable there. And I know you love it. But everything about it summons the memory of Sarah. You say the memory won't interfere with us. I'm not sure I believe it."

"We don't have to talk about Sarah when we're there, and I don't have to invite the kids," Harry importuned, feeling he had to hold on to the old home.

"You're missing the point. That house *is* Sarah. There's a memory of her in every nook and cranny. It reeks of her. I mean it, Harry. If you need to hold on to it, then you must let go of me."

So that was it. She drove a hard bargain. The choice was before him and he needed to make it.

"Well then, I'll sell it." He took a big gulp of his coffee, as though he had to push something down very hard.

"Really? Could you do that? Could you do it without resenting me, without feeling that I took something away from you that was very precious?"

"I think … you're right. It's time to let go and start a new life."

"Your children will not favor this."

"If they want it, they can have it. But then they have to pay the taxes, the upkeep, and everything else. They won't do that because they can't afford to. Besides, they're almost never there."

"They'll be angry with you."

"Amanda, I'm doing this for us. Their wishes concerning this don't matter. There is something, though, something I need to make clear. I can't rip Sarah out of me and pretend she never happened. There are photo albums and all kinds of memorabilia. I need to keep those. I'll never put them in front of your nose, but I can't throw them away either. I have a loyalty to the past I never want to let go of."

"Oh, love, of course," she said as tears reappeared in her eyes. "I wouldn't dare try to take those memories away from you. I can't do that, and I wouldn't want to do that. She's a part of who you are. I believe that. I believe that all the important people who have been in our lives are part of who we are, for better or worse. Sarah resides in a part of your mind that is reserved for her, and she'll always be there. She's imperishable. I need you to put me in another part, and to keep the two separate."

Harry felt a wave of relief. We should meet the Js in Paris, he told himself whimsically. "Do you need a tissue?" he asked.

"I can get my own tissues, thank you," she said, "and I'm still angry with you." She rose, walked into the living room and yanked a tissue from its box on an end table. He walked in after her to witness Amanda dabbing her eyes. He asked why she remained angry with him. She rolled the wet tissue into a ball and threw it at him, striking him on the forehead.

"Bitch," he said. He wanted to kiss her but thought he should wait.

"There's something I want you to hear. It's a CD that I bought for you, but then you broke up with me, asshole that you were."

Harry was grateful that she employed the past tense. She

produced a CD player, placed the CD in it, and advanced it to the seventh selection. When the female singer's smoky, alto voice began singing the words *dancing in the dark*, Amanda turned toward Harry and said, "Shall we dance?"

Grinning, all fear vanquished, filled with an unconquerable elation, he hurried into those lovely, welcoming arms.

And the dance began.